# MIDORI
by
# MOONLIGHT

# MIDORI

by

# MOONLIGHT

Wendy Nelson Tokunaga

 St. Martin's Griffin  ❧  New York

MIDORI BY MOONLIGHT. Copyright © 2007 by Wendy Nelson Tokunaga. All rights reserved. Printed in the United States of America. No part of this book may be used or reproduced in any manner whatsoever without written permission except in the case of brief quotations embodied in critical articles or reviews. For information, address St. Martin's Press, 175 Fifth Avenue, New York, N.Y. 10010.

www.stmartins.com

ISBN-13: 978-0-312-37261-3
ISBN-10: 0-312-37261-2

First Edition: October 2007

10  9  8  7  6  5  4  3  2  1

For Manabu

# Acknowledgments

FIRST OF ALL I WANT TO THANK MY FANTASTIC AGENT, MARLY RUSOFF, for her support and belief in me. And a big thanks to my wonderful editors at St. Martin's Press, Hilary Rubin and Jennifer Weis, as well as production editor Julie Gutin and copy editor Sabrina Soares Roberts.

And I am so appreciative of the following writers-teachers who have given me such insight: Martha Alderson; Frank Baldwin; Ericka Lutz; Michelle Richmond; Ellen Sussman; and Lisa Zure.

And to all the following friends, some of whom are also fellow writers, who have been so generous with their help and support over the years, which has meant so much to me: Sandy Ackers; Hiro Akashi; Irina Eremia Bragin; Margo Candela; Brigitte Claydon; Nancy Evans; Neil Evans; Sue Zisko Feigenblatt; Tracy Guzeman; Gemma Halliday; Susan Hatler; Kathy Holmes; Patria Jacobs; Ferrell Jennings; Suzanne Kamata; Sami Kaneda; Mary E. Mitchell; Gemma Nemenzo; Deborah O'Kelly; Erika Opper; Marisa Peña; Kate Perry; Bev Rosenbaum; Carter Schwonke; Kiran Sethi; the folks at the Squaw Valley Community of Writers; Karen Van Alstine; Alison Weiss; Natasha Williams; Etsuko Wright; Jennifer Wright; and Lyndane Yang.

Thanks to my mother, Nancy A. Nelson, for her love and support.

And, most of all, I want to thank my husband, Manabu Toku-naga: I am so grateful for your love, support, and faith in me. I couldn't have done it without you.

# 1

MIDORI SAITO RECEIVED THE FOLLOWING WARNING FROM HER MOTHER right before she left Japan: "Running off with a foreigner will bring you nothing but trouble," she said. "You'll end up just like poor Emiko-chan on *Longing to Hug*."

It's insulting enough to be compared to a hapless, naïve soap opera character, but it's a far greater insult to discover that your mother's prediction couldn't have been more correct.

Now, a little more than a week since her mother's admonishment, the morning sun casts a pleasing light through the curtains. But Midori's mood is far from sunny. Kevin disappeared during the party they attended the night before. She doesn't know where he went, but she does have a hunch.

"Midori?"

Kevin knocks before entering her room. They're staying at his parents' house in the Presidio Heights district of San Francisco. Midori thought it odd when Mr. and Mrs. Newbury insisted the couple sleep in separate bedrooms, but she wasn't about to raise a fuss. Instead, she accepted the rule with good cheer. "I don't want to wrestle any feathers," she said to Kevin. He laughed at that, but she wasn't trying to be funny.

As Kevin walks in, Midori is making her bed, even though Kevin's mother advised her to leave any chores for Consuelo, the maid. Midori is grateful for her presence. Fresh from El Salvador, Consuelo is the one person in the house whose English is worse than Midori's. But Midori is determined to keep her room neat without any help from a maid—she doesn't want her future mother-in-law to think of her as a lazy pig.

"Yes?" Midori says to Kevin.

Kevin is dressed not in the sweats that he always wears to breakfast, but in neatly pressed jeans and a white button-down shirt. Midori is puzzled by his appearance, but filled with relief. At least he has come to give her an explanation and apologize for what happened last night.

Kevin sits on the upholstered easy chair next to the window, perching on the edge of the cushion as if he isn't intending to stay long.

While she waits for him to be the first to say something, Midori folds the lace-trimmed, lavender-flowered sheet over the pink blanket, tucking it securely under the mattress. *So frilly*, she thinks. Midori prefers sheets with more muted earth tones. That's what she plans to select for their wedding registry. Yesterday Mrs. Newbury asked her where she wanted to register. Being in San Francisco for only eight days, Midori knows nothing about the stores here. Kevin's mother gave her two choices: Gump's or Saks Fifth Avenue. Gump's sounds like a disease so Midori is leaning toward Saks.

Since Kevin has only coughed and has yet to say a word—let alone an apology—it might be best to first bring up something pleasant before confronting him. She asks him which shop he prefers.

"Midori, I can't marry you."

"Eh?"

What did he say? *I can't carry you? I can't bury you?* Did he really say he couldn't *marry* her? It isn't possible. She must have misunderstood. Midori spins around, peering at Kevin's face.

*"What did you say?"*

"I can't marry you."

His subdued tone reminds her of a misbehaving little boy, cowering from the inevitable scolding.

"What *happened* last night?"

He averts his gaze to the hardwood floor and says nothing.

"Where were you?" Midori's voice shakes. She doesn't wait for an answer. "Kevin, I know I just arrived here and do not understand everything, but I was not born the day before yesterday."

He gives her a slight smile. "Yesterday."

"What?"

"Yesterday. The correct way to say it is, 'I wasn't born yesterday.'"


The night before, Mr. and Mrs. Newbury threw a combination welcome home and engagement party for Kevin and Midori in the Newburys' seven-bedroom home. Midori had never been inside such a huge house. Kevin didn't tell her how rich his family was. When he said they were "comfortable," she thought he meant they would be easy to get along with.

The party was held in the ballroom. Kevin had told her it was large enough to fit one hundred and fifty people, which was the exact number of guests attending the party. Already it seemed near capacity.

The decorations reminded her of an elaborate display in an exclusive store window or scenery from a stage play. Miniature trees shaped into sculpted balls of green leaves topping slender trunks lined the walls. Midori could only half remember what Mrs. Newbury called them. *Tipperaries?* That didn't sound right. Tiny white lights twinkled from each one. Swans made of ice swam motionlessly on buffet tables. Gold chandeliers bursting with clusters of electric candles shone from the ceiling, giving the room a warm yellow glow. At the base of a spiral staircase that led only to the ceiling, a young red-haired woman in an angel costume sat on a stool, plucking "We've Only Just Begun" on a harp.

The only people Midori knew at the party were Kevin and his

parents. Kevin left Midori on her own, saying he was going to get her a glass of wine. But about fifteen minutes passed and he still hadn't returned.

Most of the guests were middle-aged; the women dressed in sparkling gowns, the men wearing business suits. All Caucasian, their hair boasted a variety of colors ranging from chocolate-browns to buttery blonds. Midori, in her black hair and decidedly unglittering, tan linen dress, felt as out-of-place as a pair of chopsticks thrown in the silverware drawer.

The only nonwhite people were those serving the food and drinks, including Consuelo. But in a far corner Midori spotted a man who was clearly nonwhite and clearly not part of the help. He was a guest with black hair who looked Asian. Could he be Japanese? Speaking nothing but English for more than a week, Midori's brain was as stuck as a clogged kitchen sink. It wasn't supposed to be this way. When she first met Kevin at the Let's English Language Academy where she had worked as an office lady back in Fukuoka, the first words out of his mouth were *How do you do? My name is Kevin Newbury. So nice to meet you!* spoken in perfect Japanese. Smooth and creamy, his voice sounded like a Japanese television announcer's, but so wonderfully mismatched, coming from a six-foot-tall Caucasian man with curly hair the color of marmalade. It wasn't until later that she found out this was the only Japanese he knew.

This nonwhite man at the party looked like he could have been Japanese, and at a party in Japan one could safely assume he was. But here in San Francisco he could be Chinese, Thai, or Vietnamese. Or, perhaps, Japanese, but born in the United States and fluent only in English. As Midori contemplated whether to go up to him, Kevin finally arrived with her glass of wine.

"Where have you been?" she asked. He acted as if he didn't hear her so she tried a different question. "Who is that person?" She pointed to the man.

Kevin's face lit up. "That's Shinji," he said. "You have to meet him." He led her in the man's direction.

Kevin hugged Shinji, patting him on the back. "Shinji," he said. "I want you to meet my fiancée, Midori Saito. I never would have met her if it weren't for you." Kevin turned toward Midori. "It was Shinji who convinced me to go work in Japan."

Kevin had never mentioned a Japanese friend in San Francisco.

Shinji broke into a big smile. He looked to Midori about her own age—thirty—and his hair, cut and gelled into jagged upright stalks, reminded her of a haystack. She couldn't figure out what his job might be—even in a black suit and white shirt he looked too cool to be a regular salaryman. She was surprised to find herself thinking he was actually good-looking, at least for a Japanese guy.

"Nice to meet you," he said in Japanese. "I am Shinji Nishimura."

The reassuring sound of her native language was like hearing a favorite old song unexpectedly on the radio.

"*Saito Midori to moshimasu ga. Yoroshiku onegai shimasu,*" she said, introducing herself. Shinji was from Japan, all right, but when he bowed with a droop of his shoulders, he looked stiff, out of practice. Midori figured that would happen to her once she lived in the States for a couple of years. It was obvious Shinji had been here for quite a while—the naturalness of his Japanese was marred by a slight American accent meandering throughout his speech.

Midori continued on breathlessly in Japanese; it was like receiving a glass of water to soothe a parched throat. "Thanks for taking care of Kevin and getting him to Japan. I really appreciate it."

"It was my pleasure. Kevin's a good friend," Shinji said. "Congratulations on your engagement."

"Kevin!"

A piercing female voice cut through the din of conversation and harp music. Startled, Midori pressed her hand to her chest and turned around to see an extremely striking woman, about a foot taller than her, sliding next to Kevin's side. Interlocking her arm with his, she rested her head for a brief moment on his shoulder. Her clingy pink jersey gown hugged her breasts, cinched her waist, and caressed her hips—all in hourglass-perfect proportion—a figure Midori had always understood was the most desirable for an American woman. And the opposite of hers, she thought, which more resembled that of the stick lady on the door denoting the women's restroom.

A wave of blond curls cascaded down the woman's back. Her eyes—darting from Midori's to Shinji's and back to Midori's again—were almost as blue as Kevin's.

"Hey, Shinji," she said.

"Hi, Kimberley," Shinji said. Midori noticed the surprised look on his face; it was clear he hadn't expected her to be here.

But Kevin didn't look surprised—just embarrassed. His cheeks turned into two patches of red, like when he drank too much sake. "Kimberley . . ."

Kevin had repeatedly told Midori that she should always make eye contact with Americans so as not to be considered rude. It was never easy for her to look someone in the eye, but she made a point of it this time. Fixing onto the woman's gaze, she smiled. "Hello, I am Midori Saito."

Kimberley extended her hand. "Oh, the Japanese girl. I'm Kimberley Hobbs."

"Kimberley's an old family friend," Kevin said.

Kimberley ran her hands through her hair, tossing her curls like a salad. She laughed. "Yes. An old family friend."

Midori laughed too even though she didn't know what was so amusing about this.

Kimberley resumed holding on to Kevin's arm. "Kevin, I wonder if I might have a moment with you."

"Sure." Kevin kissed Midori's cheek. "I'll be back in a minute."

Midori watched as Kimberley maneuvered Kevin through the crowd. It seemed that every person she brushed by smiled and said hello to her.

"Who is she?" Midori asked Shinji.

"Just an old friend of Kevin's, I guess," Shinji said, frowning and raising his eyebrows. His friendly smile returned. "So this is your first time in the States, right?"

"Not exactly. When I was in college I took a two-week trip here. I saw New York, Los Angeles, Las Vegas, and San Francisco."

"Two weeks isn't too long."

"No, it isn't. Do you live in San Francisco?"

"Yeah, for six years."

"How did you come to find yourself here?"

He smiled but rolled his eyes. "It's a long story," he said. "Maybe I can tell you someday."

Midori was curious about Shinji's story, but her train of thought was disturbed at the sight of Kimberley and Kevin hovering in the corner of the room, their heads nearly touching. She seemed to be doing all the talking. Couldn't she finish and leave him alone? And why were they huddled so close together? Midori felt as if she were trying to breathe underwater.

"You're staying with Kevin's parents right now?" Shinji went on.

"Yes, while we look for a house."

"And I heard he's going to start a job at one of the colleges?"

"Yes, teaching English as a foreign language." Midori could see Kevin and Kimberley laughing. She certainly was quite a comedian. What could she be saying that was so funny?

"How great," he said. "And the wedding is soon, right?"

"Yes, June 24. I hope you'll be coming."

"I wouldn't miss it." He paused, then cleared his throat. "I know you'll probably be busy, but if you ever get homesick and want to speak some Japanese, give me a call." He plucked a pen from his coat pocket. "This is my home number," he said, writing on the back of the card.

*Sawyer & Jones Advertising*, it said. *Sean Nishimura, Graphic Artist.*

"Thank you. It's been painful to speak only English. It feels so good to talk in Japanese." Midori paused. "Sean Nishimura is your name?"

"That's what I use here. For Americans 'Sean' is easier to remember than 'Shinji.'"

Midori thought this was strange, and vowed not to change her own name, except to Midori Newbury, of course. Her head throbbed as she glanced in the direction of the garden. "Can you excuse me, please?" she said to Shinji-Sean.

Midori's heart fluttered as she headed for the sliding glass door leading to the backyard. But just as she got there, Kevin's mother rushed to her side. She was tall and slim like her son, and with the same blue eyes. Her white hair was cut in a chic short style, framing a face mostly devoid of lines or wrinkles, even though she was probably sixty. Kevin had told Midori that his mother had worked part time as a fashion model when she was in college.

"Midori, you must meet Kevin's uncle Ralph," she said, pushing Midori's arm. "He was engaged once to a gee-sha girl when he was in the Korean War."

"Excuse me, Mrs. Newbury, but who is Kimberley Hobbs?"

Mrs. Newbury blinked several times, as if she were trying to get her eyes in focus. "So you met Kimberley? She's an old friend of Kevin's. From college."

Mrs. Newbury kept Midori busy with introductions to various people. Aunt Ralph, Uncle Agnes, Mr. Church who worked for a bank. Or was it Mr. Bank who worked for a church? Midori couldn't keep anyone straight. Their faces had all blurred into a dull, doughy similarity.

Midori extricated herself from Mrs. Newbury by saying she had to go to the restroom, but instead headed toward the garden. Strings of white lights shimmered on the rosebushes and rhododendrons. Midori saw several guests enjoying the balmy evening but she couldn't locate Kevin or Kimberley.

Midori decided to go to the powder room after all. The ballroom bathroom resembled one in a department store, with a large room separate from the toilets and expansive, lighted mirrors and flower-painted ceramic sinks. Opening the door, Midori's chest burned as she recognized the back of some familiar blond curls. Kimberley stood in front of one of the mirrors, dabbing her face with a small round cloth.

"Hello, Kimberley," she said, which sounded more like *Hah-row, Kim-bah-ree*, in what for Midori was a loud voice.

As Midori had hoped, Kimberley jumped. Her compact slipped from her hand and fell into the sink.

"Oh, Mitori," she said, turning around. "What a nice party." She retrieved the silver compact and turned on the water to rinse the powder dotting the basin.

"Yes, but it has nothing to do with me. It is thanks to Kevin's parents." Midori thought afterwards that it would have been better to just have said, "Thank you" to this, but that would have seemed like bragging. She couldn't take any credit for this party.

"Of course."

Midori placed her hands under the gold faucet as water magically poured over them. "Where did you meet Kevin?"

"In high school." Frazzled, she jammed the compact into a pink, beaded evening bag.

"Do you know where he is? I can't find him."

"No, I don't know where he is," she said, her tone implying that there was no reason to believe that she would be privy to such information. She twirled her fingers through her hair, looking at her watch. "So nice to meet you, but I have to run. It's almost midnight."

"Will your car become a pumpkin?"

Kimberley gave Midori a puzzled look. Did she mix up her fairy tales? At any rate, Kimberley didn't seem to get the joke. *It had been a risk*, Midori thought, *attempting to be humorous in English.*

"Good night," Kimberley said, rushing out the door.

Back in the ballroom, the party seemed to be winding down. The angel had removed her wings and was wheeling out her harp. Midori still couldn't find her fiancé. She tapped Mrs. Newbury on the shoulder. "Have you seen Kevin?"

"No, dear," she said. "Maybe he already went to bed."

Midori didn't think that was true, but rode the elevator to the third floor anyway. At first, she couldn't believe that a family would have an elevator in their home, but after living here for a week she'd become used to it and found it rather thrilling, and handy as well.

The door to Kevin's bedroom was open, but the only occupant was Snowball, the Newburys' white Persian cat, who stretched leisurely on the bed, gripping the spread with her claws.

When Midori turned on the light, Snowball rolled on her back and let out a loud, contented meow. Midori gazed around the room as she scratched the cat's belly. Kevin's open suitcase, still adorned with Japan Airlines tags, lay on the floor; his shoes and socks were strewn about as if they were homeless. His striped cotton robe was draped leisurely over a chair. On the dresser a bottle of cologne rested on its side, surrounded by a scattered collection of pennies, dimes, and quarters mixed with 100-yen coins.

Midori grasped the handles on the dresser drawer, pulling it open. What did she expect to find? A secret diary? Mysterious letters stashed away in an old cigar box? Perhaps she was acting silly to be so nosy. It was something Emiko-chan from *Longing to Hug* might do. But that didn't stop her from rummaging through the disarray of underwear, socks, and pajamas.

All she found was Kevin's sterling silver pen. It was his favorite. When they lived in Japan he used it to correct student papers. Midori had never looked at the pen closely until now. Rolling it in her palm she noticed the engraved, swirling lines, which gave it an elegant look. But there was something else. On the other side of the clip she spotted an inscription: *K & K Together Forever.* She had to stare at the letters for what seemed like minutes before she realized their meaning. Her body, frozen and chilled like one of those swan ice sculptures downstairs, couldn't move until she heard a familiar voice.

"Looking something?"

Midori turned around to see Consuelo standing in the doorway, her eyebrows arched in surprise. Snowball jumped off the bed and bounded toward her, rubbing enthusiastically against her legs.

"Yes," Midori said, trying to put on a smile. "But I found it. Good night." She clasped the pen in her hand as she eased past the housekeeper and the cat, walking in a hurry toward the stairway to her room on the second floor. Midori gave up searching for Kevin. Still in her party clothes, she lay stiffly on the bed. Holding the pen between her fingers, she couldn't stop staring at the engraved message until she drifted into a troubled sleep.

———

Now, in the bedroom with the freshly made bed, Midori can feel Kevin looking at her as she stares out the window.

"I couldn't find you last night," she says. "You disappeared. Were you with Kimberley?"

"Yes."

She crosses her arms, holding them to her chest. She puffs out her cheeks.

"I'm sorry I never mentioned this, but I was engaged before."

"To her?" Midori says. Of course the answer is obvious, but she wants to hear it from him.

He nods.

"Why didn't you tell it to me?"

"I don't know. I didn't think it was important."

What other things has he considered too unimportant to tell her? When they first met, she asked him why he had come to Japan. He said he wanted to "get back down to earth." What was he—an astronaut?

"When she broke the engagement, I decided to go to Japan." He reaches for Midori's hand. "And now I realize that she and I . . ."

"Yes?"

"Midori, I'm sorry."

"You just realized now?" Has she been such a disappointment ever since arriving here that he suddenly changed his mind?

He shakes his head. "No. I've been in touch with her for a while."

"When we were in Japan?" Midori nearly loses her balance as she sits with a thump on the bed.

Kevin rubs his temples with his palms. "Yes."

"And you still brought me here?"

"I was confused, Midori. I wasn't sure what to do."

She stares at his blue eyes, which now seem to have turned gray—the color of mold infesting a slice of bread. How mortifying to recall that from the first moment she met Kevin, she thought he was the one. When the school administrator at Let's English introduced him to the office ladies Midori became so dizzy she thought she would faint. Gazing at his muscular frame, his blond hair, his blue eyes, and hearing his charming Japanese, she thought, *I'll put up with any of his faults, if only he'll be my boyfriend and, maybe if things work out, my husband.*

And his face had looked so familiar. Where had she seen it before? Was it Robert Redford in *Out of Africa*? Brad Pitt? Tom Cruise? Maybe, but not quite. Then it hit her. When she got home she immediately went to her room, to the bottom row of the bookshelf that held her childhood books. Spying the familiar green cover, she pulled out the picture book *Tamanokoshi*, the Japanese translation of *Cinderella*. Because it was a European story, all the characters in the illustrations had white faces, not Japanese. She turned the pages, then stopped when she saw a portrait of a man wearing a belted, bright white jacket with gold-fringed epaulets—Kevin was a dead ringer for the prince.

Now, instead of Prince Charming, Kevin seems to have turned into his evil twin, Prince Alarming or Prince Harming or *something*.

"You will marry her instead of me?"

"I'm not sure. But we found that we— we"—he is stuttering now—"we're still in love with each other. I just feel so terrible about this, Midori."

"*You* feel terrible? You cannot feel *my* terrible feeling." She sighs. It isn't how she wants to say it. She wishes she could do something dramatic to make him feel her hurt. Throw herself on the floor and beg him to take her back, rip the curtains from the rod and threaten to jump out the window. Those are definitely scenes worthy of a soap opera. But instead she grabs the silver pen from the bed table and throws it to the floor.

"Congratulations, Kevin. Now the K and K can be together forever."

It's as though Midori had been cast in *Longing to Hug*, but was abruptly killed off because her character hadn't been popular enough with viewers.

Kevin said good-bye to her that morning and left the house. She assumed he was rushing off to be with Kimberley. Now it's up to Mrs. Newbury to deal with Midori. The two women sit across from each other in the bright, sun-filled kitchen as Consuelo rinses dishes in the sink and loads them into the dishwasher.

"It's a shame, dear, but sometimes these things happen for the best," Mrs. Newbury says.

In Japan, an incident like this would have been of extreme embarrassment to the family. Endless apologies would be expressed and who knows how long it would take the affected parties to recover. And relatives would be tsk-tsking all over the place, bestowing looks of great pity toward the jilted bride-to-be. But Mrs. Newbury never says she is sorry and never apologizes for her son's behavior. To her, it seems the wedding plans had simply been a picnic that required cancellation because of a rainstorm.

At first Midori was offended and hurt by Mrs. Newbury's behavior. There's that English expression . . . *What am I? Chopped asparagus?* But, no, that didn't seem quite right. Yet as Midori sits in the kitchen staring at the bouquet of shiny copper pots and pans hanging by hooks from the ceiling, and the enormous preparation counter—they call it an island—where Consuelo is now slicing a plump purple eggplant, she feels a strange sense of relief that this transaction is turning out to be short and sweet. Yes, she is beyond disappointed; and yes, she is livid with Kevin; and, yes, she doesn't know what she's going to do with her life now. But she takes comfort in the straightforward simplicity of it all, the complete lack of decorum.

So when Mrs. Newbury says it might all be for the best, Midori simply nods.

"I've arranged for an electronic ticket to Tokyo on Japan Airlines for next Wednesday. Here's the information. They sent it in Japanese for you." She pushes a fax in Midori's direction. "And until then you can stay at one of the hotels, as I'm sure you wouldn't be comfortable staying here any longer."

Midori nods once more.

"Which would you prefer, dear? The Fairmont or the Mark Hopkins? Of course we'll pay for everything."

It reminds Midori of the choice Mrs. Newbury had given her between Gump's and Saks. She has no idea which to select. Her throat tightens as she thinks of the wedding registry that is no longer necessary.

She decides to choose the hotel that doesn't sound like a man's name. "Fairmont?" she says as she listens to the rhythmic tapping of Consuelo's knife on the cutting board.

"Fine. Mr. Newbury knows the manager so it'll be no problem getting you a nice room. I'll make a reservation and have a cab come over and take you there. By the way, they provide some wonderful tours. You can see all the sights with a Japanese guide before you go home. Just charge everything to your room." She stops for a moment and places her index finger on her temple, reminding Midori of an executive's secretary, making sure she hasn't forgotten any details. "You're all packed, correct?"

"Yes." Midori pauses. "I'm sorry, Mrs. Newbury." Kevin had warned her that she would look like a weakling if she constantly said "I'm sorry" to Americans, but it came out automatically, the way your leg pops up after the doctor hits your knee with a hammer.

"Nothing for you to apologize for, dear."

"Thank you for everything."

"You're welcome. Too bad things didn't work out." She gets up from the table. "But life goes on, doesn't it?"

Out of the corner of her eye, Midori can see Consuelo staring in her direction. As she looks to her for a comforting glance, the maid quickly bows her head and stabs another eggplant. Perhaps Consuelo had tattled to Mrs. Newbury, and figures Midori was being dismissed for stealing from Kevin's room.

Consuelo doesn't know the half of it, and perhaps neither does Mrs. Newbury—unless Kevin has told her. This is much more than a breakup for Midori. This is *a big fucking deal*, as Kevin would say.

When Midori left Japan, she planned to leave permanently and live her life in the States married to Kevin. She would have received a green card through her marriage and eventually become an American citizen, as she had no interest in returning to Japan except for an occasional visit.

"Why can't we just get married in Japan and then move to San Francisco?" Midori asked Kevin. "All we have to do is register at the ward office. We can still have our wedding in San Francisco." She had read an article in a Japanese magazine about a couple that took their vows in a picturesque village called Sausalito, with the Golden Gate Bridge behind them. It was so magnificent—it looked as if they were standing in front of a backdrop photograph at Universal Studios.

"My parents really want to meet you," he said.

So that was why Midori entered the United States on a fiancée visa. But now she wonders if Kevin had only wanted to put off the marriage because he wasn't sure what would happen with Kimberley. Anyway, it was necessary to marry Kevin to acquire the proper credentials to stay legally, but now that was impossible. And if she stays for more than sixty days, and the authorities find out she hasn't married Kevin, she'll be deported, and banished from the United States for years, if not forever.

One time, back in Japan, Kevin had been complaining to Midori about Howard, one of the other teachers at Let's English.

"He always goes round and round when he talks," Kevin said. "He's so indirect. He never gets to the point."

"He's always going in the bushes," she said.

"What?"

"He's always going in the bushes."

Kevin laughed so long and hard it looked as though he were having a seizure. He smiled warmly as he put his arms around her and kissed her lips. "I love you so much," he said. "'Cause you're so funny."

Midori liked how Kevin always said, "I love you"—so unlike a Japanese man. But she didn't know why he thought she was "funny."

"What is so funny?"

"When you say he's going in the bushes it sounds like he's taking a piss or something. I think what you wanted to say is, 'He beats around the bush.' It's just an idiomatic expression."

From then on Midori was determined to correctly learn as many English idiomatic expressions as she could. But she called them *idiot-matic* expressions, because she felt like a complete idiot when she got them wrong. She memorized dozens and tried to use them as much as possible. She was proud of her accomplishments, much like a foreigner in Japan learning to write her first Japanese characters. But still she made mistakes and Kevin would correct her when she spoke of getting egg on her eyes, or pulling the wool over somebody's face.

Now, slumped in the backseat of a taxi on her way to the Fairmont Hotel, climbing the steep hills like the Matterhorn ride at Disneyland, Midori bites her lower lip. As tears fall on her cheeks, she is oblivious to the bright blue sky and the clanging of the cable car bells. But she knows the exact idiomatic expressions to describe her situation.

*I'm in deep shit*, she thinks, *and up the creek without a saddle.*

# 2

MIDORI STARES HARD AT HER THREE SUITCASES SITTING UPRIGHT AND unpacked in her room on the seventh floor of the Fairmont Hotel. Then she throws her body on the king-size bed—beaching herself like some disoriented whale, pounding the pillows with her fists.

"How could you do this to me?" she yells.

It's surprising how her voice has the capacity to be so loud. It bounces off the walls, echoing in the room. She quickly covers her face with one of the pillows. Choking on her sobs, she attempts to muffle them. She doesn't want anyone to think she's being beaten to death. A frightened guest might call the front desk. The police would then be summoned, along with immigration officials and their German shepherd attack dogs.

"You are Mee-dorey Say-ee-toe?" a burly man in a dark blue suit would ask.

"Yes, sir."

"You are the pitiful alien dumped by your fiancé who *will not be getting married after all?*" he'd say, while another would shine a flashlight into her eyes.

"Yes, sir." Midori would only be able to squint and shield her eyes with her hand.

"You are required to vacate this room and this country at once."

Then they'd set the dogs off in the direction of her bags to sniff out the cyanide she'd hidden in an aspirin bottle. The cyanide she'd sprinkled in Kevin's coffee that morning. For that's how Emiko-chan from *Longing to Hug* got back at her American husband upon discovering his affair with their son's nursery school teacher.

But Midori hadn't been willing to risk life in prison over Kevin. She would have to try to get over her humiliation in a more mundane way: She would have to eat desserts. She would have to consume beautiful pastries, enjoy an artistic presentation of color, texture, and china to try and forget her troubles.

After perusing the room service menu, she calls and places an order for every dessert that is listed.

Over the years Midori fantasized about being a pastry chef at a top restaurant, but hadn't done too much about it other than to enroll in a few cooking classes. But whenever her mood was low, going to a fancy restaurant and ordering its best dessert seemed to get her out of the doldrums. She'd take a photo, put it in her "pastry album," and write a description, trying to guess how it was made.

She isn't up for going to a restaurant tonight; her hotel room will have to suffice. The waiter wheels in a cart with each dessert covered by a silver dome. He removes each one to reveal chocolate caramel raspberry mousse cake with raspberry coulis; caramelized apple pie with crème fraîche; lemon meringue tart with blood orange sauce; and trio of crème brûlée accompanied by cookies.

"Thank you," Midori says, opening her wallet to give him a tip. As she pulls out some bills, a card falls to the floor. It's the business card Shinji Nishimura had given her last night at the party. The man with the long story about how he came to San Francisco. *Sean* Nishimura, Kevin's friend. She still can't get used to calling a Japanese man "Sean."

Placing the card on the table next to the lemon tart, she then pulls her digital camera from her bag and snaps photos of the desserts. Taking slow, meticulous bites of each one, she notes the complexity of the flavors, colors, and textures. The fruity softness of the mousse, the tartness of the tart, the snap of the crème brûlée when she inserts her spoon. She writes descriptions on a piece of stationery embossed with *Fairmont Hotel*.

Usually she isn't too big of an eater and only consumes half of a pastry and calls it quits. But tonight is different. She wolfs down each dish in an orgasmic frenzy, and soon is more buzzed than if she'd consumed an entire bottle of whiskey. She is giddy. Who cares about getting dumped? Who cares about being illegal? Who cares if her parents will have tandem heart attacks when they find out she isn't getting married? Maybe everything will be just fine. Maybe, just maybe, everything about her messed-up life will turn out as exquisitely as a piece of raspberry mousse cake.

Her sugar haze is pierced suddenly by an electronic version of "Take Me Home, Country Roads." She jumps. What was *that*? It takes a moment to realize that it is her cell phone ringing. Midori's heart almost comes to a halt as she rummages through her handbag to retrieve it. Kevin had set her up with this phone when she arrived in San Francisco. For all she knew, he'd canceled the account by now (or his mother had). Only two parties had the number—Kevin and her parents. Maybe Kevin had changed his mind. Maybe he was calling to beg her forgiveness. "How could I have been so foolish?" he would say. "You know I love you, Midori."

"Hello?"

"*Moshi-moshi*, Midori?"

It's her mother. Midori's heart drops at the urgency in her voice. Did she somehow already find out what had happened? Had it been on the front page of the *Mainichi Shinbun*? MIDORI SAITO, 30—DUMPED: NO HOPE OF EVER GETTING MARRIED NOW.

"Hi, Mom!" Midori tries to make her voice sound cheerful, the perky tone of a young woman who has just returned from a busy day of picking out her Waterford china pattern and getting fitted for her Vera Wang wedding gown. "Why are you calling?"

"I hadn't heard from you for a while so I was worried. I wanted to see how things are going."

"Things are going just fine."

"How is Kevin?"

"He's fine too."

"Is Mrs. Newbury helping you out?"

"Yes, she's been a big help." Out of the corner of her eye Midori sees a red blotch on her white blouse. Raspberry mousse cake. She sighs as she wads up a linen napkin, dips it in a glass of water, and rubs it across her chest. The stain, which had been about the size of a postage stamp, now has increased in size, making her shirt resemble the Japanese flag.

"I'm going to buy the airline tickets today. Shall we fly out on June 21?"

Midori opens her mouth but no words come out. She has temporarily lost all language ability.

"*Moshi-moshi*," Mrs. Saito says impatiently. "Midori?"

"June 21?" Midori finally says, brushing her fingertips over the smear, hoping that will somehow make it disappear.

"Yes. June 21. Isn't that the right date?"

"I guess so. Yes, that's fine." Midori pauses again. "Are the tickets refundable?"

"Eh?"

"Yeah, June 21. You know, Mom, can I call you back later?"

"Call me back as soon as you can." Her mother's irritation comes through loud and clear seven thousand miles away.

It is probably the fact that she'd just consumed four rich desserts in their entirety and not that she had to talk to her mother, but Midori's stomach suddenly begins to rumble and belch like Mount Vesuvius.

After a couple of trips to the bathroom and putting the dirty dishes on a tray out of sight outside her door, she feels better. As she stretches on the bed, she stares at Shinji-Sean Nishimura's business card. Should she contact him? He's now the only person she knows in San Francisco, but what a burden to place on him, to ask for his help. Yet it isn't even clear how he *can* help her. Maybe Kevin has already broken the news to him. Maybe he was actually happy that Kimberley and Kevin were back together. Maybe he'd said, "Yeah, Kevin, you made the right decision getting rid of such a boring girl."

She looks at her watch. It's almost nine o'clock. Maybe it's too late to call Shinji, she thinks, but in the next instant she dials his number anyway, hypnotized by an unseen force.

"Nishimura-san, I'm sorry to bother you," she says in Japanese when he answers. "This is Midori Saito. I met you last night at the engagement party . . ."

"Oh! Saito-san? How are you?"

The friendly but formal tone of his voice makes her think that he hasn't spoken to Kevin. "I'm fine." She pauses, pulling at her hair. "I'm very sorry to ask you this, but do you think it's possible for me to meet with you sometime soon?"

"Meet? Sure." He sounds surprised.

"I know you must be very busy, but . . . do you have time tomorrow?"

"Tomorrow's a workday but . . ."

"Do you take a lunch hour?"

"Yes."

"Do you know the Fairmont Hotel?" Midori asks.

"Of course. My office isn't too far from there."

"Do you think you could meet me?"

Shinji is agreeable and Midori meets him the next day at the Fairmont lobby. He isn't as dressed up as he was at the party. He wears black jeans, a light blue shirt, and black sneakers with bright orange laces. But his hair still looks like a haystack and his high cheekbones and large eyes could have gotten him a part on *Longing to Hug*. His smile is sweet and friendly.

"Shall we have lunch here at the hotel?" she asks him. The least she can do is charge the meal to her room and have Kevin's parents pay for it.

The restaurant is quiet and dignified, just like the hotel. They are seated at a corner table with heavy mahogany chairs. Black-and-white photographs of old San Francisco hang on the walls.

"I was a little surprised to hear from you," Shinji says, his eyes bright. "I figured you must be busy with wedding arrangements and all."

Midori had planned to be completely calm in front of Shinji. She barely knows him and the last thing she wants him to think is that she is some kind of nutty, fresh-off-the-boat Japanese girl with little or no common sense, even though this is probably an accurate description. She wants to appear cool, almost blasé, with an oh-well-life-goes-on attitude, just as Mrs. Newbury had said. She wants to look in complete control. But instead, as soon as she hears his words, she bursts into tears.

Shinji immediately leans over, placing his hand on her wrist. *Such an American gesture*, Midori thinks, *and completely unexpected*. But she welcomes it.

"What's the matter?"

Midori wipes her eyes with her napkin and stares into his face. "Kevin and I aren't getting married. He broke up with me."

Shinji sits back, looking almost like a child in an oversized mahogany high chair, his eyes as wide as the bread and butter plates. *"What?"*

"I'm sorry to burden you with my problems," Midori says, her hands wringing the napkin like a wet washcloth. "But you're the only person I know here in San Francisco except for Kevin and his parents."

"I'm shocked." He shakes his head. "I'm so sorry to hear this."

"He's still in love with Kimberley. And I didn't know a thing about her until I met her at the party. I didn't know that they were engaged and she broke up with him. I didn't know that's why he came to Japan. To forget her. He never told me anything about this." Once she started talking she couldn't stop.

Shinji is silent, looking down, deep in thought.

"Please eat something," Midori says. "I know you have to get back to work."

"That's okay." He makes a halfhearted attempt at swirling some pasta on his fork, but lets the tangle of noodles rest on the edge of the bowl.

"I guess you knew Kimberley from before."

He shifts in his seat. "Kind of," he says. "I met her a few times.

Yeah, they got engaged, but I don't know exactly why they broke up."
He pauses. "I'm sorry, Saito-san. I feel bad that it was me who suggested that Kevin try and get over her by moving to Japan."

"No, no," Midori says. "Please don't feel that way. You were being
a good friend to him." Midori sips some water. "Anyway, I'm staying
here at the Fairmont Hotel. Kevin's parents are paying for it until I
return to Japan next Wednesday."

Shinji continues to look stunned.

"Are you sure you don't mind my telling you all these personal
things? Normally I wouldn't do this, but I'm in kind of a desperate
situation."

"Don't worry. Please, go on."

"I don't want to return to Japan. I haven't even told my parents
yet about what happened. I had intended to stay here forever."

Shinji nods.

"Please eat something," she says.

He dutifully shoves a few strands of pasta into his mouth.

"I don't want to trouble you with my problems. But is there somewhere, maybe I could rent an apartment, where I can stay until I de-
cide what I'm going to do? I don't want to go back to Japan next
Wednesday. I never want to go back, if I can help it. But I don't know
anything about San Francisco."

"Kevin's not helping you at all?"

"No," she says. "His mother was the one who took care of getting
me into this hotel and arranging for my ticket home."

Shinji shakes his head in disbelief. He places his hand on top of
hers. "That's terrible." He drinks some water. "So you are on your own
then. I see . . ."

He doesn't say anything further and a sudden paranoia that seems
to come from nowhere now makes Midori wonder if contacting him
has been a mistake. If Kevin wasn't willing to help her, why would his
friend? Someone she met only one time? Someone who might have
thought that Kevin was a good guy and maybe there *was* something
wrong with this Midori girl and why shouldn't Kevin have gone after
the love of his life if his only other choice had been this dull, drab of-

fice lady who could only speak broken English? Maybe it's time to face facts and get on that plane and return home. And have her parents tell her to her face what a failure she is.

Shinji leans forward, looking directly into her eyes. "I'd like to try and help you."

Back at her hotel room Midori's mood is a bit lighter. Maybe things will get better. Shinji said he would try to figure something out and would give her a call.

She gazes at her luggage. She might as well at least unpack some more clean underwear. But when she opens one of the bags, she realizes this particular one doesn't contain any underwear. It's her miscellaneous suitcase, the one that holds books and keepsakes she had wanted to bring with her, to have as part of her new life in America. There's her pastry album; her copy of *You! Take the Cake*, a baking cookbook written in Japanese that her mother had given her; and a framed picture of her and Kevin taken at Let's English.

Turning the picture over and burying it deep inside the suitcase, she reaches for a small white box stashed under a silk pouch where she keeps her few pieces of jewelry. Opening it she pulls out a music box shaped like a cable car. She turns the knob and listens to the tune that plays. It's called "I Left My Heart in San Francisco." She was eleven years old and in middle school when she received this little gold car from Miyuki.

Midori would never forget the day when her teacher Kimura-sensei had introduced Miyuki to the class. "Please make friends with Miyuki-san since she is new here," she said.

But nobody seemed to want to make friends with Miyuki. She was a *kikoku-shijo*, a "returnee" to Japan. When she was seven her father's company transferred him to California. In this situation, it was often the case that the rest of the family would stay behind in Japan so the children could continue in the Japanese school system. But in Miyuki's case, her entire family moved to California. Now, four years later, Miyuki was back in Japan and attending Midori's school as a new student.

Even though she wore the same dark blue skirt and white blouse uniform all the girls had to wear, Miyuki seemed different. Unlike the other girls she walked with a confident stride, her shoulders back, her chin forward, as if she had a purpose. When she laughed, she didn't put her hand over her mouth. Her voice was louder and she was taller than even some of the boys. Midori knew her height had nothing to do with her living abroad, but it added to her appeal. Midori was excited to meet such an exotic new friend and thought it was a good sign that the first part of their names had the same pronunciation. This meant they shared the same nickname: Mi-chan.

Despite the teacher's request, no one spoke to Miyuki. Midori guessed the other students were all too shy. But Midori didn't know the meaning of shy.

One day in English practice Kimura-sensei was having the students talk about the four seasons.

"What you wear in summer?" the teacher said slowly. "What you wear in winter?" Her English was wrapped in a thick blanket of Japanese accent.

Miyuki raised her hand.

"Yes, Miyuki-san?"

"We say, 'What *do* you wear in summer," she said, smiling and in a helpful voice. "What *do* you wear in winter?"

*Why did Kimura-sensei's face drop?* Midori wondered. *Why should she be surprised?* Miyuki was fluent in English and was just trying to help. Midori was glad that the teacher thanked Miyuki and corrected herself.

"Speak some English to me," Midori said to Miyuki afterwards.

Midori couldn't understand a word of what she said, but she was mesmerized by Miyuki's ability and the ease with which she spoke. It sounded more like singing than talking, like someone on Armed Forces Radio, the station for the Americans who lived on the U.S. Army bases in Japan. Midori loved hearing English even at that young age and listened to the radio station for hours, although she couldn't understand a word. She liked hearing the latest hits from America, but the fast-talking disc jockeys, the jingles, and commercials were her favorites. And Miyuki spoke like them.

Midori introduced Miyuki to her best friends, Kaori and Rika. At first they were inhibited, but soon enough everyone seemed to get along. Kaori and Rika acted friendly and asked Miyuki about America. *Isn't it great to add this new girl to the group?* Midori thought. It was fun to have a new friend. She couldn't wait to see Miyuki again.

The next day, Midori met Rika as usual at the corner in front of the convenience store where they always met to walk to school.

"*Ohayo*," Midori said, greeting her with the usual "good morning."

Rika didn't answer as she walked by Midori's side.

*Maybe she didn't hear me*, Midori thought. "*Ohayo*," she said once more.

Again, Rika didn't answer.

Midori tried something else. "Did you understand the math homework last night? It was so hard for me."

This time she did answer, but it was just, "Mmm."

"But my mom finally helped me so I have the right answers if you didn't get them."

Again, she didn't say anything.

"Is something wrong?"

She shrugged.

"What's the matter?"

"Don't talk to me."

"*What?*"

"I said, 'Don't talk to me.'"

"What's going on?"

Rika kept walking alongside Midori, but went silent again. Midori's stomach burned. Why was Rika so out-of-sorts? At the corner where they always met up with Kaori, Midori could see her waiting for the two of them. Maybe she could snap Rika out of her bad mood.

"*Ohayo*," Midori said brightly.

Kaori didn't answer either, but when Rika said, *"Ohayo,"* Kaori responded enthusiastically. *"Ohayo!"* she said. "Did you get the math homework?"

"No! It was so hard," Rika said. "I couldn't get half the answers."

"Yeah, me too." Kaori looked worried. "I'm gonna fail for sure."

"I have the answers," Midori said. "My mom helped me. You can read off my paper."

Without acknowledging her, Rika said, "Did you see *The Best Ten* last night?" It was a popular music show the three of them always watched.

Before Kaori could answer her, Midori blurted out, "I did. Didn't that song—"

Kaori looked right through Midori; she might as well have been invisible. "Yeah, I saw it," she interrupted. "Wasn't Matchy looking so cool?"

"I know!" Rika clapped her hands and they went on talking as if Midori wasn't there.

Midori gave up and let the two girls walk ahead of her as they approached the school. Her heart sank, but she was angry. All she could remember was the previous afternoon when they were laughing and talking with Miyuki on the way home. What had happened between then and this morning? Had she said something to hurt their feelings? Midori couldn't understand what it could be.

When she got to school the only person who would talk to her was Miyuki. Everyone else gave the two girls the cold shoulder. Midori finally realized what was happening and once she figured it out, she couldn't believe how slow she'd been to catch on. She was being bullied for talking to the new girl, the different girl, the girl who didn't fit in. And that was what Midori liked about her—that she was different. But no one else in class wanted to be associated with her.

At lunch Miyuki and Midori ate by themselves at a far corner of the yard. They didn't talk about the other students ignoring them.

"Did you do okay on the math homework?" Midori asked.

"It was kind of hard for me." Miyuki had explained that she was

behind in her studies and had been trying to catch up before she enrolled in school. The classwork in California had not been as ad-
vanced.

"I have all the right answers," Midori said, taking the paper out of
her binder. "My mom helped me."

Miyuki gave Midori a grateful smile. "Thanks, Mi-chan."

"You're welcome, Mi-chan."

They laughed.

"I have a present for you," she said. "From San Francisco. In English an *omiyage* is called a 'souvenir.'"

"Souvenir," Midori repeated. Now her happiness about Miyuki's
gift swelled with the wonderful sound of the word. *Souvenir.* Finally
something good was happening today.

Miyuki handed Midori a small white box. Midori opened it to find
what looked like a little train car.

"It's called a cable car," Miyuki said. "Look. You wind it up and it
plays a song."

She turned the knob a few times and they listened to the pretty
melody.

"Thank you! Thank you, Mi-chan!" Midori said.

After lunch, Midori carefully placed the box with the cable car
inside her book bag. She could hear the noise of the kids in the class-
room but as soon as she and Midori walked in, the class turned silent
except for muffled giggles and phony coughs. Midori glanced at the
blackboard. In big letters was written: MIYUKI-PIG AND MIDORI-PIG
PLAY TOGETHER IN THEIR FILTHY SLUT PIGPEN.

Midori's stomach dropped as she saw the sad expression on
Miyuki's face. She quickly took her seat in the back of the room.

When Kimura-sensei arrived she looked at the blackboard but
gave no indication of what she thought about the message. She said
nothing. Taking the eraser and wiping the board clean, she could
have been erasing a math problem that was no longer relevant. She
didn't seem upset and wasn't interested in finding out who wrote the
hateful words. Midori couldn't concentrate the rest of the afternoon.
Miyuki rushed off by herself when class let out, and Kaori and Rika

didn't wait for Midori. She walked home alone. What could she do? Complain to the teacher? Speak her mind to Kaori and Rika? She decided to tell her parents that night at dinner.

"Maybe you shouldn't be her friend," was the first thing her father said.

Midori couldn't believe what she was hearing. "Why not? I like her."

"She may be a nice girl, but she sounds full of herself, correcting the teacher like that." Mr. Saito took a swig of beer, then let out a satisfied sigh.

"She was just trying to help. She knows English better than the teacher."

"The other students don't like someone who is too different, you know," he said.

"I like her *because* she's different." Midori heard her voice get louder.

"Then you'll have trouble."

"Why?"

"Because that's the way things are. You need to be more cooperative, Midori. Not go your own way all the time." The tone of her father's voice told her this was a fact, not just an opinion that could be debated.

Her mother agreed with him. "Kaori-chan and Rika-chan probably feel bad."

Midori held her arms to her chest and puffed out her cheeks. "Why should they feel bad?"

"Maybe they think you like this girl better than them."

"What about Miyuki-chan? She feels really bad," Midori said.

"She should be in an international school," Mrs. Saito said. "With other *kikoku-shijo*. She would feel more comfortable there."

Midori was stunned at her parents' reaction, shocked that it was so different from hers.

"Don't be so stubborn, Midori," her father said, shaking his head. "You know, that is your problem."

Miyuki did end up transferring to a school for international students. Yes, she was technically Japanese, but she really wasn't Japanese anymore. Midori lost touch with her and gradually regained her friendship with Rika and Kaori. But it was never the same, and when Midori got to high school she made other friends. Rika and Kaori faded away, but she never could forget how they treated her and how they treated Miyuki.

The night before Midori had left for San Francisco with Kevin, she slipped the little cable car into her suitcase hoping it would bring her good luck. And now, as luck would have it, it sure hasn't.

She turns the knob and stares blankly at the little car as it plays its melancholy song. Tears well up in her eyes. When the tune is finished, she tosses the cable car in the desk drawer that holds a Bible, slamming it shut with such force that the lamp on top tips over and falls to the floor.

# 3

RIGHT BEFORE MIDORI FELL ASLEEP THAT NIGHT, SHE HAD BECOME more hopeful in anticipating Shinji's call. But when the phone rings at five-thirty the next morning, she knows it can't be him. It is her cell phone and not the hotel phone. And at that strange hour, it has to be a phone call from Japan.

"*Moshi-moshi?* Midori? Are you okay?"

It's her mother. *Again.*

"Why wouldn't I be okay?"

"Why haven't you called?"

"Mom, it's five-thirty here."

"So?"

"Five-thirty in the morning."

"Oh. Well, I need to know the date for the plane tickets, you know."

Midori's head throbs. "Yeah. The plane tickets." She takes a deep breath. She knows she has to get it over with. "I have, I have some news."

"News?"

"Kevin and I are postponing the wedding." It's the best she can do at five-thirty in the morning, and maybe the best she will ever be able to do.

Her mother's gasp is so loud she might as well be calling from a wind tunnel. *"You're canceling the wedding?"*

"Canceling the wedding?" Midori can hear her father's voice booming in the background.

"No, postponing the wedding. Postponing. Is that Dad?" Of course it's him. Who else speaks in such an annoying tone?

Mrs. Saito tells her husband to be quiet, but Midori still can hear his continuous bellowing.

"We had trouble booking it at that winery in Napa so . . ."

"I still don't understand why you would want to get married at a wine factory."

"It's not a wine factory, Mom. It's a winery. I told you before. But anyway, we can't get a spot there so we have to find a new place. Kevin says it will take time."

"How much time?"

"I hope you didn't buy the tickets yet."

"Midori," she sighs. "That's why I called. I told you I was waiting for you to call."

"Uh-huh."

"So when do you think the wedding will be?"

"Maybe in . . . ," Midori says, pausing. "September."

*"September?* Not until *September?"*

Is she unfamiliar with the word for the ninth month of the year? Had Midori said September instead of *kugatsu?* No, she hadn't been speaking English. "Maybe sooner. I'll let you know when I find out."

"Midori, what happened?" Her father's cranky voice blasts in her ear. "Is the wedding off?"

Midori sighs. "No, Dad. Just postponed. We have to find a new location and it isn't easy. Everything is crowded."

"America is a big country, there must be thousands of places."

"Yes, we'll find one."

"Are you sure you aren't canceling for another reason?"

"It's not a cancellation. Stop worrying. Let me talk to Mom."

"Maybe you should just come home."

Her father's words chill her bones. She might as well be eleven years old again. It's the same voice that had told her to stop being Miyuki's friend, complained about her less-than-stellar grades, and lamented that her teachers were concerned that she was becoming too outspoken in class.

"No," she says, feeling the sweat on her forehead. "I won't be coming home."

"Always so crazy about America. Well, maybe it's not the place for you. Maybe you don't belong there." He snorts. "But then you don't belong here either."

She turns the phone off and throws it on the floor.

Her parents hadn't been happy that she'd gone off with a foreigner, never to return to Japan, but they had been relieved she was finally getting married. Her marital status had been their all-consuming passion for years.

But her father didn't like the fact that she only dated non-Japanese men. And that wasn't something easy to accomplish when you lived in Japan. Kevin had told Midori that if an American psychologist had analyzed her, the conclusion would be that she didn't want to marry her father. Whatever the reason, even as a young person, she was never attracted to Japanese men. In middle school when all her friends were mooning over the current Japanese teen idol, Midori preferred the latest blond from England or America.

Japanese men became even more unappealing as she reached her teens. There just seemed to be no lovable Japanese men around. They didn't want romance—they wanted a mother and a servant. All she had to do was look at her own parents' marriage.

Mrs. Saito was a housewife and Mr. Saito worked for a bank. Instead of calling each other "darling" or "honey," in the endearing way an American couple would, they called each other *okaasan* and *otousan*—mom and dad, just like every other Japanese couple with kids. Mr. Saito expected to order his wife around and she expected it from him. An obedient servant, Midori's mother waited on her husband constantly, treating him like a demanding but helpless infant.

"*Oi, sake!*" he'd bark at her and she'd come running to pour more into his cup. "*Oi, gohan!*" he'd command, thrusting his bowl out, and she'd dutifully take the wooden paddle and scoop up more rice from the rice cooker, refilling it to the brim.

Only once had Midori invited an American guy she dated briefly to her house for dinner. Darryl was an exchange student at her university and wanted to see a "typical" Japanese family. He knew some Japanese and enjoyed trying to understand her parents' conversations. He witnessed her father's incessant barking and her mother running around, but didn't mention anything about that. But what he did say was, "Your mom seems to have an unusual name. I've never heard of it before."

Midori was surprised to hear such a comment. Her mother's name was Fusako Saito, which was nothing out of the ordinary.

"What do you mean?" Midori said.

"Oi. I've never come across a Japanese woman with that name."

And with that Midori burst out laughing as she explained to him that *oi* was the equivalent of "Hey, you." But the more she thought about it, *oi* truly *was* her mother's name. And Midori didn't want it to become hers.

Mr. Saito advised Midori that being a wife and mother was the best thing a woman could do. "It's the natural order of the world," he always said. "It's the way things are supposed to be." When Midori enrolled in cooking classes she let him think she was studying the culinary arts to provide good meals for her eventual Japanese husband. It was an easy way to placate him.

But Midori's own plans and Mr. Saito's plans for her did not gel. When she got to college she became a serial English learner. Not only was she studying it at the university, she constantly hung around language schools taking lessons, and worked at part-time jobs at English schools. When she wasn't studying, she spent time at English "conversation lounges."

Midori frequented them all—Hello Club, Danny Boy, Come On Inn. They weren't bars, but you could drink beer or cocktails and be guaranteed a conversation or two in English with native speakers. Japanese customers had to pay an entry fee and were required to pay stiff prices for drinks. The native English speakers, however, got in free and their drinks were discounted by 50 percent.

Not everyone was cute at the conversation lounges, but the majority of customers were foreign men who had an interest in Japanese women, so it worked out for Midori. She dated a number of gaijin (foreigners), but she had yet to fall in love.

"You're just a conversation lounge yellow cab," her best friend Akina would tease her. A yellow cab referred to a Japanese woman obsessed with gaijin men; she was as easy to ride as a taxi. Midori certainly wouldn't have used that phrase to describe herself, but she had to confess that she was as obsessed with English and foreigners as her parents were about their only daughter becoming a nice Japanese wife to a nice Japanese man.

After Midori graduated from college, her plan was to get a job that would take her to the ideal place—the United States. The place where she could live her life freely and, not to mention, a place full of gaijin men. She thought being an interpreter was a good choice so she attended a private interpretation school to get a certificate. It would be reasonable to think that a person who had spent so much time studying English would be able to pass the test to be an interpreter, but Midori was a hopeless case. She failed three times and spent way too much money and time on the school.

Her next tactic was to become a tour conductor. Surely she could get a job in America helping Japanese tourists see Yosemite, the Golden Gate Bridge, the Grand Canyon. Enrolling in yet another expensive private school, she studied to become an "international tour conductor specialist."

By the time she was twenty-nine, the years had passed and she still hadn't found her ideal man. But just as she was about to earn her tour conductor certificate, she'd met Kevin Newbury.

On their first date Kevin took her to a movie. On their second date they went to a love hotel—it had been impossible to resist him. On their third date Kevin treated her to the fanciest restaurant in Fukuoka—Il Bacio—which was on the top floor of the Seibu Sun Hotel.

Kevin ordered a bottle of Sangiovese—Midori had mentioned it was her favorite Italian red wine and he had actually remembered—and they sat at a candlelit table next to a large picture window displaying a breathtaking view of the twinkling lights of the city. Over a shared dish of exquisitely creamy tiramisu topped with a generous sprinkling of shaved chocolate, Kevin took Midori's hand.

"Midori, you're the most beautiful and sweetest girl I have ever been with."

She blushed. "That is not possible."

Smiling, he said, "I hope this doesn't shock you, but . . ." He reached for something in his pocket.

Midori's heart pounded. This was like something you'd see in a movie. One of those Meg Ryan or Sandra Bullock movies. Was he going to say what Midori thought he was going to say?

He opened a small blue velvet box and showed her its contents: a simple but tasteful diamond ring. "Will you marry me?"

Midori was stunned. Even though this had been her dream, it *was* only their third date. Wasn't it a bit rushed? Later, when she thought back to this moment with benefit of much hindsight, she realized that these circumstances should have made her suspicious, but at the time it didn't even occur to her. Her only concern was that she did not want to appear like a desperate Japanese woman ready to marry the first gaijin who asked, a yellow cab with the motor running and the driver saying, "Jump in!"

Instead she said, "Oh, Kevin! That is so nice. But isn't it a little too soon for this?"

A look of disappointment flashed across his face, but he quickly recovered. "I know it's sudden," he said. "But I hope you will seriously think about it."

The next day she'd met Akina for lunch. Her friend almost

choked on her milk tea when Midori told her what had happened at Il Bacio.

"He did *what?*"

"He asked me to marry him."

"What did you say?"

"I said I had to think about it."

Akina looked as dreamy as Emiko-chan from *Longing to Hug*, albeit before her bubble burst. "Ooh, these gaijin are fast."

"Well, I've dated gaijin before but *this* never happened." Midori leaned toward her. "He said we would live in San Francisco and that I could still work as a tour conductor if I want to. And go to cooking school. Not just stay home and be his wife. It's up to me."

"Wow, really?" Akina gulped. "Have you even slept together?"

"Oh, yes."

She stared at Midori for a moment and then said, "Well?"

"Well, what?" Midori knew what Akina wanted to ask, but she liked to play dumb to tease her.

"How is he?"

"Quite good."

"And he's, um, peeled, right?"

"Yes, of course." Midori tossed back her head as she laughed.

"Why didn't you just say yes?"

"I want to take a little time," Midori said. "I don't want to come off as desperate and I want to get to know him a little better."

About a week after Kevin's proposal, while Midori was eating breakfast at the kitchen table, her mother came in and sat across from her. She held a large brown envelope. Carefully opening it, she pulled out a photograph and set it in Midori's direction next to her cereal bowl.

"He's rather good-looking, don't you think?" she said brightly.

The picture was of a Japanese man who was probably about Midori's age, but his sober expression made him look a good decade older. His eyebrows spread across the bridge of his nose in such a continuous bushy line it would have taken a pair of heavy-duty hedge clippers to tame them. It was a shame that some of this abundant hair couldn't have been transplanted to his head, which was in desperate need of more growth. To top it off, his slight but noticeable overbite made him a viable candidate for a Bugs Bunny look-alike contest.

Midori thought her mother had truly gone out of her mind. Why was she showing her such a thing? "This is what you call good-looking?"

"Well, he's no Hiro Yamada."

Hiro Yamada was the handsome gynecologist on *Longing to Hug*.

"But," she continued, "he looks kind."

"Perhaps."

"His name is Koji Tamasaki," she said, her tone mimicking the high-voiced women on the morning talk shows who pitch exciting new products to eager housewives. "He's pretty high up in Papa's bank." When she wasn't calling her husband *otousan*, she was calling him Papa.

"So?"

"And your father knows his father."

"And?"

"Midori, you're almost thirty and you're nowhere near getting married."

Midori had been so dense that her mother was forced to draw her a picture, or at least *show* her a picture. Mrs. Saito wanted to set her up on an *omiai* with this fellow—a meeting for an arranged marriage.

"Ugh," Midori said. "Mom, you know I hate the thought of an *omiai*." Midori figured this must have been her father's idea. "Can't you tell Dad to just stop?"

"It's not just your father. I'm concerned too. You know what they say about the Christmas cake."

Midori frowned as she placed the photograph in the envelope, pushing it away with such force that it almost slid off the table. In her mother's generation, if a girl wasn't married by the time she was twenty-five, she was considered as stale as a leftover Christmas cake, languishing days after December 25. That kind of thinking was old-fashioned by today's standards, but being twenty-nine and unmarried was nothing to be proud of. Many of her classmates from high school had husbands and children by now. She'd attended her share of weddings. Midori might not have thought much of being a Christmas cake, but concluded that she was edging closer toward becoming a New Year's Eve éclair.

That night when Mr. Saito returned home from work he was actually in a cheery mood. And Midori knew exactly why. "Did your mother show you the photo of Tamasaki-san's son?" he asked.

"Yes."

"So when will we set up the *omiai*?"

"Never," Midori said.

He glared at her. "Why not?"

"He's not my type."

"Not your type? He's one of the top young executives at the bank. And he has his own apartment."

"I *don't* want an *omiai*," Midori said in as firm a voice as she could muster. "If and when I want to get married, I'll find my own husband."

"Well, you haven't found one yet and time is running out."

"Why is time running out?"

"You're almost thirty! Are you going to be an old maid the rest of your life?"

"Why does it matter how old I am? Who cares if I ever get married?" Telling him about Kevin's proposal was out of the question. She'd only hear him complain that Kevin wasn't Japanese. Besides, she wasn't even sure if Kevin was the one for her. It was best to not say anything.

After Midori made it clear she wouldn't budge, her parents didn't mention anything more about an *omiai* with Koji Tamasaki or anyone else. She was happy to again have her life back to herself. She started a new pastry-making class to master the perfect piecrust. She would get to know Kevin a little better, then make a decision. Everything was under control. But soon enough, she reflected later, the straw was about to arrive that would collapse the camel's back.

A month had passed and Mr. Saito's birthday was imminent. Midori's mother decided to plan a celebration for him. Midori was surprised; she couldn't remember the last time one of her parents had a birthday party. But since Mr. Saito was turning sixty, perhaps Midori's mother wanted to do something special. Coincidentally, her mother had arranged for a dinner at Il Bacio, the restaurant where Kevin had proposed.

Midori decided to invite Kevin, thinking it would be a good time for him to meet her parents. She hadn't told them anything about him, let alone the fact that he'd proposed marriage. She'd made mistakes in the past by introducing her parents to boyfriends who ended up not lasting very long, and this time she wanted the timing to be just right.

But before Midori even had a chance to mention this to her parents, Kevin told her he didn't want to go.

"No, Midori," he said. "Let me meet them in a little more informal situation."

"But my father can't get mad at his own birthday party."

"Maybe it will ruin his birthday. I'll meet them some other time."

Midori didn't care whether her father's celebration would be ruined or not, but she accepted the fact that Kevin wouldn't feel comfortable. He wouldn't be there, but Midori decided to bring a picture of the two of them taken at Let's English to the dinner, and introduce him to her parents that way. Then in a few weeks perhaps they would all have lunch together.

On the taxi ride to Il Bacio Mr. and Mrs. Saito were unusually quiet. It sure wasn't a very festive atmosphere. Were they really on their way to a birthday celebration? Midori's father stared out the window while her mother picked at nonexistent lint on her skirt.

"Is something wrong?" Midori said.

"No," her father snapped. "What could be wrong?"

"I don't know," Midori snapped back. After an uncomfortable silence, which seemed to go on forever she finally said, "It's certainly a beautiful night," in hopes of starting a neutral conversation.

Her mother jumped when she spoke, and her father sat with his arms folded as he continued to gaze at the passing traffic. Only the driver responded with, "Yes, isn't it?"

Once they arrived at the hotel there was more uncomfortable si-

lence as they rode the elevator to the top floor. Did some relative die
and she hadn't been informed? It really seemed they were on the way
to a funeral instead of a birthday party. But Midori was happy to be at
Il Bacio again. "You're the most beautiful and sweetest woman I have
ever been with. Will you marry me?" Kevin's words rang pleasantly in
her ears.

Midori and her father sat on a small sofa in the waiting area while
Mrs. Saito conversed with the maître d'. They spoke in such hushed
tones that Midori couldn't hear what they were saying. The dining
room was only half full. Why weren't they seated right away? She
craned her neck to search out the table where she'd sat with Kevin.
The view would be nice again tonight as well.

Finally the maître d' came over and said, "This way, please." Midori and her parents followed him past the main dining room and
down the hall to what looked like a small private banquet room.

"Why aren't we eating in the main room?" Midori whispered to
her mother. "It's only the three of us."

She didn't answer. The host opened the door to let them in. As
Midori walked through the arched entryway, she saw a man and a
woman around her parents' age facing toward her and smiling, sitting
at a small banquet table. The man was balding and dressed in a suit,
while the woman wore her hair up, and tugged at the collar of her
conservative, gray kimono. To the man's left sat a younger man, also
in a business suit. Rising as Midori approached the table, he smiled at
her with oversized teeth that suddenly looked familiar. Midori's neck
stiffened as she realized his identity—Mr. Bushy Hedge, Koji
Tamasaki.

Every drop of moisture in her mouth seemed to dry up when she
discovered she'd been tricked. This was no birthday party. Midori
flashed her eyes toward her mother who gave her a don't-you-dare-
mess-this-up look.

Mr. Tamasaki was talking as Midori sat across from him, his wife,
and son, but she was in such a rage that she couldn't comprehend
what he was saying.

Then she saw her father put on an arrogant smile as he began to speak. His manner was so formal and stiff he might as well have been addressing the emperor.

"We are so very honored that you have come all the way here to meet with us and to consider our daughter Midori," he said, bowing.

Midori knew she should just go along with the show and turn Koji down later. That would have been the rational thing to do. But she was as far from rational as Mount Fuji is from the Golden Gate Bridge. She refused to keep quiet, a trait that never did bode well for her in Japan. Her knees shook, her thighs felt like two bricks. She managed to stand up while her father continued to groan on.

"Excuse me," Midori interrupted him, her voice a croak. "I must apologize to you." Out of the corner of her eye she could see her father's jaw drop. "I had no idea I was coming here to meet you. I should have told my parents first, but . . ."

Koji, his eyes bulging, whipped out a handkerchief from his pocket and sopped up his sweat-soaked forehead. Mrs. Saito waved her chrysanthemum-patterned fan vigorously in front of her face, creating such gale-force winds they would need to be reported on that night's weather forecast.

Opening her purse, Midori pulled much too hard on the snap, causing a lipstick to fly out like a missile. Swishing through the bag with her hand, she finally located the picture of her and Kevin.

"I have already agreed to marry Kevin Newbury," she announced, holding up the photo so everyone could see it, resembling an Olympic judge displaying her score for the ice dancing competition. Midori bowed deeply. "I apologize for causing so much trouble. Excuse me." With that she rushed out of the room.

"Midori!"

She could hear her father's angry voice echoing through her ears as she ran down the hall. The elevator opened as she heard his heavy footsteps. Midori jumped in. Thankfully the door closed right after, nearly catching her skirt. Once the elevator opened to the lobby she stumbled out and rushed to the ladies' room. Bumping into a young woman on her way out, she sputtered a quick, "Excuse me," then flopped onto the couch in the lounge area. Midori grabbed her cell phone from her purse.

"Kevin?" she said when she heard his voice.

"Midori? Are you okay?"

"Kevin. Yes! I will marry you."

# 4

BACK IN HER HOTEL ROOM, RECOVERING FROM HER PARENTS' PHONE call, Midori is now wide-awake. Retrieving her cell phone from the floor, she then opens one of her suitcases and takes out a file folder that holds a large envelope. Yes, Kevin is gone, but she still has her tour conductor specialist certificate. She gazes at her name written in gold lettering and the red seal on the lower left-hand corner. Surely she'd be able to get a job at a Japanese tour company that would sponsor her for a green card, allowing her to live legally in the United States forever. After all, that was what the counselor at the school had told her.

She hums to herself as she pages through the San Francisco phone book and writes the names and addresses of four Japanese tour companies on a pad of paper. She showers, puts on her charcoal-gray business suit, and stops by the concierge desk to pick up a map of San Francisco.

She discovers that three of the offices aren't too far away to walk.

Ichiban Tours and Travel is located in a tall, modern building, but the office itself is small and cramped. In fact, when she walks in she finds herself transported back to Japan, back to Let's English. The desks are arranged facing one another and the ten or so people working all appear to be Japanese. Except for one woman talking on the phone, the place is quiet, a quiet you'd encounter upon entering a church with a congregation in prayer.

"May I help you?" a young woman asks her, speaking in Japanese.

"Yes. My name is Midori Saito. I'd like to speak to the hiring manager."

The girl gives her a blank look and turns around as a man who appears to be about forty comes to the counter where Midori is standing.

"I am Section Chief Kataoka," he says, staring at her as if she has showed up at his costume party without a costume. "May I help you?"

Midori bows. "My name is Midori Saito." She fumbles with her briefcase and takes out the brown envelope holding her certificate. Presenting it to him, she says, "I have a certificate of completion of training from the GoGo World Travel School in Fukuoka as a tour conductor. I have just arrived in San Francisco and I am looking for a job. . . ."

Section Chief Kataoka sucks in his cheeks so that his face now resembles a prune. He puts on his reading glasses and squints, peering at the certificate with the concentration of a scientist examining a specimen under a microscope. He hands it back to her. Taking off his glasses, he shakes his head. "We don't have any jobs here," he says, his voice gruff and with a tone that makes her think she should have already known this.

Both his response and his abruptness shock her as she wobbles on her high heels.

"No jobs at all?"

"No."

"Oh, I see," Midori says, placing her certificate back in the envelope. Her forehead turns moist, her face crimson. "Thank you and sorry to have bothered you," is all she can bring herself to say. The young woman glares at her as if she suspects Midori really had laced Kevin's coffee with cyanide.

She's hopeful that Fuji Tours, which is several blocks away, will bring her better luck. But when she reaches the building and peruses the directory, she isn't able to find a listing for a company with that name.

This is not looking good. Midori tries to put on a confident air as she moves on to the next agency, but a queasiness is overtaking her stomach, one that isn't related to the other night's dessert orgy.

At least Genki Travel has an office. And it's open. A friendly-looking Japanese woman greets Midori in Japanese from her seat at the reception desk. The office is light and airy, the travel posters bright and cheerful. The weight lifts from Midori's shoulders. She feels good about this place.

Midori figures she should just get to the point. "My name is Midori Saito and I'm wondering if you have any openings for tour conductors? I have a certificate from GoGo World Travel School in Fukuoka. . . ."

"Oh, I'm sorry, Saito-san," the woman says, her eyes wide. "But we do not have any openings."

Midori's face falls. "Do you know of any other tour companies I could try?" She figures she should at least take advantage of the woman's friendliness.

"Well," she says slowly. "To tell you the truth, in the past few years Japanese tourism here has gone way down. Young Japanese are traveling more on their own instead of on tours, and people in general are concerned about terrorism and such. It's not expected to get much better."

"Oh, I see."

"Do you have a green card?"

"Um, no. I thought I could get one by working at a company. . . ."

"That isn't really possible, I'm afraid. You would need to have a working visa or green card to work here, if there were any openings. And you would also need experience in the field. We wouldn't accept just a certificate." The woman gives Midori a sympathetic look. "I'm sorry, Saito-san, that I can't be of further help. Good luck."

Midori thanks the woman and tries as hard as she can to steady her quivering lower lip, but she can feel the tears on her cheeks. Why bother to try anymore? She clutches her map so tightly she's crumpling it.

Returning to her hotel room, she kicks off her high heels, letting them fly across the room. As she flops on the bed she notices the blinking light on the phone. A message. It must be from Shinji. It is.

"Saito-san? If you have some free time around five o'clock, can you come meet me at my office? There's something I want to talk to you about."

The rest of the message explains the directions to Sawyer & Jones and his phone number there. She immediately calls him back, but gets his voice mail. "Yes, I will see you at five o'clock today."

What will he have to say to her? Her heart pounds as she charts the course to his office on her severely wrinkled map. It's located not too far from her hotel, a decent walk.

After changing her clothes and taking a nap, she sets out a couple of hours early. As she walks down the steep hill, she finds herself in Chinatown. It's like a miniature version of Hong Kong, where she'd visited long ago. She can understand some of the Chinese characters in the shop signs. The middle-aged Chinese ladies are adorned in bizarre fashion combinations of baggy plaid pants and bulky flowered jackets as they clomp along in oversized athletic shoes, grasping plastic bags filled with groceries. They smile and shout to one another in words Midori can't begin to understand. She wonders how they got here, if they are legal or illegal or somewhere in between.

As the sidewalks level out, she's now left Chinatown and in the distance she can see a long building in front of the Bay Bridge. A tall, ornate clock tower rises above the structure like an elegant single candle atop a birthday cake. The bridge isn't as pretty as the Golden Gate she remembers from the tour she and Akina took of San Francisco when they were twenty-two. She thinks of the thrill she felt at dreaming she might return here someday. She remembers the young Japanese woman who had led that tour, proudly holding her flag— something Midori, it seems, won't be privileged to do.

As she gets closer to the building she can make out a sign saying WELCOME TO THE FERRY PLAZA FARMERS MARKET. Looking at her map and locating the Ferry Building she can tell that Shinji's office isn't too far from here. She still has plenty of time before she's to meet him.

Shoppers bustle around stands displaying red, green, and orange tomatoes; heads of lettuce; herbs; melons; and what look like Japanese *mikan*, but are called "tangerines." The people selling the fruits and vegetables don't look like farmers to Midori. The atmosphere is more subdued than marketplaces in Japan. There are no vendors with bullhorns shouting their *"Irrashai! Irrashai!"* welcomes as shoppers scramble for bargains.

Midori spies a stand selling jars of specialty mustards with odd flavors—aioli horseradish, smoked pomegranate, even sake and wasabi. As she picks up a jar of pineapple cilantro, out of the corner of her eye she notices a short, dark-haired woman at another stand staring at her. She wears white tennis shoes, thick nylon stockings, a black skirt, and is bundled up in a big, brown, quilted coat. She starts to stuff a plastic bag with fuzzy peaches that look as soft as a newborn baby's head, but then she stops once more to look at Midori.

Who *is* she? And how could anyone look familiar in a place where Midori has been not even two weeks? But a moment later she realizes who the woman is. It's Consuelo, the Newburys' maid.

Midori's heart seems to jump into her throat as she scans the crowd for Kevin or his mother. But how stupid is that? There's no way they would be accompanying the housekeeper on a shopping trip. Midori's first instinct is to run and hide. She doesn't want to talk to Consuelo. And she doesn't want to hear any further news about Kevin. But now the woman is walking toward her. It's too late to run away now. She looks friendly, though, with a small smile on her face.

"Señorita Saito," she says.

"Yes. Hello, Consuelo. How are you?" Midori says, wondering what they will possibly be able to talk about in their limited English.

Consuelo puts her hand on Midori's arm. "Very sorry," she says, with a sympathetic frown, her brown eyes turned downward. "Kevin. Bad man. Bad man." She shakes her head.

Yes, he certainly is a bad man. That's perfect English. Midori smiles and nods. "Yes. Thank you, Consuelo."

The woman nods in return and, giving Midori a wave, goes back to her shopping at the peach stand.

Midori's heart lifts. How nice it is to hear her words.

She walks inside the building with the clock tower, which is crowded with shops and restaurants. There are stores selling fresh breads, foreign teas, colorful pastas, exotic mushrooms—anything you can think of. But one shop immediately catches her eye. La Petite Pâtisserie with its pink-and-white-checked awning sits between a cheese shop and a wine store. The cakes, cookies, and pies in the display case ooze charm along with a meticulous design Midori can well appreciate.

It's as if her dessert orgy is a distant memory. Midori nearly falls into a trance. There are marzipan petit fours topped with delicate spring flowers and jumbo-sized cookies made out of lavender shortbread. The tarts are smothered with raspberries, peaches, and blueberries, and the chocolate-ginger cupcakes are topped with whipped white frosting that looks as delicate as meringue. Thank goodness she has thought to bring her camera. She snaps some photos, then buys some samples, tucking a printed take-out menu into her purse.

Finding a bench outside on the opposite side of the building from the farmers' market she takes in the view overlooking the bay while nibbling on her pastries. The marzipan in the petit fours has such an intense flavor that it must have a high almond-to-sugar ratio. Midori takes a deep breath as she inhales the fragrance. Why would anyone need to sniff cocaine when there's marzipan in the world?

A ferryboat sounds its horn. The seagulls flying overhead seem to answer back with their screeching cries. Midori sits quietly on the bench; the sweets and thinking of Consuelo's words give her mood a much-needed boost. She thinks about Shinji. She tries not to think about Kevin, her parents, the tour companies, or her future. The wind seems to die down and she can feel the sun warming her face.

*Splat.*

Something lands with the precision of a dart on a bull's-eye on her left shoulder. Something soft. Something wet. Twisting her neck, she attempts to look. A puddle of white-and-brown goop now drips on her coat, sticking to the strands of her hair. A seagull has insisted on providing her with a unique souvenir. She gathers her pastry bag and purse and goes off to find the nearest restroom, where she vigorously scrubs the poop with paper towels as best she can. First raspberry mousse cake. Now seagull shit. Her mind returns to thoughts of Kevin—the bad man. He's probably the one who had sent that bird, a carrier seagull with a stinky message.


Sawyer & Jones Advertising is on the twenty-second floor of a building forty-five stories high.

The reception area is fancy, much fancier than the tour companies from this morning and about as big as the whole of Let's English. The plush couches are plump and white, and a gleaming silver-lettered sign reading SAWYER & JONES ADVERTISING seems to almost jump off the wall. Next to it are framed certificates affixed with gold seals and ribbons that appear to be prestigious awards.

The receptionist looks like a twenty-year-old version of Kimberley Hobbs, with blond curls and a tight purple top showing off her ample breasts. They remind Midori of the cantaloupes she saw at the farmers' market.

"May I help you?"

"I want to meet Shinji Nishimura," Midori says. "I mean, *Sean* Nishimura."

Not too long after she sinks into the sofa, Shinji arrives.

"Thanks, Roxanne," he says to the receptionist. Then, speaking in Japanese and giving Midori a warm smile, he says, "Saito-san, nice to see you again. You found the office okay?"

"Yes. Thank you for your easy directions." Midori is glad to see him. Dressed in a crisp, striped button-down shirt with no tie and again in black jeans, he looks cool and relaxed, not as if he's at work. Kind of, well, *American*. Midori can't help but envy how comfortable and established he appears, straddling Japanese and English with ease, and enjoying an important position at a top firm.

Shinji brings Midori to a spacious cubicle. "Have a seat."

As soon as she sits down, the phone rings.

Shinji takes the call. "Yeah, okay." He turns toward her. "Saito-san, I'm sorry but I have to do something. Can you wait here just a minute?"

"Of course. I'm sorry to bother you when you're so busy."

"Don't worry about it."

Midori takes out a notebook from her bag. She hopes Shinji will give her some kind of information she can write down. She taps her foot, gazing around his cubicle. At Let's English, employees weren't allowed to keep personal items on their desks, but in addition to a computer with a huge display screen, Shinji's cubicle bursts with photographs, toys, and knickknacks, mostly having to do with outer space. A mobile of shiny, metallic moons and stars hangs from the ceiling, moving in the breeze provided by the air-conditioning. Photos of the moon in various phases and eclipses are tacked up on the walls. A miniature toy telescope sits on one corner of the desk.

Other pictures depict scenes from office parties, with red-faced people making funny faces at the camera. Another photo shows Shinji in the middle of two pretty blond women, one kissing his cheek. He looks half-happy and half-embarrassed, as if he weren't used to that kind of attention. Another picture is of him standing with his arm around a Caucasian woman with long, tan-colored hair. They're wearing shorts, tank tops, and sunglasses. The trees and mountains in the background make it look as though they were on summer vacation.

Midori pulls a few strands of her hair toward her nose. Unfortunately, they still smell vaguely of seagull poop. She nervously eyes her watch. But what is her hurry? To rush back to an empty hotel room?

Glancing toward the opposite cubicle wall, she spies another picture. She puts her hand over her mouth, trying to stifle a gasp. She hopes no one heard her. It's a photo of Shinji with Kevin. *Kevin the bad man.* Both are grinning and holding *masu*—square, wooden sake cups—in a toast to the camera. They look to be at a sushi bar—Midori can see the chef in the background wearing a blue-and-white bandana tied around his head. Midori's stomach turns upside down and it isn't due to the pastries from La Petite Pâtisserie. Her eyes fixate on Kevin's red cheeks, the same red cheeks that were on display when Kimberley Hobbs came sashaying into their engagement party on her way to ruining Midori's life. She can't stop staring at the photo, her anger rising. Just then Shinji returns.

"Sorry to keep you waiting," he says. Then he looks worried. "Is everything okay?"

Does her upset show on her face? How embarrassing. Midori is about to answer that she's all right when Shinji suddenly notices the picture of Kevin. He pulls it from the bulletin board and promptly rips it up in little pieces, depositing them in the garbage can under the desk. "I'm sorry, Saito-san. I should have noticed that." His eyes are warm, concerned.

Midori can't believe what he's done. "You didn't have to do that," she says, but she's so grateful that he did.

Shinji doesn't respond but smiles, looking at her notebook. "Did you plan to take notes or something?"

"I thought maybe you were going to give me some information, but . . ." Midori's face turns red as she fumbles with the notebook, dropping her pen on the floor.

Shinji grins as he picks it up and hands it to her.

"Thank you for calling me back so quickly," Midori says.

"I called you because I have an idea, but I don't know what you'll think about it."

His relaxed manner puts her somewhat at ease, but she still feels nervous. She doesn't know him, but she has to rely on him. And that makes her uncomfortable. "Idea?"

"I live in a two-bedroom apartment in Pacific Heights. And I just kicked my roommate out last week."

"You kicked your roommate out?"

"Yeah, he was too messy. I mean, I'm not weird or anything, but somehow he had a different attitude about cleanliness than I do." He pauses for a moment to collect his thoughts. "He didn't always pay the rent on time. And he was always forgetting to take off his shoes when he came in the house. I don't care about much else, but I don't like to have people wear shoes inside. Old habits die hard."

"I see." It had been strange to wear shoes in the house at Kevin's parents'; she found herself always taking hers off and putting on slippers.

"Anyway, now I need a roommate and you need a place to stay."

"Yes . . ."

"So I thought maybe you might want to rent the room in my apartment."

Midori stares at him. Did he really ask her to move in with him?

"Of course, it would be a roommate situation," he goes on. "I'd give you complete privacy. I'm busy a lot of the time and I don't eat at home very much. And I stay at my girlfriend's place sometimes." He leans forward in his chair. "If you're interested, all I ask is you pay the rent on time, and be neat. Your business would be none of my business and vice versa."

Midori is so shocked that she can't speak. She closes her mouth when she realizes it must be hanging open like a panting dog's on a hot summer afternoon.

Shinji looks worried again. "Are you all right? I'm sorry if I offended you with this plan."

"No, I'm not offended." Midori puts her hand on her chest. "I'm just so, so surprised that . . ." She knows she must look idiotic to him, but it's not something she would expect to happen in Japan. Yet maybe in America this is a common occurrence.

"Well, it sounds like it would suit both our needs, right?"

"Yes." She bows her head. "I only wanted some advice from you. I never expected something like this."

He laughs as he leans back in his chair so that it rests up against the desk. "Saito-san, you look like you're going to die."

There's only a slight teasing in his voice and the tone is friendly instead of condescending or showing irritation. She likes the comfortable feeling she has with him.

They talk about the rent and Midori explains to him that she has a savings account and that she hopes she can get some kind of job soon. She doesn't mention the account's pitiful balance and doesn't mention her bad luck that morning with the tour companies. Shinji doesn't appear to be too worried about money, though it sticks in her head that he mentioned that the previous roommate was often late with the rent.

Concerning Midori's job prospects, Shinji sounds like the friendly woman at Genki Travel. "It's going to be hard," he says. "Because you can't legally work here."

She nods. "I'll try to figure out something."

"Well, some people work 'under the table.'" He says the last phrase in English.

"On the table?"

"Under the table. It means their employer just pays them cash. I've heard sometimes people can work at restaurants that way. It's illegal, but . . ." He smiles. "Anyway . . ."

Midori lowers her head again. "Thank you so much, Nishimura-san. I would like to take you up on your offer."

"Great. When do you want to move in?"

"Tonight."

# 5

A LARGE TELESCOPE SITTING GRANDLY IN THE LIVING ROOM IS THE FIRST thing Midori notices when she walks into Shinji's apartment. It's positioned directly in front of the expansive picture window overlooking the jutting rooftops of Pacific Heights. She remembers the photos of the moon and the outer space toys on Shinji's desk at his office.

"You like to look at the moon, don't you?"

He smiles. "I'm kind of an amateur astronomer."

Photographs on the walls show the different phases of the moon, like the pictures tacked up in his cubicle. "Did you take those?" she asks, gazing at them.

"Yeah," he says. "It's easy to attach a digital camera to the telescope. Tonight's not a very clear night but when it's nicer I'll let you look if you want."

"Thanks. I'd like to."

Midori thinks of the autumn harvest moon festival in Japan. Her mother would always put out a vase filled with pampas grass and make rice dumplings as an offering to ensure a good harvest. Midori's parents, of course, were far from being farmers, but Mrs. Saito's grandparents had owned a peach farm near the Japan Sea, and the harvest moon festival brought back pleasant memories. Her mother liked the moon so much that she collected figurines of rabbits pounding rice cakes. Midori knew that Americans thought the craters of the moon looked like the face of a person, which they called "the man in the moon." But as hard as she looked she couldn't see a man, she only saw a rabbit making rice cakes.

Shinji helps wheel Midori's suitcases to her room. "Here it is," he says. "I hope you'll feel comfortable."

He explained that when he'd moved into this apartment three years ago there had already been some furniture. The room has a single bed, a chest of drawers, a small closet, and a side table. The floor is wood, with no carpet. Any messiness from the past roommate has been obliterated. Everything is neat and clean like a room in a model home.

"It's perfect," she says. And it is. Her own room in an apartment with a roommate. It's not something most young women in Japan can afford to do. They're stuck living with their parents until they get married, or make their escape by some other route.

"I'm glad you like it. And over here is the kitchen."

The stocky refrigerator is nearly the size of a small car, and the stove is almost as big as the one in the kitchen at Kevin's parents' house. There's a white wooden table surrounded by four matching chairs, a generous number of cabinets, and a closet pantry. A small portable television sits on the yellow-tiled counter next to a microwave.

"Go ahead and buy any food you want for yourself," he says. "I'm not home that much."

"Where's the market?"

"There's a grocery store on California Street, off Fillmore."

"Can you show me on this?" Midori digs out the map from inside her purse.

Shinji laughs. "This is kind of a mess, isn't it?"

The map is now beyond decrepit from Midori crumpling it in frustration during her own ill-fated tour of Japanese tour companies.

"Actually, I think I have one." Shinji leaves the room and quickly returns with a crisp map of the city that looks like it has never been unfolded until now. Spreading it out on the kitchen table he begins circling landmarks with a pen. "Here's where the market is," he says. "And we're not too far from Japantown if you want to buy Japanese food."

"Is that where you shop?"

"No way," he says. "I don't buy Japanese food to have in the house. And I never go to Japantown unless my girlfriend drags me there."

"Your girlfriend likes Japanese food?"

He smiles, nodding. Suddenly his cell phone rings with a tune Midori doesn't recognize. "Yeah, I'll be there soon," he says in English. "Uh-huh. Bye." He gives Midori a smile. "And that was her."

"Speak the devil," Midori says in English. Shinji laughs; it must be the correct idiomatic expression.

"There's a TV here and in the living room. Use them whenever you like. There's a station with Japanese programming. I think it's mainly on the weekend. I've never watched it. I can ask my girlfriend about the details, if you're interested."

"She watches Japanese TV shows?"

He rolls his eyes. "Yeah. She's addicted to all things Japanese." He gives Midori a friendly smile. "But I suggest you watch shows in English. It's good practice for you."

Midori nods in agreement.

Shinji drums his fingers on the kitchen table. "So I guess I'll leave you to your unpacking. Your house key and the key to the mailbox are here on the counter. I'll be staying at Tracy's—that's my girlfriend, I'll be staying at her place tonight. Do you need anything before I go?"

His girlfriend Tracy. Is this the woman in the picture in his cubicle? Does Shinji only date American women? American women who like Japanese things? "No, I'll be fine. Go ahead. Thanks again."

"You have my cell phone number and my work number, right? So don't hesitate to call if you need any help. I'm not home much, but I'm sure we'll run into each other sometimes. Feel free to use any of the kitchen stuff."

"Thank you, Shinji-san." She smiles—she is glad for all his help, but wishes he weren't running off so soon.

After he leaves she returns to her room. Flopping on the bed, she stares at the dark wooden plank beams attached to the ceiling. She imagines Shinji kissing the woman with the long, tan-colored hair who had been in the picture tacked up in his cubicle. What had he said at the engagement party? Oh, yeah. That it was a long story, how he got to the United States. Midori's is a short story: Girl meets fake prince; girl escapes forced marriage meeting; girl arrives in gaijinland; girl gets dumped.

The ceiling has turned into a movie screen; the only thing missing is a tub of popcorn. Shinji and Kevin are at the sushi bar—it's the scene from the picture Shinji had ripped up. Does he hate Kevin now as much as she does?

She must be going crazy, to lie on her bed, thinking all these weird thoughts and watching imaginary films on ceilings. But even if you know you're crazy, it's best to pretend that you're of sound mind, rational. Midori decides to inspect the rest of the apartment.

Shinji's bedroom is next to hers. How often does he sleep here? Does Tracy ever spend the night in his room? The door isn't shut. She knows she should respect Shinji's privacy and not be a snoop. But she walks in anyway, first on her tiptoes, as if that somehow makes it less intrusive.

His large double bed is neatly made, covered with a gray-and-white duvet. A pile of magazines called *Sky and Telescope* are stacked neatly on a side table next to the bed topped with a silver lamp in the shape of a rocket ship. The floor in his room is also hardwood, but there's a small red-and-black throw rug with white fringe. On a sleek metal desk sits a computer and a radio, a stack of bills marked paid, and a few credit card receipts, mainly from computer stores. There's a closet with sliding doors and a bureau. There aren't any toys or knick-knacks like she'd seen on his desk at work, perhaps because he doesn't spend much time here.

Everything looks normal, in order. But something that doesn't quite fit, sitting in the corner of the room, catches her eye. Atop a small wooden pedestal sits a pair of athletic shoes. But they aren't an ordinary pair of shoes. They're made of metal. Bronzed.

Midori had heard of people turning baby shoes into bronze to keep as a childhood memento. And her mother had saved imprints of her hands from when she was five years old and had hung them on the wall next to photographs of her grandparents. But these shoes aren't baby shoes; they're the size Shinji probably wears. They're obviously something special, to be enshrined like this. Had Shinji won some kind of athletic event wearing these shoes? Although she barely knows him, somehow she doesn't think he's the type to show off his achievements. He doesn't even strike her as particularly athletic, although he's in good shape. And there aren't any trophies or medals in his room. But what else could it be?

Midori jumps when she hears the noise of a door opening, and flies out of the room. It certainly wouldn't make a good impression if Shinji caught her sticking her nose in his business. He might kick her out like his last roommate. Not only would she have been dumped by her fiancé, but also dumped by a platonic roommate who was just trying to help her. Then she'd surely be hungover. No, that's not it. No, she'd be hung out to dry.

She's frozen as she stands in the entryway to her room. The front door remains shut; the noise must have come from the hallway outside. She puts her hand on her chest, sighing with relief.

She looks at her watch. It's early afternoon in Japan. She decides to call her friend Akina.

"You have to be joking—it can't be true!" is her reaction when she hears the sad tale of Midori Saito and the Bad Man.

"It's pathetic, isn't it?" Midori says.

"Mi-chan, it's so horrible. So when are you coming home?"

"Coming home? I'm not coming home."

"But you said you can't work or go to school without having the right status. So what can you do?"

"Well, I did manage to find a place to stay." She explains to Akina about Shinji, the guardian angel.

"At least you got something out of Kevin—his friend has been nice to you. But how are you going to pay your rent if you can't work?"

"I'll just have to figure it out."

"I'm sorry to say this, Mi-chan, but maybe you'll just *have* to come back home."

"No! Anything is better than going back to Japan."

"Of course you're right. You don't want to be in my shoes." Akina pauses, then her voice becomes strained. "My boss keeps asking me when I'm going to quit and get married. It's obvious they want some younger, *pichi-pichi* office lady instead of a thirty-one-year-old bag like me."

Midori laughs in sympathy; she knows the scenario all too well and doesn't envy Akina one bit. But at least she has a boyfriend. "So how's it going with Yuichi?"

"Arghh! Don't ask! He's *so* immature, and so *not* husband material." She snorts. "Not that he's asked or anything."

"Still addicted to video games?"

"It's getting worse, if you can believe it. And he's still only working part time at 7-Eleven. He says he could never survive a rigid salaryman life, even if he could get such a job."

"I guess you can't really blame him in some ways, though."

"I know. What choice does anyone really have these days with this kind of economy? But I just wish he'd get a full-time job. You know, maybe a trade. He loves to eat bread so I thought maybe he'd want to be a baker. But he hates getting up early." Her sigh is heavy. "But why should he change? He's got a comfortable life; his mother does everything for him."

"Poor Akina-chan."

"No, poor Mi-chan! I'm so sorry for you. Do you think you can find someone else to marry so you can get a green card?"

"That would be ideal, but I want to fall in love. Is that too much to ask? I don't want to marry someone just so I can be legal. But I'm not sure how I'll even meet someone."

"Yeah, there sure aren't any English conversation lounges in San Francisco."

Midori laughs but it's the kind of laugh that could dissolve into tears at any moment.

"Don't worry, Mi-chan. Things will work out. *Gambatte!* Do your best."

Midori can't quite get used to the idea of sharing a washer and dryer with the other three apartments in Shinji's building, but there's not much she can do about it. It's not common in Japan since each family usually has its own. On the other hand, this washer and dryer are about twice the size of the ones at her parents' house. She knows it's silly, but as Shinji has said before, old habits die hard.

The laundry room is in the basement. It's dark and dank, not the kind of place you'd want to spend a lot of time. Midori opens the lid of the washer to see a pile of wet clothes. Did someone forget they were doing their laundry? Or are they just lazy? Ugh! It's so rude to leave your clothes for the next person to see.

Midori doesn't want to wait to do her washing so she begins to take the clothes out of the washer, then places them into the dryer, holding each one with the tips of her fingers, as if they'd been sitting in a garbage can instead of a washing machine. There are T-shirts, briefs, socks—all men's things. There don't seem to be any women's clothes.

"Oh, sorry!"

It's a man's voice. She turns around to see a guy standing in the doorway who looks to be in his thirties with brownish blond hair, wearing a plaid shirt hanging over torn jeans. Normally she would think this looks sloppy, but because the man is so good-looking, his ensemble comes off as fashionable, cool. He grins. She quickly notices his eyes are blue.

"Sorry about that. Let me get this stuff out of your way."

"Thank you." Suddenly this laundry doesn't seem so offensive.

"I'm Graham," he says, shutting the dryer door and pressing the Start button. "Graham Striker."

"Midori Saito."

They shake hands.

"Hey, Midori, nice to meet you. Didn't you just move in?"

"Yes."

"You're the wife of the guy in number three, right?"

"*Wife?* No, no, no. Not a wife. Just roommate. Roommate."

Graham laughs. "Oh, sorry. My mistake. Where did you move from?"

"Japan."

"Wow, that's a pretty long way. So what do you do?"

Midori gives him a quizzical look. "Doing laundry."

He laughs again. "No, I mean your job. What's your job?"

"Job?" She doesn't want to tell him that she's employed at absolutely nothing. That makes her a worse slacker than Akina's boyfriend. She might as well say what she would like to do. "Um, I am pastry chef."

"Wow. Really? Where do you work?"

"Restaurant."

"Yeah? Which one?"

She likes that he's continuing the conversation, but it also means she has to lie even more. "Oh, just small one. What is job for you?"

He scratches his head. "I'm a cook."

A cook? How stupid she looks now that she's lied about being a pastry chef. "Oh, that is nice." She turns to put her clothes in the washer.

"Yeah, I work at Lupine over on Hyde Street. You know, on the cable car line."

Midori nods even though she doesn't know what he's talking about. He looks friendly still, but at this point he must think she's lost her nuts. Or, rather, her marbles. "Which apartment you are living?" she asks.

"I'm in number one."

"Number one. That is best." She laughs but knows her joke is pitiful.

"Maybe so. Well, nice to meet you," he says. "See you again."

"I like that."

Maybe her luck is beginning to turn. Graham the cook. Here she was just telling Akina how she thought it would be so difficult to meet someone and now a guy just appears, as if conjured by a fairy godmother. And he wasn't wearing a wedding ring. And he didn't have any women's clothes in his laundry.

They'll fall in love and get married, then open a restaurant together. She'll say they'll call it Graham's, but he'll insist on calling it Midori's. After the grand opening, they get nothing but four-star reviews. A little while later they have a baby. A girl they name Gwyneth—no—Reese. The three of them pose for a portrait, all wearing their white cotton chef's clothes. Baby Reese holds a whisk in her cute, fat, little hand; a puffy white hat perched on her head.

The picture-perfect all-American family.

# 6

"UNDER THE TABLE."

Midori repeats the phrase to herself as she walks down Fillmore Street toward Japantown, passing through several blocks of upscale boutiques, restaurants, and coffeehouses. People glamorous enough to be in magazine ads shop and walk their golden retrievers and Labradors, their cell phones attached to their ears like an additional body part.

The plan is to find a Japanese restaurant where Midori can work as a waitress and where they won't mind her shameful illegal status. She's never worked as a waitress before, but that's not going to stop her. It's always best to be optimistic. And how difficult can it be? She's taken lots of cooking classes—both Western and Japanese. She understands food and restaurants. And, anyway, being a waitress isn't her end goal. She pictures herself quickly being promoted to line cook, then to master chef. Once her English improves she'll switch to a Western restaurant, become an assistant to the pastry chef, then a chef in her own right. Then her lie to Graham will actually be true. She'll design desserts that rival those of the Fairmont Hotel's room service, La Petite Pâtisserie at the Ferry Building, and anything else in her pastry album. There'll even be an article in one of those Japanese women's magazines for ladies over thirty, about Midori Saito, a girl who survived being dumped in the United States and who became a top pastry chef at a restaurant she owns with her husband, Graham.

As she approaches the intersection of Fillmore and Post she sees a group of buildings that make up the Japan Center. She walks into the first Japanese restaurant she sees—Sumida-ya. It's almost eleven-thirty and already there are lunchtime customers.

A middle-aged Asian lady stacks menus behind a small podium.

"Excuse me," Midori says in English, not wanting to assume the woman is Japanese.

"Table for one?"

"No, thank you. I'm sorry. Do you have any waitress job?"

"Waitress job?" The woman looks Midori up and down, as if she's unsure whether her clothes fit properly.

"Yes."

"You have green card?"

"No."

She shakes her head firmly and goes back to her menu stacking.

"No 'under the table'?"

"*What?*"

The woman's contorted expression makes her look as though she's been forced to eat something unpleasant, but is too polite to spit it out. Obviously it's not the right thing to say. Midori is careful not to utter that term again, but the story is the same at the next four restaurants she tries. Just like at the tour companies, no one is willing to hire her without a green card.

Despite the disappointing turn of events, Midori still has an appetite, but is too embarrassed to eat lunch at any of the restaurants where she'd inquired. And it's better to save money anyway since it looks as though a job is not going to materialize any time soon. Instead she wanders into a Japanese grocery store and buys a small package of sushi. As she walks out she notices an expansive bulletin board that takes up the whole wall, bulging with ads for babysitters, Japanese lessons, and motorcycles for sale.

Most of the ads are written in Japanese but there are a few in English. Teach me Japanese, one says. But how could she possibly explain Japanese to Americans? She can't even explain it in Japanese. And she's never taught anything before. Even the teachers at Let's English were required to have a four-year English degree.

Another ad written in English is for a housekeeper, a person who'll clean and prepare meals. Just like Consuelo. Midori doesn't want to be someone's maid, but it might be the kind of job where they wouldn't ask if you had a green card. Does Consuelo have one? And how much money would Midori's mother earn for waiting on her father if he'd hired her instead of married her?

Out of the corner of her eye she can see an Asian woman also perusing the ads. It's obvious the woman is staring at her, but Midori tries to act like she doesn't notice.

"Are you looking for work?" The woman speaks to her in Japanese.

Does she look that desperate? Couldn't she be looking to buy a motorcycle?

"Yes," Midori says, but in the next instant wonders why she feels the need to be honest with a stranger.

The woman appears to be in her forties. With her tight jeans and red chunky-heeled sandals, her legs resemble two bamboo stalks. Her black tank top has the words YES, I AM A MODEL emblazoned across her chest in gold glitter. She doesn't look like a model. For one thing, she's heavily freckled, and her eyelashes seem to be coated with automobile oil instead of mascara. Her long black hair is a mass of split ends, permed wavy and streaked with auburn. Who does she look like? Ah! She looks like Namie-san on *Longing to Hug*. After her divorce from debonair gynecologist Hiro Yamada, poor Namie had been forced to work as a "masseuse" at a questionable bathhouse to make ends meet.

"Do you know the Miki Lounge?" the woman asks.

"No."

She turns and points toward the corner. "It's right across the street. It's a bar with karaoke. Mostly Japanese clients. They need hostesses." She raises her eyebrows. "And," she says in a low voice, "you don't have to be legal."

"Oh, really?" Midori says, trying not to be rude, but thinking this woman is a bit strange to be talking to her all of a sudden, and a bit psychic for correctly guessing that she's fresh off the illegal alien boat. It's as if Midori is wearing a shirt proclaiming, YES, I AM AN ILLEGAL ALIEN.

"If you're interested, come by any evening after six and ask for Taffy."

Taffy. Isn't that a type of stretchy candy?

The woman takes out a pack of cigarettes from her purse and offers one to Midori, who firmly shakes her head no.

"I'm Crystal," she says, lighting up and taking a long drag.

"Midori." Midori can tell Crystal is from Japan by her speech and her mannerisms. This can't be her real name. It's like Shinji "Sean" Nishimura. Taffy is no doubt Japanese as well.

As Crystal puffs on her cigarette she says her good-bye with, "*J'ya, ne*," and saunters away, teetering gingerly on her heels like a highly skilled stilt walker.

A bar hostess. Not a very respectable position, but something apparently one can do without a green card. And it sounds better than being a maid.

After eating her sushi and mulling over the prospect of working as a bar hostess, Midori is still not satisfied. A good pastry is in order. She walks back up Fillmore Street and stops in a café called My Sweet Heart that she noticed on her walk to Japantown. A piece of Hippodrome sponge cake—bright orangey red, filled with apricot preserves, sliced almonds, and cream, and covered in a light apricot glaze—calls out to her. After taking a photo, she lets the sweet, fruity flavor swirl in her mouth.

"Are you a restaurant critic?" asks an elderly lady sitting at the table next to hers.

Midori's cheeks turn warm. "No. I just take a picture of a beautiful pastry."

The lady smiles and returns to her coffee.

Midori composes her notes, and then begins to write a grocery list. She stops at the market and buys as many baking staples as can fit in one bag. Butter. Eggs. Sugar. Flour. Milk. Baking chocolate. Shinji had hardly anything in the refrigerator or the cupboards. On the way to the market she'd seen a kitchen supply store. She'll have to return there and buy some cake pans, a spatula, an electric mixer—she's sure Shinji doesn't have any of these in the house.

It's a relief to finally get home and dump the heavy grocery bag on the kitchen table. The room feels homey, the sun pouring through the window; it's not even too much to expect a pair of Disney cartoon bluebirds to perch on the sill and start singing. Midori gazes at the oven, the sink, the cupboards. She finally has her own kitchen, and one that's three times the size of the kitchen at her parents' house.

After putting away the groceries, she treks to the kitchen supply store. Prices are expensive and it takes some time to figure out what to buy within her budget. It's not too smart to spend so much money on baking supplies when you don't have a job, but it sure feels good.

Returning to the kitchen—*her* kitchen—Midori takes out her *You! Take the Cake* book and pages through it until she finds the recipe for vanilla cupcakes topped with chocolate buttercream frosting. It's a simple enough dessert to make, but she plans to spend most of her time perfecting the decorations.

The cupcakes can serve a dual purpose—she can bring some to Graham and the rest will be a thank-you to Shinji, although it's true that he's rarely home. In the almost two weeks that she's been living at the apartment she's seen him only three times and briefly at that. But he'd left her a note one morning, which she found on the kitchen table.

Hope you're doing fine. Be sure and call me if you have any problems or questions. Work is very busy for me right now . . .
Shinji

Maybe she should freeze some cupcakes to save for him when he'd be home. They won't taste as good as fresh, but that can't be helped. And, as for Graham, he may wonder why she's baking cupcakes all day at home when she works as a pastry chef. But she'll worry about that later.

She's not sure why Shinji has a portable television in the kitchen since there's a large one housed in an entertainment center in the living room. But as she mixes the ingredients in a bowl, she decides to press the remote, turning it on. A soap opera is in progress, one she soon learns is called *Farrington Falls*. It's a perfect opportunity to practice understanding English. And perhaps an American soap will be of higher quality than *Longing to Hug*.

It turns out that *Farrington Falls* isn't too difficult to understand if she concentrates hard. The actors speak slower than real people in regular conversation, and they often repeat what they say, which is quite helpful.

A couple lays in a bed covered with red silky sheets and plump white pillows. The man is handsome—he almost looks like Graham— and with roughly the same color hair and eyes. The woman next to him, wearing a pink-and-black negligee, has dark fluffy hair the same shade as the frosting that will top Midori's cupcakes.

The woman looks upset. "Who told you?" she asks the man. "Who told you that I'm—that I'm carrying Damian's baby?"

*Carrying Damian's baby.* How would she be carrying it? Midori pictures a woman walking down the street holding an infant in her arms like a sack of groceries.

The man looks at the woman, his eyebrows knit tightly together, for what seems like a long time. Dramatic music plays. "Sheridan," he finally says.

The woman doesn't believe him.

"Sheridan told me you're pregnant," the man continues.

Oh! She's pregnant. She's *pregnant* with a baby. *Well, what else would she be pregnant with?*

Midori encircles the bowl with the spatula at a higher speed, scraping it along the edges to get at the batter sticking to the sides.

The woman on the TV begins to cry. The man puts his arms around her, holding her close. "Kendall," he says. "Kendall, you know I can pretend the baby is mine. I can do that much."

"Oh, Bent!" she exclaims. "You would really do that?"

"Yes, Kendall. Yes, I would."

"Oh, Bent! I love you!"

Everyone has such unusual names. Damian. Sheridan. Kendall. Bent.

They kiss passionately, almost swallowing each other. The music, heavy with saxophones, approaches a crescendo. Midori stops her spatula movement for a moment, taking in the scene, her jaw dropping. Just when it looks as though they're going to get down to serious business, a commercial comes on. The old song "I Can See Clearly Now" plays, but it sounds different since it's the soundtrack for an ad for a window cleaner. Now that's clever.

Midori places pink paper cups in the two cupcake pans, then pours cake batter into each one. She places the pans in the oven and sets the timer. Now she can start creating the frosting. In the end she'll make several kinds to concoct a variety of flowers. Using sprinkles and piping, she'll create different flowers on each cupcake, to make them unique.

When she again hears the theme to *Farrington Falls*, her eyes return to the screen. A woman in her thirties sits at a big desk. Her light brown, straight hair moves and sways like a gentle waterfall. Midori has never seen a more perfect turned-up nose—it even surpasses Kimberley Hobbs's. The woman is extremely busy, looking through files and signing documents. It's obvious she's important, with important work to do. Her phone rings.

"Yes?" she says impatiently. "No. I told you. I told you we're not going with the entire picnic spread for the cover. We're going with just the bottle of wine, the cheese, and the loaf of bread. Right." She hangs up.

Just then a young woman with curly red hair, who looks like she might be an office lady, rushes in. "Did you approve this copy, Sheridan?" she asks breathlessly.

So this is Sheridan. The one who told Bent that Kendall is pregnant with Damian's baby. It's a monumental event: Midori is actually following a story told entirely in English.

"Yes, Ashley," Sheridan says. "This is a go."

Midori doesn't know what a "go" is, but that's okay. It doesn't seem important. The office lady leaves. Sheridan picks up a magazine that's called *Elegant Lifestyle*. She concentrates on it intently, as if she's searching for mistakes. There's another phone call.

"Sheridan Hamilton." Suddenly Sheridan's demeanor changes from a busy professional businesswoman to someone softer, someone more vulnerable. "Oh," she says in a demure voice. "Hello, Bent."

"Sheridan." The screen now splits in two, showing both Bent and Sheridan on the phone.

"Sheridan, I told Kendall. I told Kendall that I know."

Sheridan looks upset. "Not about us, I hope."

"No, of course not. Not about us. About her being pregnant with Damian's baby."

"I see." She pauses. "But you're sure she has no clue about us?"

Bent looks pensive. Music plays. "No, Sheridan. And she never will. Not if I have anything to do with it."

Sheridan nods, smiling self-assuredly and maybe even a little evilly.

"What does she have up her butt?" Midori murmurs to herself. No, that's not right. "What does she have up her *sleeve?*" Yes, that sounds more like it. Next a commercial comes on; a calico cat dances in a litter box accompanied by a hip-hop beat.

So Bent and Sheridan are having an affair? And Kendall doesn't know, but she's pregnant with Damian's baby anyway, and Bent said he'll pretend it's his? Is this what is really happening? As *Farrington Falls* ends, Midori sets to work on her frosting flowers.

# 7

AFTER DINNER, MIDORI GAZES AT THE CUPCAKES SHE MADE THAT AF-ternoon. They look pretty displayed on a yellow platter she found in the cupboard, sort of like a pastry flower garden. She puts four on an-other plate and goes to give them to Graham. She rings his doorbell, but there's no answer. How dumb. It's seven-fifteen—he's probably at work. He'd been home doing laundry during the day so he probably works the dinner shift.

She's not back more than a minute when the front door opens. How unusual for Shinji to come home on a weeknight at this time. Or even to come home at all.

"*Okaeri nasai*," she says automatically when he walks through the hallway and sees her in the kitchen. It's a typical greeting that's said when someone comes home, but why couldn't she have kept quiet? It sounds like she's his wife.

He laughs. "*Tadaima*," he says, giving the correct response, mean-ing "I've just come in." "Oh! Cupcakes."

"Did you eat dinner already?" Again her conversation continues in a spouselike vein. *Can't you just shut up?*

"Yeah," he says. "I grabbed something." He points to the cup-cakes. "Did you make these?"

"Yes." Midori smiles. He really does look excited.

"They look so professional. Can I?"

She hands him one with blue flowers.

He peels off the paper wrapper and takes a bite. His eyes grow wide. "Mmm," he says. "This is really good."

"You think so?"

"Yeah. I'm not just saying that. It's really delicious. So fluffy." He takes another bite. "And light."

It's like he's on a commercial. "Thank you. Take more. Bring some to work if you like. I can't eat them all. I was going to give some to Graham, our neighbor. I met him in the laundry room the other day. He lives in number one. He's a chef. He seems very nice. Do you know him?"

Shinji smiles. "Guess he made quite an impression on you."

Midori blushes. Did she sound that ditzy, going on about Graham as if she were a teenager hopped up about the cute lead singer in the latest boy band?

"Um, not really. Just want to be neighborly."

"Sorry, I've never talked to him. I'm not sure who he is." He pauses. "Anyway, you sure you want me to take them to work?"

Midori nods.

"Thanks. I can put them in the break room. I'm sure people will go crazy for them." He sits down across from her. "What's this?" He points to her pastry album splayed on the table.

"My pastry album," she says. "I take pictures of desserts I eat at restaurants." She pushes the album in his direction. "To remember them and to get ideas for what to bake next."

"So you write down what it is and where you ate it?"

"Uh-huh."

He slowly turns the pages, studying them with great interest. "Where's the stuff you've made?"

"What?"

"Where are *your* pastries?"

"Mine? I don't take pictures of mine."

"Why not? You should. These are really good." He wolfs down another cupcake.

It's such a simple concept, to take pictures of her own creations. Why *hadn't* she done it?

"So is everything going okay with you?" he asks. "Any problems?"

"I'm fine," she says, grateful for his concern. "I found out about a job today."

"A job?"

She looks in amazement as he gobbles a third, then a fourth cupcake.

"I can't stop eating these," he says, grinning.

"Have you heard of the Miki Lounge?"

"No."

"It's a karaoke bar in Japantown. They need hostesses. And apparently you don't need to have a green card."

He whistles, then laughs. "A bar hostess? I know it's none of my business, but are you sure you want to do that?"

"I don't know. I can't seem to get anything else. I think I'll at least check it out."

"But you have a savings account so you don't have to be that desperate, right?"

Yes, her savings account. The one without much of a balance. Shinji obviously thinks that money is no problem for her, but why shouldn't he? She hasn't told him otherwise.

"Well, anyway, if you end up working there make sure you take a cab home," he goes on. "Japantown's not that far from here but you shouldn't walk by yourself late at night."

"Oh, I know," she says, even though it was something she hadn't thought about.

"Okay," he says, patting his stomach. "I'm going to stop now even though I could eat about three more."

"I'm so glad you like them." She gets up and takes a box of aluminum foil out of the drawer. She wraps all but two. "These are all ready for you to take to work. I'll save these two for taking a picture."

"Thanks." He smiles and stretches, raising his arms toward the ceiling. For the first time she notices how lean his body is—lean in a muscular way. She can see his flat stomach as his shirt creeps up slightly above his belly. She can't stop looking at it.

He doesn't seem to be rushing off to visit Tracy. But maybe she's coming over and Midori will finally get to meet her. It would look bad to pry or be nosy, but she's curious as to what kind of girl he goes for.

"Bring some cupcakes over to Tracy," she says.

"Tracy has a big test tomorrow so I'm not going to see her tonight."

"She's in school?"

"Yeah. She's getting her B.A. in Japanese."

A B.A. in Japanese? Tracy's Japanese is probably better than Midori's English. "Oh, I see." So it looked as if Shinji would finally be spending the night at his apartment for the first time since Midori moved in. In addition to Tracy, there is another thing Midori has been dying to know. "When I met you at the party, you said it was a long story as to how you came to live in the United States."

"Oh, yeah."

"What happened?"

"You sure you want to hear about it?"

She nods enthusiastically.

"Well, basically I came here because of my older brother, Toshi." He takes another cupcake from underneath the foil cover, looking like a mischievous little boy. "Just one more, okay?"

Midori laughs. Shinji is her pastry kindred spirit. It would have been no problem for him to eat all four of the Fairmont Hotel's room service desserts in one sitting.

"Anyway, Toshi's dream was to go to Waseda University, major in finance, and work for a big bank," he continues. "Don't ask me why. We were total opposites—I liked more artistic stuff and didn't have much aptitude for math, but he was a numbers geek. So of course from the time he got into junior high, most all his energy was put toward that, studying for tests that would prepare him for the big exam to get into Waseda."

"My father works for Bank of Japan," Midori says.

Shinji nods. "I knew Toshi wanted this, but my parents really pressured him too. It would be prestigious to have your son go to Waseda and get a big banking job. They told all the relatives. All the neighbors. My mother centered everything around Toshi to make it easy for him to concentrate."

"A real 'education mama,' huh?"

Shinji smiles. "You got it. All Toshi seemed to do was eat and study. My mom even made me bring him his dinner. He ate by himself in his room so he could have more time to study. He was like a ghost to me. We'd been close before, even though we were four years apart. He was the one who taught me how to look at the moon through a telescope. But once he got into this mode I hardly interacted with him. He didn't have time for anything else."

"He didn't complain about it?"

"Oh, no. He was the perfect son. Unlike me. I complained all the time about everything." Shinji shrugs. "Anyway, to make a long story short, after all this hard work and all this preparation the big day came. He took the exam, and he thought he did okay. Then a few weeks later we all went with him to school to get the results."

This was a typical story Midori knew well, though she had not been an ambitious student herself. The intense pressure to succeed to get into a good college and to then get a good job held no appeal for her. She'd avoided it by going to a mediocre college. And she'd had other priorities, such as learning English, making pastries, and dating gaijin men. But young women still didn't have quite this type of pressure as young men, though they had the pressure to marry. It was no wonder so many young guys these days were happy to just graduate from high school, live at home, and work part time at the 7-Eleven, just like Akina's boyfriend Yuichi. Who needed all the stress? Even the jingle for the store's Japanese commercial made it clear: "7-Eleven—Good Feeling!"

Shinji gets up, pours water into the teakettle, and turns on the burner. "So," he continues, "I'll never forget the day we went with him to his school. He and my dad walked over to look at the test results posted on the wall while my mother and I waited behind. And they couldn't find his name. And, of course, that meant he didn't pass."

Midori slowly shakes her head. "That's tough."

"He was devastated. We were *all* devastated. I mean, this was of course everyone's big expectation. A big assumption. I never imagined he wouldn't pass. It didn't even occur to me. We went home and I can't remember what I did the rest of that day. It's a blank."

Shinji drums his fingers on the table and glances at the teakettle.

"So I got up early to go to school the next day, still in shock of course. And when I get home my father was there, which was very unusual. He'd always get home from work around nine or ten and it was only around four-thirty."

Midori nods. Just like her father.

"And even more strange, there were two police officers talking to him." He pauses and looks directly at Midori's face.

What is he going to say?

"They came to tell him that Toshi had thrown himself under the Tozai line subway train at Waseda Station. He was dead."

Midori gasps, clasping her hand over her mouth. She jumps as the teakettle gives off a shrill whistle.

Shinji slowly rises to fix the tea, then puts the teapot and two cups on the table.

"How awful," Midori whispers. "Your poor brother. How awful for you and your family." The kitchen that had felt so homey and warm now feels distant and cool.

"They brought us his shoes. He'd taken them off before he jumped. He left them sitting on the platform. Sometimes I'd ride the subway and when it stopped at Waseda I'd look at the platform and imagine I saw his shoes."

"The shoes," Midori murmurs. "The shoes in your room." Now he'll know she'd been snooping. You couldn't see the pedestal just walking by when the door was open. Her face turns hot like it always did when her father scolded her, but she can't take back what she said.

Shinji looks a little surprised but only replies, "Yeah. I kept them. I brought them with me here to always remember him, and to remind myself why I'm here and why I'm no longer in Japan. All that crap, all that pressure, all that bullshit. Toshi didn't feel he had any recourse. I had to get out. I never felt like I belonged in Japan anyway."

Did Shinji's father also advise him not to be too different, no matter what he felt deep inside because he would have trouble? And that his problem was that he always wanted to go his own way?

Shinji pours tea into her cup. "When I told Tracy this story and showed her the shoes, she said I should have them bronzed. I didn't know what that meant, but when she explained it to me, I thought it was a good idea."

Midori nods, warming her hands on the hot teacup.

"Anyway, Toshi being dead wasn't the end of it. About a week later, some officials from the Tozai subway line came over."

"They came to your house?" She'd never heard of such a thing.

"Yeah. They explained to my parents that their son jumping in front of the train caused a thirty-three-minute holdup on the subway line that delayed fifteen trains and led to seven more being canceled. Can you believe my parents had to reimburse them the amount of money they lost because of the delay?"

"They made them *pay?*"

"Yeah. I didn't find this out until I was older. And my father said that if Toshi had jumped at rush hour, the charge would have been even more."

His voice is bitter. After all these years, he has remembered exactly how many trains were delayed and canceled, and the length of the holdup. It's something you'd never forget. She could only imagine that she would feel the same way. And having to pay money because your son committed suicide—it seemed an inconceivable punishment.

"So this had a major effect on me. After losing Toshi I just seemed to sleepwalk through the next few years. I never got over it, but things gradually got more back to normal. I graduated high school. I went to an art college and majored in graphic arts. I worked for a couple of advertising companies. Through a very lucky break I found out that Sawyer and Jones in San Francisco needed people to work on a Japanese-oriented campaign for some American companies and they needed someone who spoke Japanese. My English wasn't too bad and I ended up getting the job and coming here. That was six years ago. They sponsored me for a green card and I also applied for one during the lottery. I ended up getting both. I was extremely lucky."

There's silence except for the ticking of the kitchen clock, the humming of the refrigerator.

"I don't know why Toshi couldn't have had some of that luck," Shinji finally says in a low voice.

Midori immediately puts her hand on his, patting it gently. It's the same gesture he'd made when he met her at the restaurant in the Fairmont Hotel. "I'm so sorry that had to happen."

He gives her a small smile, but it's a sad one.

"So you don't plan to return to Japan?" she says, pulling her hand away.

"No. I never felt like I fit in Japan. I knew it ever since I was little, way before what happened with Toshi. I resisted everything my parents and teachers told me."

Midori nods. "I was the same way," she says. "Do you go back to see your parents?"

"I've only gone back a couple of times to see them."

"Weren't they upset that you left?"

"Yeah, but they couldn't really say anything. They'd pressured Toshi and look what happened. They knew I was always the hothead and by then they let me do whatever I wanted." He pauses. "I'm really happy here. I can't imagine ever living in Japan again."

Midori thinks of her own parents. They just have her cell phone number and she doesn't know how long the phone will keep working. She knows she should tell them where she's living now, but how can she admit to them that Kevin has dumped her? Maybe she should write them a letter. That would be easier. But maybe they don't need to know anything, just yet.

"So that's the story," Shinji says, sipping his tea. "Not a very happy one, but . . . hope I didn't depress you too much."

"It's very sad, of course," Midori says. "But I guess it has given you strength."

"I guess so. It's a little like your story, Midori-san. You'll be the stronger for it too."

# 8

THE MIKI LOUNGE IS ON THE CORNER OF POST AND BUCHANAN, BUT IS actually located at the end of a stairway below the street, as if it were hiding from the world.

At six-fifteen the evening sun is still shining, but walking into the Miki Lounge it's so dark you would have thought it was almost midnight. Midori blinks, waiting a moment for her eyes to adjust to the poor light. Finally able to look around the room, she doesn't see any sign of Crystal, the woman who had spoken to her at the Japanese supermarket. All she sees are black booths, small tables, a few wooden chairs, and a stage with a karaoke monitor and some microphones. A vague scent of disinfectant tickles her nose; the odor a mixture of pine and strawberry, the same brand her mother uses.

She's never been inside a hostess bar in Japan, but she's certain most would look more elegant than this. On the other side of the room is a long bar with a mirrored shelf displaying bottles of whiskey, sake, and other spirits. A middle-aged Japanese man, his hair greasy from applying too much pomade, emerges from the restroom and takes his place behind the bar. He looks in Midori's direction.

"Yes?" he says in Japanese.

"My name is Midori Saito. Is Taffy here?"

"No, she isn't." His tone is abrupt.

It's as though she's stumbled into a roadside tavern in the Japanese boondocks where the locals aren't used to seeing strangers in town.

"Do you know when she'll be in?"

"Soon."

"Well, maybe I'll—" At that moment a petite, fifty-something Japanese woman wearing a black tulle pillbox hat with a net over her face, a red feather boa wrapped around her neck, and a sleek black top and miniskirt finished off with high black boots sweeps into the bar and immediately begins chattering in Japanese to the bartender.

She seems to be talking about a mutual friend but stops short as the pomade man points to Midori and says, "She's here to see you."

The woman turns toward Midori, smiling. "What can I do for you?"

"My name is Midori Saito. I heard from someone named Crystal that there might be a job opening here."

"Ah! You're a friend of Crystal-chan's?"

"Well, I just met her the other day and—"

"Oh, yes. I'm sure you'd love working here. All the girls love it, don't they, Jiro-kun?" she said, addressing the bartender, who seems to be the only one with a Japanese name.

Jiro doesn't say anything but gives a slight smile, which could be construed as a smirk, as he turns to dump a bucket of ice into the sink.

"Have you been a bar hostess before?"

"No, but I've worked as a waitress in Japan," Midori lies.

"Oh, well, you're so pretty and fresh-faced I'm sure you'll be very popular here. Do you sing?"

Midori doesn't consider herself particularly pretty and her face is probably more stale than fresh, but she *can* carry a tune. "A little."

"Always helps with tips if you can sing with the customers since we, you know, have karaoke here. But the most important thing is for you to make the men feel pampered and comfortable so they'll order lots of drinks. Flatter them, tease them, and act interested even if you're bored out of your mind. You know?"

"Yes, I think so."

"Well, we have an opening for someone who can work Thursday, Friday, Saturday, and Sunday nights from nine to two o'clock in the morning. Is that something you think you can do? We pay you five dollars an hour, but you get to keep all your tips. How does that sound?"

"I can start this Thursday." It comes out before she's even finished thinking about it.

"Wonderful! And do you speak English?"

"Yes." Another lie.

"We sometimes get English-speaking customers, so that's a real plus. Good tips, you know?"

"Thank you, Taffy. I'll see you this Thursday at nine o'clock," Midori says, not quite believing that it could be so easy to get a job.

"Wear something a little sexy, you know?" She winks. "They like that."

"Yes. Well, I'll see you then."

"Welcome to the Miki Lounge, Midori-san."


"I got a job," Midori says to Akina on the phone.

"Really? I thought you needed a green card to be able to work."

"Not for this one. It's working 'on the table.' I mean, 'under the table.' It's not legal."

"Ah!" she says. "Are you going to make pastries?"

"No."

"Oh. Then are you going to be a tour conductor?"

Midori sighs. "No."

"An office lady?"

"No." She pauses. "A bar hostess."

"A *bar hostess?*"

"It's the only thing I can get. They were so happy to have me. It's in the Japanese section of San Francisco. I start this Thursday."

"Well, Mi-chan, I think it's better to be a bar hostess in San Francisco than an office lady in Japan."

"Maybe so."

"Guess what? I have news."

"What?"

"I broke up with Yuichi."

"*Wah!* Sorry!"

"No, it's for the best. I came to the decision because I read this book that changed my life."

"What book?"

"You know *Howl of the Loser Dogs?*"

Midori had heard of this book but hadn't read it. Written by a single Japanese woman in her thirties, it proclaimed that unmarried older women should resist society's criticisms about their shameful single status and, instead, hold their heads high. They only needed to take back the term *loser dog* that had been foisted upon them by society and turn it into something positive, something of which to be proud.

"I've decided I'll join the ranks of the loser dogs," she goes on. *"Ah-woo! Ah-woo!"*

Midori giggles. "Your howling is very impressive."

"Thank you. I'd rather be single than settle for someone like Yuichi. He's the real loser—not me, even though everyone else might not think so."

"Good for you, Akina-chan. Too bad you can't come here, though. Shinji-san would be just perfect for you."

"But he has an American girlfriend."

"Well, someone *like* Shinji-san."

"Maybe Shinji-san is right for you." Akina's voice has a teasing tone. "After all, you live together."

"Well, he prefers gaijin and so do I. Besides, I've already met someone."

"*Wah!* So fast!"

"He's a neighbor. And he's a chef."

"A perfect match!"

"Isn't it?"

The doorbell rings. "Akina-chan, I have to go. Someone is at the door."

Midori looks through the peephole. Just like in a movie, it's Graham. What is he doing here?

"Hi, Midori," he says, smiling. "Some of your mail got put in my box by mistake." He hands her several envelopes, none for her of course. She's usually the one to check the mail, hoping for something that will magically be addressed to her. But that's impossible since no one knows who she is or where she lives. That's what happens when you're illegal and a nonentity. But it's better being a nonentity in the United States than an entity in Japan. Anyway, it's always the case that the mail is either addressed to Shinji or someone named Occupant or Resident.

"Thank you, Graham. Would you like to come in for a moment? I have something for you."

"For me?"

He walks in and closes the door behind him.

"Oh, I'm sorry," Midori says. "But do you mind take off shoes?"

He looks surprised, then smiles. "Sure. No problem." He's dressed in his clothes for work—a white chef's coat and baggy white-and-black-checked pants. He's wearing clogs so it's easy for him to slip them off. "Wow, this is a nice place. Bigger than my apartment. Guess it's a two bedroom, right?"

"Yes."

"Nice telescope. Are you a stargazer?"

"Not me. My roommate."

"Your roommate. Not your husband." He chuckles.

"Yes." Midori goes to the kitchen and pulls out a plate with a new batch of cupcakes. "I wanted to give these to you."

"Wow, thanks. So you bake even at home? You're dedicated."

Midori isn't sure what he means.

He seems to note her blank look. "I mean, you bake at work, right? And you do it at home, too. I don't feel much like cooking once I get home."

"Uh, yes. I just am crazy pastry girl."

He laughs and bites into a cupcake. "Very delicious. I can tell you're a professional."

Midori beams.

"Where did you say you work again?"

"I'm not working now," she says, realizing she can't go on with the lie anymore. "The restaurant closed."

"Oh, really? Sorry to hear that. Too bad there's no opening at my place. We already have a pastry chef. You should come by sometime. Lupine on Hyde and Pacific."

It's not exactly a date, but it is an invitation. "Thank you. What is your working schedule?"

"I work from four to midnight Wednesday through Sunday." He looks at his watch. "Which means I have to get going. Thanks again for the cupcake."

"Please take them all," she says.

"Are you sure?"

Midori nods.

"Okay, I will. Be sure and come by the restaurant sometime. You can sit at the counter. It's an open kitchen so you can watch me in action."

For her first night at the Miki Lounge Midori puts on the sexiest dress she has, which isn't saying much. Instead of clinging to her body, the material droops, in search of curves that aren't there and won't show up anytime soon.

She arrives promptly at nine o'clock. Again only Jiro the bartender is present.

"Where is everyone?" Midori asks.

He shrugs. As usual, a man of few words.

After too long of a silence he finally says, "How long have you been here?"

"Just a few minutes."

"No, I mean in the United States."

Midori blushes. She must be nervous. "A little while." She had decided ahead of time to be vague, and divulge her sad situation to as few people as possible.

"Are you studying here?"

"Yes." So many lies. But it sounds a lot better than saying her fiancé had tossed her in the recycling bin like last week's newspaper.

"What are you studying?"

"Um, cooking. I go to culinary school." If only she could have afforded to actually do this. If only she had a student visa.

Just then, high-pitched female voices cackling in Japanese fill the room. It's Crystal and another woman.

"It was so huge," Crystal is saying. "As big as a pepper mill."

"No way!" shrieks the other woman.

"Yes! I was in absolute shock! So he gets in bed next to me and I say, are you really going to put that—" She stops when she notices Midori sitting at the bar.

"Ah! It's you."

"Yes, thank you. I am Midori." Midori assumes she has forgotten her name.

"Hi, I'm Britney," says the other woman.

"Nice to meet you," Midori says.

Britney wears a sparkling burgundy-colored dress. She's small-waisted and slim-hipped, but sports an enormous chest. It has to be fake. Crystal's red-streaked hair is pulled into a bun, long strands framing her face. Her fuchsia lipstick matches her skirt, which covers only about three inches of thigh. In comparison, Midori might as well be wearing a McDonald's uniform.

She had wanted to buy something special to wear, but she'd spent so much money on baking ingredients and supplies that she didn't feel she could afford a new dress. Besides, her savings account has been set on permanent dwindle. On the other hand she isn't expecting to stay at this job long. Somehow something else will have to materialize. Her bar hostess days will be a long-ago memory she'll reminisce about with some slight embarrassment, but a little fondness as well. *Remember that time I actually had to work at a hostess bar? Ha-ha!* But, on the other hand, Midori knows she may be just kidding herself. It's possible that her only other occupational choice will be working as a "masseuse" in a bathhouse like Namie-san on *Longing to Hug.*

Taffy bursts into the bar, talking on a cell phone, giving everyone a wave at the same time. She speaks in English but Midori can't understand much of what she's saying. She talks a lot faster than the people on *Farrington Falls*. Behind her another Japanese woman saunters in.

"Hey, Amber," Crystal says. She introduces her to Midori.

Midori stares. The girl looks familiar, but she can't place her. Her mouth is slightly skewed to the side, as if maybe she'd been injured in an accident. Still, she looks pretty, but seems quiet and sullen, suggesting she would rather be having her wisdom teeth extracted than spend time at the Miki Lounge. Had she been a classmate? Midori doesn't think so—she looks too young. Maybe she's from Midori's hometown, though the chances of that seem remote.

"Are you from Fukuoka?" Midori asks her in a friendly voice.

Amber shakes her head. Her thin lips remain in a straight line, as if it would take too much energy to coax them into a smile. "I am Japanese but I was raised in Singapore." Her voice is low, a bit of a croak. She chews on her words as though her mouth is stuffed with marbles.

"Oh, I see. Do you speak Chinese too? And English?"

She shakes her head no again and looks down, grasping a strand of her hair to examine it for split ends, though it's so dim it would be impossible to see any. Her black slinky dress isn't as elaborate as the other women's getups, but it still looks better than Midori's burlap sack. Midori wonders how Amber got to be in San Francisco, but she isn't exactly brimming with information about herself.

"Where are you girls from?" Midori asks Britney and Crystal.

"Tokyo," they both say quickly and at the same time. They giggle.

Britney turns serious. "Don't you want a different name?" she asks Midori.

Was this something she was supposed to have thought of ahead of time? "Different name?"

"You know," Crystal says. "An American name."

Midori understands now. Maybe it would be better to have a pseudonym—a bar hostess stage name. It does make sense to be anonymous at a place like this. She thinks for a moment. "I'll be Sheridan."

"Sounds good!" Taffy says brightly. *"Sheridan!"*

A few minutes later a balding Japanese man who looks about Midori's father's age walks into the bar.

"Imamura-san! Imamura-san." Britney gushes like a schoolgirl brought face-to-face with her favorite to-die-for movie actor. "You're back!"

The man stares at her breasts as if he's pleased at seeing two old friends. He grins as she, Taffy, and Crystal all descend upon him like circling hawks readying to pounce on a rabbit. Amber, however, remains sitting forlornly at the bar. Britney helps Imamura-san slip out of his trench coat and tosses it to Midori, who nearly drops it.

"Where do I put this?" Midori asks Jiro. He points to a closet near the bathrooms. Midori hangs up the coat as she notices Crystal receiving a drink from Jiro, then serving it to Mr. Imamura.

Midori isn't sure what she's supposed to do next. She looks in Amber's direction, but the girl only continues with her split ends procedure.

Imamura-san sits in a large booth with Britney and Crystal on either side of him. Midori is about to sit next to Britney when another man who looks like he could be Imamura-san's twin brother walks in. She'd never paid too much attention to it in Japan, but here it does seem that all Japanese businessmen can look nearly identical in their blue suit, white shirt uniforms.

Taffy greets this customer with an enthusiastic, "Teraoka-san!" She looks at Midori and motions for her. As she hands over his coat she whispers, "Sheridan, you really should wear something shorter, you know. Show more legs."

Midori dutifully hangs up Teraoka-san's coat. Is she only going to be relegated to coat-check girl? Though she's not exactly looking forward to sitting with a customer, she's relieved when Taffy calls for her and Amber to sit with Mr. Teraoka.

"This is our new girl—Sheridan," Taffy says. "And I think you know Amber."

Amber nods in his direction, but appears to be under sedation.

Teraoka-san turns his attention to Midori. "You're a pretty one," he says, patting her knee.

This is startling enough, but she jumps when his hand suddenly finds itself on her thigh in one swift movement. It's rather like being felt up by your father. The musty smell of this guy's cologne reminds her of her dad, and he even wears similar eyeglass frames. The only major difference between Teraoka-san and Mr. Saito is that Teraoka-san is completely bald, the shape of his head resembling that of an octopus. Midori decides to nickname him Tako.

Taffy brings a whiskey and water for Tako and glasses of what look like orange juice for Midori and Amber. Midori sips the juice, wondering what kind of alcohol is in her drink. Is it a screwdriver? A tequila sunrise? But as the liquid slides down her throat it's obvious that it's straight orange juice and nothing more. Bar hostesses aren't supposed to get drunk, she figures. That means more liquor for the customers.

Midori thinks hard for something clever to say to Tako since Amber seems unlikely to start any conversation. She finally comes up with a feeble, "Are you in San Francisco on business?" It's the best she can do.

"No, I work for a Japanese company here," he says, winking at her.

Midori then politely inquires about his work and receives a long, sleep-inducing spiel on the life insurance industry, from compensation structures to needs-based protection selling. It isn't easy to pretend to be interested, but instead of looking bored out of her wits like Amber, Midori thinks that maybe she'll earn a better tip if she convinces Tako that the finer points of life insurance are as fascinating to her as the finer points of creating the perfect consistency for a crème brûlée custard. It seems to work. Tako becomes more lively and animated, perhaps experiencing one of the best dates of his life. It's pathetic, but the service Midori is providing at least seems to be appreciated.

After imbibing several more drinks, Tako lights up further as a Japanese song plays over the sound system. It's vaguely familiar but old, a tune that might have been popular long ago when Midori's parents were young.

Tako grabs Midori's hand. "Sing with me, Sheridan," he implores, gulping his drink and grabbing another Taffy hands to him with perfect timing. "You must know 'Matsumi no Onna'—'The Woman Who Waits,'" he says. He drags Midori by the hand over to the little stage. Taking one of the microphones, he passes her the other.

"Even though I have to keep you hidden away, you know I want you more each day," he sings.

The song is a duet. Midori only knows this because the lettering of the lyrics on the karaoke TV screen is blue for the man's part and changes to pink for the woman's. Midori doesn't know the song, but fakes it as best she can.

"I don't mind that we can't walk through the town together," she warbles. "Because we'll be together forever."

"I'll take you in my arms, lose myself in all your charms."

"I'm the woman who waits, always waits for you."

Then together they sing, "Yes, we keep our love secret, it's a secret forever, a secret that will never be told."

Midori imagines her parents' reaction if they walked in and witnessed the scene. "Look, it's Namie-san on Longing to Hug," her mother would say. "She's moved up from the bathhouse to the hostess bar." Then, "No, wait! It can't be! It's Midori." Her mother is frozen in shock as her father rushes over, punches Tako in the face, and pulls Midori's arm, yanking her off the stage.

Or what if Shinji paid a visit? He knew the name of the place, she'd been sure to tell him. How smart was that? But he'd said he never went to Japantown anyway, unless Tracy dragged him there. And a girl getting her bachelor's degree in Japanese is unlikely to visit the Miki Lounge, Midori is relieved to think.

Tako leans against Midori as he puts his arm around her shoulders. She has to use all her strength to lean against him to keep from toppling over. She's woozy and light-headed, as if she's getting drunk on his whiskey breath.

What is she doing here? It's beyond humiliating. Although she's earning some much-needed money, she doesn't know if it's worth it. Maybe she should make this her first and last night at the Miki Lounge. She cringes as Crystal, Taffy, and Mr. Imamura clap in time to the music, yelling, "*Gambatte!* Do your best!" Only Amber sits motionlessly in the booth, oblivious to the amateur hour performance on the stage. At least she has good taste. Midori still can't shake the feeling that she's seen her before.

The night drones on with more Tako and Imamura clones arriving, more drinking, more singing, and a bit more thigh-groping, but at least nothing worse.

By two o'clock it's finally over. The women gather around Taffy to collect their take for the night. Midori—hanging back so as not to appear too anxious—is surprised to see Amber collect her money, then leave on the arm of one of the customers who'd discreetly waited for her.

Midori's neck is heavy, stiff. She suppresses a yawn, and feels even more exhausted knowing she's only going to get five dollars an hour plus tips for such work. And she's the new girl so her tips are likely to be even less than the others'. How demeaning. How low she has fallen. Just a couple of months ago she was a bride-to-be living in a seven-bedroom house in San Francisco's ritziest neighborhood. Successful Sheridan Hamilton would be disappointed in her namesake.

But this line of thinking quickly changes when Taffy hands Midori her earnings for the night—one hundred and fifty dollars.

She remembers Akina's words, "I think it's better to be a bar hostess in San Francisco than an office lady in Japan." *Maybe working at the Miki Lounge isn't so bad,* she thinks, now awakened from her stupor. After all, she has kicked the jackpot.

# 9

"I CAN'T BE JUST FRIENDS," ASHLEY IS SAYING TO CASSANDRA. "I CAN'T keep these other feelings bottled up inside anymore."

"But do you think Kyle has . . . ," Cassandra says. "Do you think Kyle has those same feelings for you?"

Ashley shakes her head. "I don't know, Cassandra. I just don't know."

It's another episode of *Farrington Falls*. It's Monday, and it will be Midori's first night off since she's started working at the Miki Lounge. She doesn't think she'll quit any time soon. Already she's earned more than five hundred dollars. Now she's attempting to make her version of the Hippodrome cake she'd eaten at My Sweet Heart.

She'd seen Kyle on another episode and thought he was especially good-looking. He and Ashley would make a cute couple. But when the show returns, it's back to Sheridan and Bent. They're in bed together, and it looks as though they have just finished making love.

"Sheridan, I have to go," Bent says.

Sheridan frowns. "Bent, are we ever going to be able to spend a whole night together?"

Bent sighs. "You know how difficult that would be for me, Sheridan. Since I'm married to Kendall."

"But she's pregnant with Damian's baby, for God's sake! Your own brother . . ."

Bent shakes his head. "Sheridan, please. It's not something I want to deal with right now."

"I'm sorry. You know I love you, Bent."

*Bent.* Was this really his name? All the characters' names on *Farrington Falls* are unusual, but Midori has thought all along that Bent sounded odder than the others. Was his name actually *Brent*? She listens carefully when Sheridan says his name again as he moves closer to her. Yes, that's it.

Brent (formerly Bent) takes Sheridan in his arms and kisses her.

Midori is so engrossed that she jumps at the buzzing of the oven timer, signaling her cake is ready. After letting it cool, she'll drizzle it with apricot glaze.

Midori's Hippodrome cake sits regally on the yellow platter in the middle of the kitchen table that evening. It looks as good as the one at My Sweet Heart and she's hoping it tastes even better. She'd tried to cut the sweetness and make a thinner, less syrupy glaze. She has just taken a picture when she hears the front door open.

She recognizes Shinji's laugh, but there's also a female voice. Maybe she'll finally meet Tracy.

The girl who walks in, her arm around Shinji's waist, is the same one in the photograph in his cubicle. Her hair is shorter now, though, and lighter—more blond than tan. She looks to be in her twenties and wears simple jeans, sandals, and a black-and-blue striped shirt. Thin and about the same height as Shinji, she has brown eyes and a bright smile. She isn't beautiful like Kimberley Hobbs or Sheridan Hamilton, but she's cute. She wears little if any makeup. In essence she looks like a wholesome American college student—not a model, but a down-to-earth, friendly girl.

"More cake! Wow, I feel like I'm living in a bakery," Shinji says, sitting down at the table. "Midori, this is Tracy Harris. Tracy, this is Midori Saito."

"*Hajimemashite. Yoroshiku onegai shimasu,*" Tracy says, giving her introductory greeting in stellar Japanese.

She bows like a Japanese person at the same time that Midori extends her hand to shake it. It's confusing. Should Midori return her bow? She does. "Nice to meet you," she says in English.

"Midori is a great baker," Shinji says in English, eyeing the Hippodrome cake.

"Not so good," Midori says, blushing.

"I heard about your cupcakes," Tracy says, smiling, continuing in Japanese. "You're going to make my boyfriend fat if you keep this up." She grabs Shinji's belly, trying to pinch it, but of course there really isn't anything to pinch.

"I'm not going to get fat," he says in English, pretending to be mad. He playfully grabs at her sides. "But, oooh, what's this I feel? Are these love handles?"

Midori doesn't know what love handles are but her heart is heavy as Tracy giggles, tells him to shut up, and grabs his hands, pushing them away. By now they're tickling each other, like two little kids, a couple of happy playmates. If things had gone differently she'd be in that palatial kitchen with the island at Kevin's house, laughing with him about her funny English while he kissed her and told her how much he loved her.

"Do you want cake?" Midori asks Tracy.

Tracy shakes her head. "Oh, I don't eat anything with refined sugar," she says matter-of-factly.

She's still speaking in Japanese, but has said the words "refined sugar" in English, but with Japanese pronunciation. Midori takes this all in, wondering about refined sugar, when Shinji says, "But I'll have some."

Midori smiles and goes to get the cake knife she'd bought at the kitchen supply store.

"Did you take a photo?" Shinji asks, his eyes on the camera.

"Yes."

Shinji explains in English to Tracy about Midori's pastry album.

"How interesting," Tracy says in Japanese.

That's how their conversation goes, with Tracy speaking in Shinji's native language and Shinji speaking in Tracy's. And Shinji speaking Japanese to Midori. Midori wonders why Tracy and Shinji haven't decided on a mutual way to converse.

"Have you been to Japan?" Midori asks Tracy, switching to Japanese.

"Yes," Tracy says. "I taught English in Tokyo for a year."

*Just like Kevin*, Midori thinks.

"Thank you, Midori-san," Tracy goes on, "for speaking to me in Japanese. Shinji won't do it." She directs her pout at him, but it's in a teasing way. "He says when he sees a white face, the Japanese just won't come out."

Midori smiles. She understands how that could be a little disconcerting. Someone speaking nearly perfect Japanese who isn't Japanese can seem strange, though she isn't exactly sure why. She hadn't thought it strange, though, when her old classmate Miyuki had spoken English. And she loved it when Kevin spoke his few lines of Japanese when she first met him.

"Don't you think Midori-san wants to practice her English?" Shinji says, again with a teasing voice. "She hasn't been here that long, you know."

"*Sumimasen. Yurushite kudasai,*" Tracy apologizes to Midori. "I mean, I'm sorry. Forgive me, Midori-san."

"Maybe we can speak sometimes Japanese, sometimes English," Midori says, trying to be diplomatic.

Shinji digs into his piece of cake, making a smacking noise with his lips. "Midori-san, this is really good."

"Really?" She immediately responds in Japanese because that's what he's spoken to her. She hopes it doesn't make Tracy feel bad. It's difficult to keep track. Midori cuts a piece of Hippodrome cake for herself and takes a bite. She's happy again that the flavor is even, the glaze subtle. "Are you sure you don't want a piece?" she asks in Japanese, looking at Tracy.

"No, thank you," Tracy says.

Midori gets up to make some tea. "So did you like living in Japan, Tracy?" Midori says.

"Yes! I can't wait to go back."

"I don't know why you like it there so much," Shinji says in English, shaking his head. "It's so much better here."

"Oh, here we go again." Tracy playfully pinches his arm, and he returns the favor. "Stop it, *Sean*." She laughs and looks in Midori's direction. "Can you believe someone with such a wonderful name as Shinji asks people to call him Sean?"

"Of course Tracy would love to be called Teruko or something, I guess," Shinji says, tapping her nose with his index finger.

Midori sighs to herself as she continues to observe their affection for each other. Would Shinji follow Tracy back if she went to Japan? It seems unlikely after what he'd told her, but you never knew where life would take you; Midori's experience could testify to that.

Midori pours tea into their cups. At least Tracy isn't refusing a cup of tea. "What do you like about Japan?" Midori asks.

"It's such an exciting place. Full of cool things. I love all the young people who dress up in outrageous clothes. I love sumo, kabuki, tea ceremony, sushi, Hello Kitty—just everything," she says. "And everyone's so nice and polite."

"They're nice and polite until you wear out your welcome as a gaijin," Shinji says. "Then you're old news."

Tracy sighs. "He just doesn't want me to go," she says, winking at Midori.

"I guess not," Midori says with a smile. *Maybe they want to be alone,* she thinks. She should get out of their way. And she has to admit that their playfulness toward each other is making her feel more and more depressed. "Shinji-san, have another piece of cake," she says, cutting him a slice, then covering the rest of the cake with foil. "I'm a little tired. Have a good evening. Nice to meet you, Tracy."

"Don't you want to see the video I brought?" Tracy asks, taking a tape out of her purse. "It's a Japanese documentary on Sen Rikyu, the father of the tea ceremony."

"Tracy has to watch this for one of her classes at school," Shinji explains.

"How interesting," Midori says, though she finds the subject dull.

Is this girl also an expert on tea ceremony? She's more Japanese than Midori could ever hope to be.

"And Shinji is supposed to help me with the parts I don't understand." Tracy sticks out her lower lip. "Since it's all in Japanese."

Shinji rolls his eyes. "Tea ceremony. My favorite subject."

She punches him again and there's more tickling and laughter.

"Thank you, Tracy, but I really am kind of tired," Midori says. "Good night."

Midori isn't really tired but it's a good enough excuse. She goes to her room and shuts the door. She can hear Tracy and Shinji talking, then laughing again. She lies down on her bed and reads from *You! Take the Cake*. A little later she hears the video playing in the living room, though it isn't on too loud. Soon she finds herself dozing off; maybe she really is tired. But she wakes up with a start when she suddenly hears voices. Shinji and Tracy are in the room next door. She looks at the clock—it's after midnight. She's surprised she's been asleep for that long.

Midori is also surprised how thin the walls are. Shinji and Tracy might as well be in bed with her. She can hear their sighs, their moans, the slight creaking of the mattress springs. She sighs, closing her eyes, and cupping her hands over her ears. She doesn't want to hear Tracy's orgasm or Shinji's either, if he is indeed the type of guy who expresses himself verbally when he comes.

Still, after a while she can't help but get excited as she hears them. She imagines a big movie screen, the scene playing out in the multiplex with an audience watching. She thinks of Graham. She thinks of stroking his silky blond hair as he unbuttons her blouse, snapping off her bra with ease. As she touches herself she imagines him sucking on her breasts, putting his hand in her panties just like her hand is now. One minute he's kissing her between her legs, the next he's pushing himself inside her. Soon enough Midori hears the muffled but distinctive cry of Tracy having her orgasm. And she has hers right after, careful not to make a sound.

# 10

SHINJI HAD TOLD MIDORI THAT SHE COULD USE THE COMPUTER IN HIS room. She wondered if this meant he had accepted her nosiness. After all, it hadn't been too difficult for him to put two and two together and realize she'd gone in his room and seen Toshi's bronzed shoes. Perhaps he recognized that she would be snooping in there again anyway so he figured he might as well give her something to do.

At any rate, Midori can't stop thinking about how Tracy had refused a piece of her Hippodrome cake, saying that she didn't eat anything with "refined sugar." What did she mean by that? Once on the Internet she soon discovers it is possible to make pastries without refined sugar for people who don't think it is a "natural" food. She figures there must be such people in Japan too, but she's never met any. However, honey is apparently considered a natural sweetener and Midori is able to find a recipe for a honey-rum cake that looks intriguing and uses no sugar. She's not sure when she will next see Tracy, but she decides to make the cake anyway. Hopefully Shinji will be around and can bring her a piece. She will leave him a note.

In the midst of preparing the batter, she watches *Farrington Falls*. Damian is with his brother Brent. This is the first time she's seen Damian, the father of Kendall's baby. He's even better looking than his brother, with chestnut-colored tousled hair, blue eyes, and a cleft in his chin. A small earring dots his right ear. The brothers stand on the porch of a beautiful house overlooking a beach. They quarrel and then Brent punches Damian in the face.

Damian falls, hitting his head on a bench. It's obvious the blow has knocked him unconscious because of the dramatic music that plays and the closeup of his face, showing blood trickling from his cheek. His eyes are closed, his body limp like a rag doll. Midori hopes Damian won't die—he *is* nice to look at.

The scene changes. Now Ashley gazes longingly at Kyle—wearing only shorts—while he plays volleyball on the beach with his girl-friend, Mandy. When will Ashley tell Kyle how she really feels? Besides, Mandy isn't that pretty or smart. If Kyle knew, he'd surely choose Ashley over Mandy. Midori's thoughts are interrupted by the sound of music coming from the other room. Her heart sinks. It's her cell phone.

Although she was tempted several times to just throw the phone in the Dumpster parked outside the Miki Lounge, she felt too guilty knowing how much her parents would worry if they couldn't reach her. But somehow she hasn't been able to bring herself to call them or even write a letter. She has continued to charge the cell phone to keep it in working order, while secretly hoping the account will finally be canceled. It hasn't.

"Midori?!"

It's her mother's familiar voice, filled with maternal concern.

"Hi, Mom. How are you?"

"How am I? Well, I've been worried sick since we haven't heard from you. September will be here so soon. Have you been able to find a place for the wedding? Have you set the date?"

In the background Midori can hear the dramatic theme music to *Farrington Falls*, a personal soundtrack that seems only too appropriate.

She has to tell her. There's no use putting it off any further. She's an adult—why should she be so worried about what her parents think? It's her life, right? She takes a deep breath.

"No, we haven't found anything yet, but I think we will soon."
She closes her eyes. She is truly a chicken with its head cut off. No,
that isn't it. No, she is pure chicken feed. No, not that either. Wait.
She has chickened out. Yes, that's it. She has chickened out.

"Well, I certainly hope so. But why is it such a problem?"

"It's really complicated, Mom."

"How complicated can it be?" Her irritated sigh seems to swallow
Midori's ear. "So how is everything else going? Have you been fitted
for your dress?"

"Everything else is going very well. In fact, I've been so busy that
I haven't had time to call. But, you know, Mom? I'm going to be getting a new phone number so I want to give it to you." This is the least
she can do if the cell phone conks out. She gives her mother the
number of the phone in the apartment, Shinji's number. "But call the
old number first. If you can't get through, call this one."

She promises to telephone more often, keep her mother apprised,
then tells her to give regards to her father, and hangs up as quickly as
she can. What could she have said? *Mom, Kevin dumped me, the wedding's off, I'm living with another guy, and I'm working illegally as a bar
hostess.*

No, that just wouldn't have been the prudent thing to say.


The honey-rum cake is a success, but after eating a piece Midori
thinks that if she made one again she would have to experiment further to bring out a more balanced flavor from the honey. This version
is overly sweet for her taste. But still she has eaten two pieces this evening, not expecting Shinji or Tracy to come. But around eight o'clock
they walk in the door.

"Midori-san, so nice to see you again. How are you?" Tracy says in
her perfect Japanese.

"Wow, I'm so lucky to have a master pastry chef as my roommate,"
Shinji says, smiling at Midori and looking at her cake with an expression of great anticipation.

Midori smiles back, then answers Tracy in Japanese. "I'm fine.

How are you? I hope you'll have a piece of this cake. It's made with honey, not refined sugar. It's a honey-rum cake."

"Oh, really?" Tracy looks surprised. "But is it made with white flour?" she asks now in English.

Midori is puzzled. "Yes . . ."

"I'm sorry, Midori-san, but I only eat whole wheat flour."

"Oh, I see."

Shinji looks a little perturbed. "Tracy doesn't mind eating white rice when it comes to sushi, though."

"Yeah, yeah," she says to him, sighing. They are obviously not in a tickling mood tonight.

"Well, I'll have a piece, Midori-san," Shinji says, brightening. "And I'll have Tracy's piece too."

Tracy goes off to the bathroom as Midori puts on the kettle to make tea.

"I'm sorry, Midori-san," Shinji says quietly. "Thanks for going to all this trouble for Tracy. That was really nice of you."

"Oh, it was no trouble," Midori says. "I guess I just didn't understand."

Shinji doesn't say anything further and doesn't wait for the tea to be ready before diving into his first piece of honey-rum cake. "Midori-san, you should work in a restaurant."

"Maybe someday," Midori says. "Are you sure it's not too sweet?" She pours the tea.

"It's perfect." He happily stuffs his face and makes appreciative noises that make Midori smile. "Tracy bought a new computer tonight so I'm going to help her set it up," he continues. "We just came by here to pick up some software I want to install on it."

Shinji starts on his second piece of cake as Tracy returns to the kitchen.

"Looks like you have another hit, Midori-san," she says as Shinji shovels cake into his mouth, competing in his own personal dessert-eating contest. "Guess I better take some cooking lessons."

Midori is surprised at the sarcastic tone in her voice.

"Do you know the English expression," Tracy goes on, " 'The quickest way to a man's heart is through his stomach'?"

Tracy doesn't say this in a lighthearted way, but Midori is more interested in the expression than to wonder if there is any hidden meaning behind Tracy's words. She hasn't heard this expression before. "No, I don't know that one," she says.

Tracy looks at her watch, then shoots a glare at Shinji. "It's getting late," she says. "Shall we get what we came here for?"

Shinji gives her a twisted smile, takes his last bite of cake, and washes it down with a gulp of tea. "Yes, *ma'am!*" he says, giving her arm a squeeze that seems to mean "Lighten up."

"Good night, Midori-san," Tracy says.

As they leave the room, Midori looks at Tracy's cup of tea. It's also been left untouched.

Lupine is a perfect San Francisco restaurant. Or a perfect restaurant anywhere. Housed in a Victorian storefront, there are about twelve tables and a counter that seats eight, which overlooks the open kitchen, as Graham had mentioned. It would be the perfect place to work, to work with your husband and partner. Vases offer delicate flowers on each table. The walls are painted a warm yellow and the dimmed lights give off a golden hue. A huge flower arrangement sits in an alcove, bathed in a subtle spotlight.

It's nine o'clock on a Wednesday night and the place is full except for a couple of open seats at the counter. She can see Graham bustling behind it.

"Midori!" He looks glad to see her and her heart feels full. "So great that you came. Have a seat. Chloe," he calls to one of the servers, "bring Midori a menu, please." He winks at her. "Order anything. It's on the house."

*On the house.* For a moment she thinks of "on the table." *Under the table.* This can't be what he's referring to. Instead she just nods and smiles. All the dishes on the menu are tempting—grilled yellowfin tuna with fingerling potatoes, chicken braised in wine with bacon, mushrooms, and pearl onions—but her eyes quickly move to the dessert section, which has everything from a bittersweet chocolate pot de cream to a maple syrup tart. She wonders if she'll be able to meet the pastry chef.

She doesn't want to bother Graham since he's so busy. She watches him move, his body graceful, as he grabs a pan here, a whisk and a bowl there. He has only one assistant helping—it's a small operation.

Midori orders the Pacific bluenose sea bass with spinach mousseline and chanterelle mushrooms. Graham is a talented chef—she can't remember the last time she's eaten something so succulent. There are three servers, two men and Chloe. They rush around with purpose, giving her smiles and asking how everything is, if she needs anything. There's a wonderful spirit about the place, with everyone working in unison, seemingly glad to be there. How perfect it would be to have a job at a restaurant like Lupine.

When it's time for dessert, Midori knows it will be bad form if she orders each one on the menu so she chooses the warm Dutch apple pie with caramel praline crunch ice cream. By that time things have died down and Graham has some time to talk to her. He pours her a glass of dessert wine and he drinks some chardonnay.

"Everything taste okay?" he asks.

"So wonderful," she says. "I am so impressive."

He chuckles. "Well, thank you, Midori." He swirls the wine in his glass, then sniffs inside. "So any luck finding a new job?"

She's about to mention the Miki Lounge but stops herself. How stupid would that be? *Oh, yes, my bar hostess job.* That sure would make a good impression. "Not yet," she says.

"You should come back a little earlier next time and I can introduce you to Danielle, our pastry chef. She had to leave early tonight."

"I like to meet her." Midori sips her wine. The golden light ambiance, the candles flickering in little white glasses are all too romantic.

"So you're from Japan?"

She nods.

"I've always wanted to go there. See Mount Fuji, the castles. Maybe someday." He pauses. "So what did you do? Just pack up and leave?"

"Not really." Before she can think about it, she blurts out the entire story about meeting the bad man, the engagement party, and Kimberley Hobbs. Graham's warm blue eyes and sympathetic expression as her sad tale unfolds make her feel comfortable talking to him.

"That's tough," he says. "But I hope you don't think all American men are like that."

She shakes her head vigorously. "Oh, no!"

Once the last customer is gone and everything is cleaned up, Graham drives Midori home. There are no garages in the apartment building so he has to rent one two blocks away. As they walk his arm gently brushes hers more than once. Is it on purpose? But their conversation is only about cooking and Japan and nothing more.

When they get to the building, he tells her to come back next week to Lupine. "I want you to meet Danielle and, if you don't mind my cooking, have dinner again."

She laughs. "Your cooking is so, so beautiful."

They say their good nights and go their separate ways. Midori was hoping for a handshake, maybe even a kiss. But it's okay. Maybe it's better to take things slowly. With Kevin everything went so fast and look what happened there.

# 11

IT'S NOTHING TO BRAG ABOUT, BUT AFTER WORKING AS A BAR HOSTESS for a little more than a month, Midori has come to learn the trade rather well. She is now able to fend off amorous advances without insulting her customers, and feign great interest in a variety of dull topics, from the mechanics of heavy construction machinery to the Shizuoka Mushroom Growers Association's annual trip to the Beppu hot springs. Her karaoke singing has improved and she's added several songs to her repertoire. And she has learned to react to a suggestive joke with the correct amount of embarrassment coupled with a but-I've-been-around-the-block attitude. It isn't something to exactly take pride in, but it *is* some kind of accomplishment.

"Amber's called in sick," Crystal says, frowning one Sunday evening right after the lounge has opened. "So we're short tonight."

Midori has continued to wonder why Amber looks so familiar, but has come up with nothing. And any conversation with her consists mainly of "Uh-huh," "Maybe," "I don't know," and the occasional shrug. Why does this girl continue to work at the Miki Lounge when she clearly seems to hate it so much? And why hasn't she been fired? She's always taking breaks, puffing on endless cigarettes outside. But

Taffy is the ideal boss, always cheerful and never outwardly displaying any dissatisfaction with Amber or anyone else.

And some of the men seem to like Amber's quiet demeanor. She's young and pretty, despite that crooked mouth. And she always leaves at the end of the night with a waiting customer. Midori doesn't want to ask what type of arrangement this is, but it isn't difficult to guess. But as long as *she* isn't expected to offer some kind of extra "service," it's none of her business what the other women do. It's a relief that no one has ever suggested it to her.

"Do you know anything about Amber?" Midori asks Crystal.

"Not really. I don't ask too many questions here."

Midori nods. It's true that no one talks much about their lives outside the club, why they left Japan, or how they got to San Francisco. It was only that one time with Jiro the bartender that Midori lied and said she was enrolled in culinary school, which wasn't as bad as the lie she told Graham, though now she'd straightened that out with him.

But at the Miki Lounge she hasn't had to fib again because no one else has asked her anything. Taffy, Crystal, and Britney aren't unfriendly—they just seem to keep their private lives private. And Amber is, well, basically just plain noncommunicative. Midori would love to know these women's stories, but has received the unspoken message that she just shouldn't ask. But she wishes there was some way they would open up. They must all be illegal, though, and that's probably one reason why they keep to themselves.

"Amber just looks so familiar to me," Midori continues. "But I can't place her."

"She looks a little bit like Rie Ando, the singer. Maybe that's who you're thinking of." Crystal primps her hair with her fingers, then plucks at the blobs of excess mascara from her lashes.

"Maybe," Midori says, but there's really no way that Amber looks like Rie Ando.

"Sheridan!"

Midori turns around to see Tako, who has become one of her regular customers. Her workday is about to begin.

It's almost eleven. Tako has left by now, having been replaced by another customer named Murata-san. Midori has just decided to dub him "Possum" because of his beady eyes and shaggy salt-and-pepper hair, when she hears Taffy and Crystal cry out with excitement. They always behave this way when a regular customer comes in, but this time they seem more worked up than usual.

Not wanting to deflect her attention from Possum, but curious as to who could be causing such a commotion, Midori takes a quick glance in their direction. The customer in question is Caucasian, the first non-Japanese she's seen at the Miki Lounge. She recalls Taffy telling her that they sometimes get English-speaking customers and Midori's supposed fluency in English was bound to bring her good tips. But why would any American want to get ripped off by coming to the Miki Lounge?

Still, maybe there would be a way to change from Possum over to this American. It would be nice to get more money. She stares at the guy. She squints. She stares again.

It can't be. But yes, it is.

It's Kevin.

Midori freezes for an instant, but then just as quickly defrosts.

"Sorry to be rude, but can you excuse me for a moment?" she says to Possum as Britney hurries over with a drink for him. Kevin hasn't seen her and she wants to keep it that way. Rushing to the bathroom, she locks herself in a stall and perches on the toilet.

What the hell is Kevin doing here? She wondered a few times if maybe Shinji would come to the Miki Lounge to check it out. That would be embarrassing enough, but she never imagined she would see Kevin walk in. In fact, she never imagined she would see him again anywhere. It would be mortifying to bump into him on Fillmore Street or at the Ferry Plaza, but to run into him at the Miki Lounge where she works as a lowly bar hostess? It's beyond humiliation.

She sits on the toilet, hugging her chest. Maybe her absence will go unnoticed, but that's doubtful. Yet she is determined to stay in the bathroom for the rest of the night, even the rest of her life, if necessary. But sure enough, she hears the restroom door open only a few minutes later.

"Sheridan?"

It's Taffy.

An idea suddenly pops into Midori's head. Why hadn't she thought of this before? She pulls a paper seat cover from the dispenser, places it on the floor in front of the toilet, and drops to her knees. Then she begins making retching noises, the kind that can only mean one thing: a major stomach upset. She can't recall doing anything more disgusting than this. Flushing the toilet for effect, she moans in fake pain, then begins her deceptive heaving once more.

"Sheridan, what's wrong? Are you okay?"

"Taffy?" she says weakly. "Taffy, I don't know what happened. Suddenly I got so . . . so sick."

"Oh, you poor thing! Maybe you have what Amber has."

Thank goodness Taffy is such a kind boss. What would it be like to work at one of the tour companies she'd visited? That horrible man with the prune face would be telling her to buck up and get back to work immediately. She couldn't possibly let down all those waiting tourists who need to get their butts over to Yosemite.

"Maybe I just ate something that disagreed with me, but . . . ," Midori says. "I'm sorry, Taffy, but . . . I think . . . I have . . . to go home."

"Oh, dear. And just when I thought you'd be perfect for this American customer who speaks nothing but English."

Midori makes more hideous noises. It's some kind of talent, she supposes.

"And now we're so short-staffed tonight . . ."

"Please forgive me, Taffy."

"Don't worry, Sheridan. Yes, you go on home. We'll manage somehow."

Midori gags and flushes the toilet again. She hears Taffy shut the door. Waiting a few minutes more, she cautiously walks out of the bathroom and grabs her coat and purse from the closet. How lucky that Kevin has been seated in the booth the farthest away from the ladies' room. She sees him smiling and hears his familiar, deep ho-ho-ho laugh as Crystal and Britney attend to him. What a good time he's having. The lump in Midori's throat is turning into the size of a cantaloupe. She sees that Taffy has taken over at Possum's booth. Now she has to make her goaway. That's wrong. "No, silly, it's *getaway*," Kevin would say. Who cares, *Kevin*.

She's about to rush out the front door, hoping that no one will notice, when she realizes for the first time that there's an exit door down from the coat closet. Pressing on the metal bar, she steps out into the cool night air. She looks up toward the sky and finds comfort gazing at the moon. It looks like a huge apricot.

"Home so early?"

The voice is Shinji's and she's surprised to hear it. Tracy must be with him. How wonderful. Being a witness to their playful affection or listening to their enthusiastic lovemaking are not high on her agenda tonight. But when she gets to the living room she sees that Shinji is alone, looking through his telescope.

"Did something happen?" he asks, turning toward her. "You look like you've seen a ghost."

She plops on the sofa, her coat still on, and tosses her purse on the coffee table. "You'll never believe what happened tonight."

"What?"

"Kevin came in to the Miki Lounge."

Shinji's expression is one of disbelief, the same shock that had registered on his face when Midori told him Kevin had dumped her. "You're kidding!"

"I wish I were. I had to say I was sick in order to go home," she says. "There was no way that I was going to stay."

"Did you talk to him?"

"No! Thank goodness he didn't see me." She goes on to explain how she pretended to vomit in the restroom.

Shinji shakes his head, then gives her a sympathetic laugh.

She laughs too. "I guess it *is* kind of funny."

"It's like a TV show," Shinji says. *"The Misadventures of Midori Saito."*

Midori nods. "That's for sure." Her emotions are all mixed up. She can see the humor in it, but part of her is also in a rage and another part wants to cry.

"But why are you so afraid to see him?"

It's a straightforward, pointed question. She thinks for a few moments. "Well, if he sees me still here struggling and working as a bar hostess, that kind of means he's won."

"He's won?"

She nods.

"Won what?"

She shrugs her shoulders.

"He didn't win anything. He lost someone very nice. He's a loser."

His words stun her, though she's not sure why. He's said it in a matter-of-fact manner, like anyone with one-quarter of a brain would know this. It's obvious, something you'd find in a dictionary of common knowledge: Ke-vin New-bury, n. 1. Loser. 2. Bad man.

"Let's go in the kitchen," he goes on. "I'll make you some tea. Or maybe you'd rather have a beer."

"Tea is fine. Thank you." Midori slips off her coat and follows him in, sitting at the table. "Why on earth would he come there?"

"I don't know," Shinji says. "Maybe he misses you and wanted to be around Japanese women. Or maybe he broke up with Kimberley." He pauses. "Or maybe she broke up with him."

Midori had thought of this very scenario during the cab ride home. She is glad to think that perhaps Kimberley had split up with Kevin, but she still has no desire to go back to him. Suddenly she's thrown into a panic. Has Kevin contacted Shinji? Does he actually know something but hasn't told her? "You haven't heard from him, have you?"

"No," Shinji says. "And I don't want to." He sits across from her.

"I still can't help but feel partially responsible for all this. Sending him to Japan."

"That's silly. Stop blaming yourself." She pauses. "I hope he doesn't start coming every night."

"Don't worry. I don't think that will happen." He leans back in his chair and cups his hands behind his neck. "So do you like working at the Miki Lounge?"

"I did until tonight," Midori says. "It's okay. The money is pretty good."

"It's not too, um, sleazy?"

Midori appreciates that his tone isn't judgmental, just concerned. "No. Nothing creepy. Although I think some of the women go home with the men. Maybe they make extra money that way. But I don't know for sure. That's certainly not for me." She sighs. "All I do is make conversation, sing karaoke, and get them to buy lots of drinks at high prices. The worst thing about it so far is having to listen to the customers' boring monologues and pretend to be fascinated."

Shinji rises to retrieve the teakettle.

She hopes she's not boring him, acting like one of her customers. But she can't stop talking about it, and goes on to tell him about Crystal, Britney, Taffy, and Amber.

"So what's *your* pseudonym?" he asks, smiling, as he pours tea in their cups.

"Sheridan."

"That sounds rather glamorous. How did you come up with that?"

It would be too embarrassing to admit her addiction to *Farrington Falls*. "Oh, I heard it somewhere." She blows on her tea to cool it. "You know, this Amber girl is so strange. I don't know how she got a job there."

Shinji is amused when Midori explains how Amber seems to be a bar hostess who can barely carry on a conversation.

"And she looks so familiar to me, but I can't place her."

"Maybe she's an old classmate. Once I ran into a guy I went to junior high with at a Giants game. That was weird."

"No. Doesn't seem to be." Midori sips her tea. "Anyway, I'm just so glad it's Sunday," she says, sighing with relief. "I don't have to go back until Thursday. I just wish I could forget about the Miki Lounge and be a pastry chef at a place like Lupine."

"Lupine?"

"That's where Graham is the chef."

"Oh, that's right. The neighbor you're so impressed with." Shinji raises his eyebrows.

"He's such a good cook! I had the most wonderful bluenose sea bass. The place is so pretty, with flowers and candles. You can hear the cable car ringing outside. Very romantic."

"So, are you going to see this guy again?"

"He's invited me to come back to the restaurant."

"So, another date?"

"Date? I *wish*. I'm not sure. He wants to introduce me to Danielle, the pastry chef." She runs her hand through her hair. "I'd love to be a pastry chef somewhere like that. Instead I have to settle for the Miki Lounge." She sighs. "I just hope I won't see Kevin there again."

"I wonder," Shinji says. "Does he have a thing for Japanese women now that he actually has to go to hostess bars? It's kind of strange." He stretches his arms across the table. "But I guess I shouldn't be so critical. I always had a thing for gaijin women."

"Oh, really?"

"It's all my mom's fault," he says, laughing. "After my brother died she went crazy for all the gaijin television stars. She even kept scrapbooks about them. I guess it was some kind of comfort to her. Do you remember Thomas Thompson? She loved him."

Midori remembers him well. He was a Mormon who spoke perfect Japanese, having studied it at Brigham Young University. He could even pull off a decent rendering of a downtown Tokyo dialect. Because he had a vast knowledge of obscure Japanese history trivia, he repeatedly took the top prize on the *Think Quick* quiz show.

She makes a face. "I thought he looked like a complete nerd."

Shinji laughs. "Yeah, with those thick, dorky black glasses."

"Did you like Alessandra Tachikawa?"

"Not really," he says, sticking out his tongue. "But my mom did."

Alessandra Salavati was an Italian who married a famous Japanese baseball player named Kazuo Tachikawa. After he died in a car accident when she was twenty-seven, she became an instant celebrity as a TV chef on a show called *We Love Cucina with Alessandra*. It didn't matter that she'd had no training in professional cooking.

"My mom liked her too," Midori says. "Sometimes she made her recipes."

"The one I liked was Gina Torrance. And she was my mom's favorite too. Every time she was on TV my mother would say, 'Shinji, come here! Gina's on!'"

"Oh, yeah—'Kissing Lips.'"

Gina was a blond American who spoke Japanese and had one hit record called *Kissing Lips* in the late 1980s. She was sexy with large breasts—the Kimberley Hobbs of her time. Midori had never paid much attention to her.

"I went pretty crazy for Gina Torrance," Shinji says. "Typical thirteen-year-old boy's fantasy, I guess. It was amazing to me to see a blond woman speak Japanese. From then on, I was pretty America crazy."

Yes, Shinji is America crazy and how nice that his dream has come true of having a homegrown American girlfriend who speaks Japanese. He's sure kissing lips with Tracy. Still, isn't it odd that someone like Shinji would be so attracted to a girl who is so crazy about Japan when he seems to want nothing to do with anything Japanese? And isn't it even stranger that he refuses to speak to her in anything but English?

"Did you listen to Armed Forces Radio?" Midori asks. It's fun to reminisce with him, especially now since this has caused the Kevin incident to almost completely escape her mind.

"Oh, yeah," he says, sitting up straight. *"American Top Forty!"* He sings the jingle.

It makes Midori laugh. What would it have been like to know Shinji back then? To have a friend with this in common? "Well, you may have been America crazy," Midori says, pouring more tea in his cup. "But you must have dated Japanese girls, right?"

"Yeah."

"Well, I've never dated a Japanese guy."

He looks surprised. "Really?"

"I was crazy for gaijin men. My father was furious with me. He kept trying to set me up with Japanese guys."

"Oh, I see," he says. "Then Kevin came to your rescue?"

Rescue? She doesn't like how that sounds, but she supposes it's true. "I guess so." Now the topic has turned back to the bad man again. Her shoulders slump as she stares at the kitchen clock, not knowing what to say next.

Shinji immediately seems to realize he's said something that's upset her. "I'm sorry, Midori-san. I shouldn't have said that."

She gives him a little smile. "It's nothing." But it stings.

They are silent.

Shinji claps his hands. "Oh, you know what?" he says brightly. "It's a clear night tonight. You want to look at the moon?"

"Okay. I saw it when I left the Miki Lounge tonight. It looked like an apricot."

He smiles. "Always thinking about food, huh?" he teases, making her laugh.

There's a large, oversized easy chair in front of the telescope, big enough for both of them to sit together. Shinji looks through the lens, turns a few knobs and dials, then tilts it in Midori's direction. It's not easy to breathe normally with him sitting so close to her, feeling his shoulder, his leg pressed against hers. It's obviously never exciting to sit close to Tako or Possum or any of the other customers at the Miki Lounge—they're so unattractive that a hand on the thigh is gross rather than thrilling. And she hasn't thought of Shinji in this way. Only Graham. It's puzzling, but it's a nice feeling.

"Take a look," he says, smiling.

She gazes through the viewer. The moon is less orange and whiter now. She's never seen it so sharp, so clear and close. It's like she can almost reach out and grab it.

"Is it a full moon tonight?" she asks. "It looks like it."

"Not quite. Almost," Shinji says. "Do you see the man in the moon?"

"I've heard of that," she says. "But I only see the rabbit pounding rice cakes."

He laughs. "Yeah. Some people see the rabbit. Some people see a man carrying sticks. Some people just see a face. I guess I can see them all if I try hard enough."

"What is it about the moon that you like so much?"

"I don't know," he says. "It's just so majestic. So peaceful. After my brother died, I used to look at the moon and wish I could just fly there. Just go far, far away."

Shinji had said that his brother had taught him how to look at the moon through a telescope. Midori thinks of the bronzed shoes sitting in Shinji's room. The shoes that had been sitting on the Tozai line subway platform at Waseda Station.

"Ah," he says suddenly. "It's past midnight. Guess I should go to bed. Some of us have to get up early for our jobs."

She knows he's teasing her. He stands up and stretches.

"Don't worry about Kevin too much," he says. "I'm sure he won't be back."

"Thanks for showing me the moon," Midori says.

He smiles. He doesn't leave right away.

"Anytime," he finally says. He puts his hands in his pockets, gently rocking back and forth on his heels. Then he lightly touches her shoulder with his fingertips. "Good night, Midori-san."

"Good night." She watches him as he walks down the hall and into his room, shutting the door gently behind him. She leans back in the chair and lets out a sigh as she notices a bright ray of moonlight shining on the hardwood floor.

# 12

DOING THE LAUNDRY HAS NEVER BEEN ONE OF MIDORI'S FAVORITE tasks, but now she seems to be in the basement every other day, hanging around the washer and dryer as if they're her best friends. Maybe she'll run into Graham. She tries to be there in the late morning, because that was the time when she first met him there.

She finally catches him taking his clothes out of the dryer. She likes the way he fits into his jeans, his black T-shirt just tight enough to show off his chest.

"Hey, Midori! How are you doing?" he says in a cheery voice, throwing some socks into his laundry basket. "When are you coming back to Lupine?"

"Soon! I want to eat more delicious food."

"Good. Then you can meet Danielle."

"Yes, that is nice." She's hoping for Graham to suggest going somewhere together afterwards, but he says nothing. She wonders if she should say something, but decides to hold back. It's best to take her time. But there's no reason not to offer a more subtle suggestion. As she begins to load her clothes in the dryer she says, "If you are not busy now, would you like to have cake and tea?"

"Sure."

Once her clothes are tumbling in the dryer, they go to her apartment. She's made a chocolate-caramel hazelnut layer cake. They sit at the kitchen table.

"Midori, this is exquisite," Graham says, closing his eyes as he takes in the flavor.

"*Exquisite?*"

"It means excellent." He smiles. "You're very talented. I'm sure you'll get another job soon."

She shows him her pastry album, which now has photos of some of her own creations.

"You're so dedicated. To be studying like this. And you only studied on your own in Japan?"

She nods. "Some classes I take."

"I went to a cooking school in Chicago," he says. "And your pastries taste just as good as the students' there."

It's like someone turned on the oven inside her. "Thank you. You are born in Chicago?"

"I grew up there. Went to school there. Got my first restaurant job there."

"Why you come to San Francisco?"

"A bad breakup," he says, frowning. "Sort of like you and your Kevin."

"Ah! I'm sorry!"

"Anyway . . ." They continue talking about pastries. He asks her about traditional Japanese sweets, which she knows little about, but she knows more about them than he does.

After two cups of tea, he says he has to go. "Be sure and come to Lupine. How about Wednesday night again?"

"Okay!"

He gives her arm a squeeze. "Thanks, Midori, for the wonderful cake. I'll see you then."


Midori dreads returning to the Miki Lounge. What if Kevin shows up again? But she has an idea. She'd noticed a beauty salon supplies shop near the grocery store on California and Fillmore. On Wednesday she decides to stop in.

The shop is called Hair Apparent. She likes the sound of the name but isn't sure what it means. They sell shampoos, conditioners, and gels, but in the back she sees several rows of Styrofoam mannequin heads displaying a variety of wigs.

"Can I help you?" asks the man behind the counter as she examines them. He looks to be around forty, with short, almost shaved brown hair and a closely trimmed beard. On his form-fitting purple T-shirt it says THY QUEERDOM COME, THY WILL BE DONE in gothic lettering. Midori doesn't understand this either. "Looking for a wig?" he asks.

"Yes. I want to look . . . I want to look unlike myself."

He smiles knowingly. "Oh, I see, honey. You mean you need a disguise?"

"Yes, I think so." How nice that the man has understood her. Maybe her English is getting better, though it's not really possible. Yes, she can understand a lot of *Farrington Falls* by now, but she speaks English to virtually no one except shop clerks and Graham. And the only other American she's gotten to know so far—Tracy—requires their conversations to be in Japanese.

"Well, let's pin your hair up, put it in a cap, and you can try some on."

The man is helpful. When she puts on a short, red, curly wig, it makes her look like Ashley on *Farrington Falls*. Cool blond waves give her the appearance of a Japanese Kimberley Hobbs, while a fringed, pink shag seems to turn her into a female impersonator. But Midori prefers a shoulder-length light brown wig with thick blond streaks. It's more subdued than over the top, giving off the right amount of mysteriousness without causing undue attention. Dare she say it? It even makes her look a little like Sheridan Hamilton.

"*Très chic*," says the man.

Midori isn't sure what this means, but she can tell by his voice and smile that he's giving her a letter of approval. "Thank you," she says.

The man takes a small card from a drawer and slides it into a hole puncher. "Here, honey," he says. "It's a supersaver card. You buy enough stuff here and you'll get a free compact and blush brush."

"Very nice," Midori says.

It's a relief to have bought something that will hopefully make Kevin look right past her, if indeed he ever sets his leg into the Miki Lounge again.

However, she isn't about to wear her wig to Lupine that evening; she wants to look the most like herself as possible. She wears her favorite black pants that make her legs appear longer, and a mint-green cotton sweater that makes it look as if she actually has a bustline. She brings her pastry album and a pear tart for Graham and Danielle to try.

"Midori!"

Even though Graham is busy he takes the time to give her a warm greeting.

"How are you?" he asks, sipping on his requisite glass of white wine.

"I'm fine. How are you?"

"Busy. Busy." He takes a kerchief and wipes his forehead. "Would you like a glass of wine?"

As he pours her a glass, Midori takes a plastic tub out of her tote bag. "Here's a pear tart I made. I would like to give to Danielle."

"That's so sweet of you." He opens the top to peer inside. "This looks wonderful."

He calls to Danielle, and a woman with short dark brown hair comes out from the back. She looks around Midori's age, and her hands are bathed in flour. She wipes her hands with a towel before she shakes Midori's hand.

"Danielle is the pastry queen," Graham says.

"Maybe I can be pastry princess then," Midori says.

Danielle's smile is friendly. "Graham has told me you're a pastry chef too."

"I am trying to be pastry chef." Midori hands her the pear tart.

Danielle cuts a slice and takes a bite. Midori holds her breath as she waits for the verdict.

"This is so delicious, Midori." She offers the plate to Graham, who also takes a bite.

"Mmm," he says. "Exquisite."

The comments seem sincere, not just polite. "Thank you."

"Where did you get these pears? At the farmers' market?" Danielle asks.

"No. A store near my apartment. On California Street."

"Anjou pears?"

"Yes."

"They're so sweet. You know," she says, taking another bite, "I know this woman named Kate who runs Kate's Katering and she sometimes needs extra help with desserts. It would just be work from time to time. Shall I give her your phone number?"

Graham winks at Midori. She can't believe her good fortune. She gives Danielle her number.

Graham presents Midori with a bowl of perfectly al dente linguine with olive oil, tomatoes, and basil. Before she picks up her fork to sample it, one of the male servers rushes over with a hunk of fresh Parmesan that he grates over the bowl, dusting the noodles like a light snowfall.

Graham refills Midori's glass with chardonnay. It's a dreamy combination: the buttery taste of the wine and the romantic lighting along with the clanging of the cable car's bell outside. It'll be just a matter of time before she quits the Miki Lounge since she'll be in such high demand from that catering business Danielle mentioned.

As Midori watches Graham toss a bundle of green beans in a copper pot sprinkled with olive oil, she pictures him kissing her outside her apartment door. They won't be able to stop, and Midori will have to fumble for her keys. The two of them will make their way into the apartment, but she'll barely be able to close the door because their passion is so frenzied. It's just like Sheridan and Brent or Kendall and Damian as they tumble onto her bed, ripping off each other's clothes until . . .

"Taste okay?"

It's Graham's voice.

"Yes. So good."

It's already closing time and the last of the customers have filed out, satisfied with their perfect meals. Midori's on her third glass of chardonnay, and wolfing down some lime sorbet with housemade cookies as she watches Graham clean up. They chat about how he mixes semolina flour with unbleached white flour to make it easier to handle when he makes fresh pasta. He pours himself another glass of wine and he seems to be leaning in closer to her as they talk. Her head feels light and puffy, she's not used to drinking so much.

It takes her a moment to realize the front door has opened. She thought they'd already locked up. Who could be coming in so late? Graham turns his gaze to the entrance and his eyes light up.

"Ah, there he is. *Finally*," he says, grinning.

Midori turns to see a dark-haired man in his thirties wearing a fashionable trench coat, a plaid muffler wrapped tightly around his neck. He walks quickly behind the counter as if he's familiar with the place. Then he takes Graham in his arms and kisses him full on the lips. "Sorry I'm late," he says.

"It was worth the wait," Graham purrs.

Midori's chair now feels off-balance, like it would take a wadded-up linen napkin under one of the legs to steady it.

"Midori," Graham says, his eyes sparkling and his arm still around the man's waist. "I'd like you to meet my boyfriend, Eric Randle. Eric, this is my neighbor Midori Saito. She's a wonderful pastry chef."

"Midori," Eric says in a pleasant and friendly voice, extending his hand. "So nice to meet you."


"He's *gay*," Midori tells Akina on the phone, spitting out the word like a piece of rotten Anjou pear.

Akina gasps. "You're kidding!"

"I don't know how I could have been so stupid, but I just never imagined it. It never occurred to me."

"So sorry, Mi-chan. Is there anyone else in the picture?"

She sighs. "No. My only other prospects are fictional—on a home drama called *Farrington Falls*."


On Thursday night at the Miki Lounge, Midori dons her Sheridan Hamilton wig.

"Sheridan!" Taffy exclaims. "Is that really you?"

Midori blushes.

"I didn't recognize you at first. Very nice. Very nice." She smiles. "Are you feeling better?"

Midori nods. Maybe, just maybe, with her fake name, wig, and uncharacteristic lavender lipstick, sunlit copper eye shadow, and ivory foundation, which make her look more geisha than bar hostess, Kevin will fail to recognize her.

Midori goes to check on her appearance in the restroom. Crystal and Britney primp in front of the mirror, but stop and let out simultaneous shrieks when they see her.

"Is this a new girl?" asks Britney.

"Sheridan! So glamorous!" Crystal raves.

"I can't believe how different you look! Gorgeous!" Britney fingers a few strands of Midori's wig.

"Thank you."

"You were sick last week, weren't you?" Crystal says.

"Uh-huh."

"You were throwing up, right?" says Britney.

"Yes."

The two women exchange meaningful glances. Britney pokes Crystal with her elbow.

"Sheridan," Crystal whispers. "Are you— are you *pregnant?*"

"No!"

"Are you sure?" Britney's eyes are wide.

"Yes, I'm sure."

"Too bad you had to go home. You missed such a cool American guy," Britney then says, bending over to flip her hair.

"Yeah," Crystal says. "So handsome! He lived in Japan before. He even spoke some Japanese."

Would it be inconsiderate to rush to the toilet and throw up for real this time? She tries to keep her face devoid of any expression. She doesn't want them to become suspicious. "Oh, really?" she says, powdering her cheeks. "Do you think he'll be back?" She keeps her tone blasé, disinterested.

"I hope so," says Crystal.

"Maybe not." Britney sighs in disappointment. "He said he's getting married."

Midori's shoulders go numb. *Married.* She'd been hoping that Kevin and Kimberley had broken up. Now apparently it's official— they really are going to become husband and wife. She imagines the two of them in miniature, standing atop a three-tiered yellow, vanilla-frosted wedding cake. In fact she sees two more cakes—one topped with Shinji and Tracy, the other with Graham and Eric, all of them happy, happy couples. And there's Midori the old spinster, all by herself, bent over and leaning on her cane atop a stale cream puff.

If only she could rush out of the bathroom, run home, and never return to the Miki Lounge. Well, she can. If she really had to, she could just leave. She'd never have to face these people again. They don't have her phone number, they don't know where she lives—they really don't know anything about her. She's just a warm Japanese body that gets customers to pay a steep admission charge and buy drinks at exorbitant prices.

She'll be able to get another job. Won't Danielle's catering friend call her? Perhaps. But she certainly wouldn't make this much money. Oh, let Kevin come back. She can face him. After all, he's the loser, right?

"Then I guess you girls are out of luck with that guy," Midori says to Crystal and Britney, finding some composure. "Besides, don't you have boyfriends?"

This is the first time she's asked them a personal question, but it certainly isn't any worse than being nosy enough to inquire whether you're carrying a baby. So what if this is supposedly against the Miki Lounge rules?

Crystal rolls her eyes at Britney. They both laugh. "Maybe," Crystal says as they leave the bathroom. Midori sighs. She isn't going to get anything out of them.

Amber arrives as they leave and immediately bumps into Midori because, as usual, when she walks she looks more at the floor than in the direction where she's headed.

"I'm sorry," Midori apologizes. "Are you feeling better?"

Amber at first looks puzzled, her smooth forehead now creased, but then says, "Oh, yeah."

"I was sick on Sunday too."

"Oh, really?" Amber slinks into the stall and shuts the door behind her.

Throughout the night Midori holds her breath as she watches each customer walk in the door, praying that Kevin won't come in. The night seems completely normal, with visits from Tako, Possum, and a few new customers. But around eleven-forty-five in walks Kevin to a flurry of squeals from Britney and Crystal. The Miki Lounge must have been a hit with him. He's back for more.

"Kay-van, Kay-van," Britney cries out, rushing over to him. Taffy meets Midori's glance and nods her head in the bad man's direction. Midori is ready. Taffy escorts her to Kevin.

"Newbury-san," Taffy says. "So nice to see you again. This is Sheridan. She speaks English!"

Midori is trembling inside, but she manages to bow while extending her hand to shake his. "So nice to make your acquaintance."

Taffy stares at her. Midori has sweetened her voice into that of a six-year-old in an attempt to disguise her identity. If it's made such a difference to Taffy, surely it will work on Kevin. And it seems to. While enchanted by her presence, he gives no indication that he's recognized her.

"Sheridan," he says in his booming voice. "That's a lovely name."

"Thank you. What is your drinking desire tonight?"

He chuckles. "Vodka martini. Shaken not stirred."

Midori hopes Taffy knows what this means, because she doesn't. Taffy nods. "Of course! Just like James Bond!"

Midori slides into the booth next to Kevin. She wonders if he'll perform a thigh grope like Tako or Possum, but he keeps his hands to himself. "So what is nice American boy like you being in place like this?"

Again he cracks up. "You're so cute."

*Yeah, I'm really cute*, she thinks, gritting her teeth. *So cute that you dumped me for some snippy, full-of-herself, melon-breasted American.*

"But why you like Japanese bar?" She bats her eyelashes.

"I used to live in Japan."

"Really? That is so interesting."

Taffy brings him his drink. Midori can see Britney, who is sitting with another customer, lean over every so often and stare in her direction, seemingly consumed with envy.

He goes on to tell her about how he taught English there and how sweet he thinks Japanese women are.

"You date lots of Japanese girl?"

He leans back in the booth, his arms stretched out along the back edge. "Some. I was engaged to a Japanese girl."

Midori can feel the sweat trickling down the back of her neck. "Really?"

"Yes. She came here, but we broke up. Now she's back in Japan."

"Oh! Too bad for her. She not like America so she went back?"

"Not exactly. It's a long story."

"I like stories." She can't believe she's saying this.

He throws back his head and laughs. "I bet you do. Anyway, I'm about to get married."

"To a Japanese girl?"

"No. An American."

"Your fiancée lets you go hostess bar?"

He sips his drink. He laughs and leans in close to her so she can feel his breath on her cheek. "She doesn't know I'm here," he whispers.

She remembers how exciting it was to be this close to Kevin, to even make love with him, but she feels none of that now. She wants to spit in his face, but smiles instead. "Oh, it is secret?"

"Yes. My little secret."

His cell phone rings. "Excuse me," he says to Midori. "Hello? Hey, babe."

Is it Kimberley? Kevin never called Midori *babe*.

"I told you. I'm with Rob." He gives Midori a wink. "Yeah, he's dealing with some shit. Just having a couple of beers. I'll be back soon. Uh-huh. Yeah. Love you too, babe."

He tosses the cell phone on the table and gets up. "Will you excuse me, please, Sheridan? I'm off to the john."

She watches as he walks away in an arrogant stride, stopping first to talk to an enchanted Britney. What *did* she ever see in him? He's so crass, so boorish. The way he calls Kimberley *babe*. And going off to the *john*. It's all so tacky, unrefined. Well, she thought he was great because he was a gaijin and he looked like Prince Charming. How could she have been such an idiot?

Once she sees him enter the men's room, she picks up his cell phone and is quickly able to understand how she can ring the last call received.

"Kevin?"

It's Kimberley. Midori keeps her breathy little girl voice. "No, this is not Kevin," she says.

"*Who is this?*"

Midori keeps an eye out for Kevin. "Sorry, but I guess he still like Japanese woman. He's at the hostess bar in Japantown. The Miki Lounge. You better be careful."

"*What?*"

"Kevin. Bad man. Bad man."

Midori hangs up and turns the phone off, just in case Kimberley calls back. She hopes Kevin won't notice. He doesn't.

"Well, Sheridan. It's been a pleasure. But I must be going."

"So soon?"

He kisses her hand. "Maybe I'll see you again sometime."

"I like that."

"That Newbury-san," Taffy says when she hands Midori her pay at the end of the night. "He liked you. Gave you a big tip! Maybe he'll come back."

Midori smiles. Perhaps Kimberley will see that he doesn't.

# 13

IT'S THE END OF ANOTHER NIGHT AT THE MIKI LOUNGE WHEN MIDORI stops in the bathroom before catching her cab home. When she enters the stall that had been the scene of her great fake vomiting performance, she notices something on the floor. It's a wallet. Bright blue and made of plastic, it's embossed with a picture of Hello Kitty, jaunty in a French beret, the Eiffel Tower looming behind her.

There isn't much to find when she opens it—twenty-three dollars in cash, a discount card for the Japanese grocery store in Japantown, a BART subway ticket worth two dollars and fifty cents, and some bus transfers. There are no credit cards, but tucked behind a receipt for Sunshine Dry Cleaning is a California driver's license for someone named Li Mei Yang. Midori looks at the photograph—it's a picture of Amber. So she's Chinese? She'd said she was Japanese and raised in Singapore. It doesn't quite add up, but nothing about this girl results in a neat sum.

Midori reads the address: 213A Sixth Avenue, San Francisco. Then she looks at the other information on the license: Amber is twenty-five, has brown eyes and black hair, and weighs one hundred and three pounds.

Midori places the wallet in her purse. She knows Amber has al-

ready left. She'll see her the following night and can return it to her
then. But Amber may panic if she discovers her wallet is missing, and
she might need it before Saturday night. Besides, Midori is curious to
see where this girl lives and whether she can find out anything more
about her. A better plan would be to go to her house and return the
wallet the next day.


Midori quickly showers and dresses the next morning, then looks at
her map to chart her course to get to Sixth Avenue. She discovers
that Amber's place is in the Richmond District. She can walk down
Fillmore Street and catch the number one California bus, which will
take her right there.

Maybe Amber will be more personable outside of work. Maybe
she'll be more relaxed, perhaps invite Midori in for a cup of tea.
She'll finally learn all about her and, perhaps, all about Britney, Crystal, and Taffy and how they ended up in San Francisco and at the
Miki Lounge. Then Midori can tell Amber her Kevin story. It would
be nice to have a friend.

After getting off the bus, Midori walks down Sixth Avenue and
easily finds the simple white house with gray trim with numbers
painted on tiles that say 213. But the address on the license had said
213A. Looking to her right she notices a narrow alleyway next to the
house. A small gate has a sign with wooden numbers that read 213A.
Midori opens the gate and walks down the lane to find a yellow door.
It seems to be the entry for a basement apartment that's attached to
the main house.

Midori knocks on the door and waits. She knocks again.

The door finally opens slowly, but only a crack. Peering out is an
Asian man, barefoot, probably in his late twenties, wearing a white
T-shirt and gray sweatpants. A dark green knit cap clasps his head.
His eyes only seem half-open. Did she wake him up?

"Yes?" he says tentatively. His voice is almost a whisper.

Midori doesn't know who to ask for. Should she say Amber or Li

Mei Yang? But Amber probably uses her American name only at the Miki Lounge.

"Is Li Mei Yang here?" she says in English.

"Who?"

"Li Mei Yang?" Her pronunciation of a Chinese name must be just short of atrocious.

The man shakes his head.

"Or, um, Amber? Is Amber here?"

"You have the wrong place," he snaps. Midori can hear an accent when he speaks English, but isn't 100 percent sure if he's Japanese. Suddenly Amber appears next to him, and the man disappears, as if he's in a hurry.

Amber is nearly unrecognizable out of her bar hostess clothes, her face free of makeup. She's dressed in baggy denim overalls with a beige tank top. Looking skinnier, her bony arms appear longer than you'd expect. Midori is struck by how young she looks, like a high school student. The Hello Kitty wallet seems to fit and yet somehow it doesn't. That slightly crooked mouth is the only thing that keeps her from looking like a knockout, even in such a plain state.

"Eh?" Amber says, looking surprised to see Midori.

This is the most expression Midori has ever seen on her face. She tries to look unobtrusively over Amber's head, hoping to peer inside the tiny-looking apartment, but she can't see much. She can, however, discern the scent of what smells like boiled cabbage.

"Uh, I just came because . . . ," Midori says, digging into her purse. "Because you left your wallet at work." She hands it to her. "I found it in the bathroom."

"Ah!" Amber says, her face turning red. "Thank you."

Midori hopes Amber will ask her in, but no invitation seems forthcoming. Midori stands there in an awkward silence, noticing for the first time that her shoes are pinching her toes. "So, um, I guess I'll see you tonight."

"Uh-huh," Amber says, giving her a tiny smile, then quickly looks toward the ground. "Thank you." She shuts the door.

What a strange girl. It's disappointing to find out nothing more about Amber other than where she lives. And how odd that the barefoot guy didn't seem to know her by either of those names. Is he one of her "customers"? Midori didn't recognize him as being from the Miki Lounge; she gets the feeling that the guy lives there too. She knows, though, that Amber will never be forthcoming. It's best to give up on finding out anything further about her or anyone else at the Miki Lounge.

"Nice party, isn't it?" Kyle says, his eyes gleaming.

On *Farrington Falls* Ashley sits at a table by herself at an elaborate function for the people who work for *Elegant Lifestyle* when Kyle comes over to her. Midori is unsure what the occasion is, but it's a fancy affair in a luxurious hotel with dinner and dancing. More extravagant than even the Newburys' engagement party for Kevin and his doomed fiancée.

"Sheridan has gone all out this time," Ashley says.

"Yeah, she's not only the queen of magazine publishing, she's also the queen of parties."

Midori presses hard on her piecrust dough with a rolling pin. Will Kyle finally profess his love for Ashley? And will Ashley finally be able to be more than friends with him?

The music starts and couples flock to the dance floor. Now it's Kyle's chance to ask Ashley to dance.

"Ashley—" he says, but is interrupted when Mandy rushes to his side.

"Kyle! You know this is my favorite song! Come on!" Mandy grabs his hand and pulls him toward the other dancers.

The camera focuses on Ashley's disappointed face. Cassandra comes over to her, handing her a glass of champagne. "You know you've got to tell him," she says.

Midori's concentration is interrupted with the sound of the front door opening and closing. It's only two-forty-five—it can't be Shinji. But then who else could it be?

"Oh, what's this?"

It is Shinji, of course. And he's caught her watching *Farrington Falls*. Midori blushes. She would have turned off the television immediately if only the remote hadn't been lying on the counter on the other side of the kitchen.

"*Farrington Falls?*" Shinji says as the theme song plays behind the fancy scripted logo, which resembles a neon sign. It even blinks. He smiles. "A soap opera?"

"Just a silly show," Midori says, walking over and grabbing the remote to turn off the TV.

"Actually I used to tape *Love Finds a Way* when I first came to the States," he says. "It was good for practicing English." In a dramatic announcer voice he speaks in English, "Extortion? Kidnapping? Murder? You'll never see such pure evil as Wyatt Dupree on *Love Finds a Way*."

She laughs. So he isn't making fun of her. "Yes, I think it's good for English practice."

"What are you making?"

"Lemon meringue pie."

"Mmm. That sounds good."

"What are you doing home so early?"

"There was a big celebration in honor of Sawyer and Jones acquiring another company. So we had a party and then they let us go home early."

Shinji begins looking through the mail that Midori has left on the corner of the kitchen table. "Just bills," he sighs. "Nothing interesting."

Midori carefully places her dough into a glass pie plate, spreading it gently with her fingers to keep it from tearing.

The phone rings. She has rarely heard Shinji's phone, and the one time she'd picked up a call, it had been the wrong number. Shinji doesn't talk much on the phone at home, preferring to use his cell phone.

Shinji goes to the hallway to answer it.

Midori can't understand what he's saying, but she can make out that he's speaking Japanese. Maybe he's talking to his parents. Calculating the time in Japan, it could be a call from there, but it would be early in the morning the next day. She pricks her pie shell with a fork to prevent it from blistering or puffing up too much when it bakes. She no longer hears Shinji talking, and when she looks up and sees him standing at the doorway to the kitchen, his face is in a grimace.

"Midori-san," he says in a serious voice. "It's your father."

"Eh?" Midori drops her fork to the floor, then quickly picks it up and tosses it in the sink.

Her father? How idiotic she'd been to give her mother this number. But what else could she have done? The cell phone must have perished by now.

Walking to the hallway she might as well be on her way to stand before the judge who'll be handing down her prison sentence. She tries to remain calm, but she knows she's guilty. She'll have to confess everything now. Yet it's her life and she shouldn't have to make excuses for it any longer.

"*Moshi-moshi.*"

"Midori?!" That voice. It's the one that brings to mind a disapproving teacher, an unreasonable boss, an overly demanding coach.

"*Otousan,* how are you?"

He doesn't answer her question. "What the devil's going on over there? We never get a call from you, and your mother has been driving me crazy with her worry about when you're ever going to get the hell married. It's the end of July and she hasn't heard a thing from you. How selfish can you be, Midori? Can you think only of yourself?"

Is he speaking into a bullhorn? It's about that loud. Shinji can probably hear each word all the way from the kitchen.

When Mr. Saito doesn't immediately receive an answer, he goes on. "And who the hell was that Japanese guy who answered the phone?"

Okay. Let's see. What else would she rather be doing than hearing this litany? Meeting Eric Randle, her once-upon-a-time husband-to-be's boyfriend? Pretending to throw up in a toilet stall? Perhaps. Why on earth did Shinji start conversing with her father? What had they said to each other? Her heart drums way too hard against her chest.

*She is thirty years old.* There is no rational reason why she should be transported back to middle school every time she receives a phone call from her parents.

She takes a deep breath. "That was Shinji Nishimura," she says. "My roommate."

"Your *what?*"

"My roommate. I'm living at his apartment."

"You're living with a guy while you're engaged to be married to another?"

"Dad, listen to me." Midori is surprised at the forcefulness that's overtaken her voice. "Kevin and I broke up. We're not getting married."

In stark contrast to the previous outburst, there is now only silence on the other end of the line. Midori has no problem imagining the look of disgust on her father's face, the snorting, the smacking of his lips in disdain. She clears her throat. "*Moshi-moshi.* Are you still there?"

She hears what always has made her think of a human vacuum cleaner—the sound of her father sucking in his breath. "I give up," he finally says, a war general admitting defeat. "Talk to your mother."

On cue, she hears Mrs. Saito's voice. "*Moshi-moshi,* Midori?"

Now she'll have to repeat herself. "Mom, Kevin and I broke up. We're not getting married."

"Eh?! Not getting married?!" Her mother is close to hysterical. This is definitely the scandal of the century, destined to be the lead story on NHK News: "Tonight, live by satellite from San Francisco, we bring you the shocking, heart-wrenching, and explosive tale of the breakup of Kevin Newbury and Midori Saito."

"What happened? Where is Kevin? Midori, then where are you living?"

"I'm living with someone named Shinji Nishimura and—"

"You have a boyfriend?"

"No. He's my roommate."

"You have a *male roommate?*" Her tone implies that this could very well be against the law. "What does that mean?"

"It means that—"

"You need to come home right now, Midori. I told you from the beginning that this wasn't going to work out. I always had a bad feeling about the whole thing."

"Mom—"

"Give me a few days and I can take care of everything. I'll set up the marriage meetings for you. This time we'll find someone you'll like better than Tamasaki-san. Just leave it to me and—"

"Mom, be quiet for a minute! Listen to me." Midori's tone continues to be assertive, confident. She hears her father blustering in the background, but unlike every other time, she's determined to not let it affect her. "I'm not coming home. I'm staying here."

"But Midori—"

"I'm doing fine, Mom. I have a job."

"A job? Doing what?"

"Doing translation work." At least she's able to be about 95 percent truthful. And her mother doesn't know enough to figure out that without getting married to Kevin Midori is illegal.

"Oh, Midori! *What happened with Kevin?*"

Midori would rather be head baker at Mr. Donut than tell her mother about Kimberley Hobbs. Can she please at least retain a few deep-fried morsels of dignity? "Things just didn't work out."

"Didn't work out? What do you mean?"

"That's all you need to know."

"But, Midori—"

"I'm fine, Mom. Don't worry. And tell Dad not to worry either. I'll talk to you later. Bye." The calmness she has felt during the whole ordeal evaporates. Her hands tremble as she hangs up the phone. Her knees turn squishy, but she's done it. It's over.

Back in the kitchen she sees Shinji paging through her pastry album. She collapses on the chair across from him. "I'm sorry, Shinji-san, but I guess you couldn't help but hear."

"Are you okay?"

"Yes," she says, smiling. "Yes, I think I am."

"At least you told them."

"Did you talk to my father in Japanese or something?"

"Yeah. I think he was so confused when you didn't answer the phone that he just started saying 'Moshi-moshi' and the next thing I knew I was speaking to him in Japanese. It was automatic. Then I realized who it was. I'm really sorry, Midori-san, if it made him even more upset."

"It's okay." Midori stares at her piecrust. "I can't believe I told them. But it's all out in the open now. Well, at least most of it."

Shinji smiles. "Congratulations. You've finally severed the seven-thousand-mile umbilical cord."

She gives a hearty laugh that emanates from deep within her belly. She can't remember the last time she's laughed like this. She is now positively lighthearted. Free. "Will you celebrate with me?"

"What do you mean?"

"I'll take you for dessert at My Sweet Heart."

He raises his eyebrows, giving her a devilish grin. "My motto is to never say no to dessert."

On their way down Fillmore Street, Shinji convinces Midori to get the pastries to go and have them at Alta Plaza, a small neighborhood park between Jackson and Clay. They sit on a bench next to flower beds of pink morning glories and purple pansies that look out on vast lawns. The sun is out in full force. Children play, dogs scamper on the grass.

Midori treats Shinji to six desserts: two gingerbread cupcakes with cream cheese frosting, a white chocolate brownie with pecans, a piece of princess cake with pale green icing topped with a red rose, a banana crème tartlette, and a chocolate mousse cup.

"Good. You brought your camera," he says when she takes it out of her purse and places each pastry on the bench.

She crouches down and snaps a photo of each one.

"Now you can eat," she says, smiling.

They share everything. Midori relishes the pleasure from the sweets, the sunshine warming her cheeks, and the fact that she isn't keeping a deep, dark secret from her parents any longer. Watching Shinji wolf down a big bite of brownie she asks, "Which is your favorite?"

"They're all good," he says. "But it's between the princess cake and the chocolate mousse."

"Yes, their mousse is especially creamy and thick. You can't add too much whipping cream or it gets runny. But this texture is just about perfect."

"I think your stuff tastes just as good, though, if not better."

"That's so nice of you to say."

"It's the truth." He leans back against the bench and closes his eyes, taking in the sunshine. "It's been so busy at work. It's nice to be able to just sit and relax."

She gazes at his cheekbones, his eyelashes, his mouth. His face looks sculpted, like a Noh mask—traditional, classic. Why hasn't she noticed this before? It's weird, but she suddenly feels the urge to kiss him, but instead crams the remaining gingerbread cupcake into her mouth.

"How's work with you?" he asks.

"Okay. But I'm wondering how much more I can take of the Miki Lounge."

"You mean because Kevin showed up that time?"

"Actually he showed up again."

"What?"

Shinji can't stop laughing while she tells him how she carried out her bar hostessing duties to Kevin without his knowledge, and called Kimberley back on his cell phone.

"I didn't come all the way from Japan to end up being a hostess at a Japanese bar, though," Midori finally says. She pauses. "But the money is too good to give up."

Shinji seems to note her worried face, giving her a sympathetic look. "I understand," he says. "But you have your savings account, right? You can wait to find something else."

Her savings account. Shinji probably thinks she has thousands of dollars, though she has never let him think otherwise. Without the Miki Lounge income she wouldn't be able to pay the rent.

"But it's too bad you can't get work related to your desserts," he goes on.

"Well, the pastry chef at Graham's restaurant gave my number to a caterer who may call me."

"Oh, really? That sounds good." He bites into the brownie. "So how is *Graham?*" Shinji says the name as if their neighbor is a famous movie star.

Midori shrugs. "I don't know . . ." She's not in the mood to share her embarrassment about her failure at picking up on Graham's sexual persuasion.

"You haven't been back to his restaurant?"

"No."

Shinji's cell phone rings. The relaxed expression on his face, the affectionate tone of his voice all point to the fact that's he's talking to Tracy.

"No, I'm in Alta Plaza Park," he says. "We got a little time off today for good behavior." He doesn't mention he's with Midori. "That's fine. Good luck. Study hard. Call me if you need any help. Love you too. Bye." He returns the phone to his pocket. "She's got a big test tomorrow," he says, assuming Midori knew exactly who had called.

"Oh, I see," Midori says. She dips her spoon in the cup to retrieve the last remnants of chocolate mousse. "So how did you two meet?"

He grins, as if he relishes the opportunity to tell the story. "There was a party at work and she came to meet her friend Carly who works in accounting. They were going out for drinks. She came up to me and started chattering away in Japanese. Somehow she knew I would understand." He laughs. "She'd just gotten back from living in Japan. I guess her Japanese guy radar detector was still on."

Radar detector. That must have been what used to guide Midori when it came to gaijin men. An antenna went up and sent a signal to her brain whenever one was in the vicinity. However, her radar had not been accurate enough to detect homosexual signals.

"How long have you been together?" Midori asks. It would be better to change the subject, but she can't stop herself. In reality, she doesn't want to hear any more about the two of them, yet at the same time it's imperative to hear every single detail.

"About two years. Before that I dated a woman named Julie. That was her American name. She was from Hong Kong. She ended up marrying a Chinese guy who has his own telecom company."

Now he'd even brought up another woman. And now she had to know every detail about her too. How they met, why they broke up, but it was better to stick to Tracy.

"Where does Tracy live?"

"In the Sunset District," he says. "Close to school."

"Does she live by herself?"

"No, she has a roommate."

Why didn't Shinji invite Tracy to live with him after he kicked his roommate out? Or maybe he did and she refused. It isn't easy, but Midori stops herself from asking any more questions. "Here," she says, handing him the banana crème tartlette. "Please finish this. I can't eat any more."

# 14

MIDORI CONTINUES TO WEAR HER WIG TO WORK, YET KEVIN HAS NEVER returned. Perhaps Kimberley saw to that. She's so relieved that she can almost say now that she actually half-enjoys her job. But that feeling does not last long.

It's a Sunday night when Midori is assigned to a new customer named Fujioka-san. She immediately nicknames him Bulldog in honor of his jowly face and wide-set eyes. While most of the customers are in their forties or fifties, Bulldog looks to be well into his seventies—old enough to be somebody's grandfather, which he probably is. He wears a suit, but it's shabby, the material thinning at the knees. It could be the only one he owns.

"Sheridan!" he exclaims after Taffy introduces him to her. "You're the most beautiful vision I've ever seen."

Midori has grown accustomed to receiving compliments from her customers. Flattery is in abundant supply at the Miki Lounge. But Bulldog won't stop. He doesn't want to talk about himself, he only wants to talk about her. He pays no attention to Amber, and that suits the girl just fine as she sips her orange juice and gazes straight ahead at who knows what. Once back at the Miki Lounge Amber has never mentioned Midori's return of her wallet. Not even a thank-you.

"Are you from Hokkaido? You look like a Sapporo beauty to me," Bulldog says to Midori.

"No, I'm from Tokyo." Her name is a lie so her hometown might as well be one too. "Where are you from?"

"Nagoya," he says. "But we don't have women there as pretty as you."

"Are you in San Francisco on business?"

He laughs. "No, I'm here for pleasure. Some pleasure with you."

"We're very flattered that you picked the Miki Lounge." She's really good at this by now. Smooth.

"You seem too beautiful to be working in such a place. Are you sure you aren't a model or an actress?"

"I don't think so," Midori says, laughing. She's heard lines like this often. "Have you been in San Francisco for very long?"

"No, but now I might have to stay forever, now that I've met you."

This old guy is really something. She might have let herself enjoy some of his compliments if he'd looked more like Shinji Nishimura than a wobbly-cheeked elderly dog.

"Maybe you'd like to sing a song?" she suggests, hoping this will steer the subject in a more mundane direction.

He chuckles. "Karaoke? No, I'm afraid I'd scare you with my terrible voice. Besides, I'd rather just be here with you." He sips his drink. "You know, your skin is the softest I've ever seen." He whispers in her ear, "How I'd love to see your entire body—in the flesh."

Ugh. His tone is more serious now. Must this conversation continue down such a sordid path?

"Fujioka-san, that's quite a compliment," she says, throwing in a giggle for good measure.

"You know what I want to do?" he says.

Now what was he going to say?

"I want to lick every inch of your perfect body."

She's heard suggestive comments before, but this is turning into something more than simple, albeit vulgar, flirtation. Could it be the wig? She hadn't received anywhere near this kind of reaction since she'd started wearing it. Something else is going on, but Bulldog hasn't tried to lay a hand on her. Not even a thigh grope.

"I bet you have the most perfect tits," he goes on. "Suckable tits." He purses his lips. "Now, wouldn't you like me to suck them?"

She can't remember the last time she's been more grossed out. Actually she can. It was when she was on her hands and knees in the toilet stall. "Now, now. Stop embarrassing me, Fujioka-san," she says, trying to sound lighthearted, pretending he'd paid her a compliment on her cupcakes with buttercream frosting. "Now, what kind of work did you say you do?"

If he tries anything funny she can summon Jiro the bartender. But Bulldog still keeps his hands to himself. Perhaps he's all talk, but she isn't sure how much longer she can stand to listen to such disgusting scenarios.

He laughs. "I don't think you want to hear about my line of work," he says, gulping his drink and motioning for Amber to retrieve another.

It's when he raises his left hand to gesture to Amber that Midori sees it. His little finger is about half the size of a normal one. This means only one thing. *Yubitsume*. You don't need to be an expert on the Japanese criminal element to know about this. Every home drama and soap opera refers to it at one time or another. Even Emiko-chan's uncle on *Longing to Hug* suffered a *yubitsume*. Fujioka-san had cut off part of this finger to ask forgiveness for some disobedience to his crime boss or, perhaps, to pay a debt to him. There's no doubt he's a *yakuza*—a member of the Japanese mafia. Midori shudders. He probably has tattoos of dragons and tigers all over his body as well—droopy dragons and tigers hanging on for dear life on his sagging skin.

The majority of the customers at the Miki Lounge are fairly conventional businessmen and most are here working in the States, at least temporarily. How could a man like this even get into the country? Yes, Midori is illegal, but Bulldog is most likely guilty of all sorts of nasty things. What is *he* doing here?

"So, Nagoya? I've never been there before. Isn't there—"

He moves so close to her, she can nearly inhale the scotch on his breath. "Then after I lick your pussy," he interrupts, "I'll put my enormous cock inside and—"

As if on cue, the lights go out. The music is silenced. The Miki Lounge is dark enough, but this must be a power failure because the room is now as black as night. Has Taffy neglected to pay the electric bill? Or has Bulldog rigged the lighting system? The women shriek, Midori included. But Midori's cries aren't just due to the sudden darkness. Bulldog is forcing his tongue down her throat, running his hand under her dress, and vigorously massaging her crotch with his fingers—including that horrible, stubby one.

"Stop it!" she yells, pushing him with all her strength, as she tries to balance herself into a standing position. Thankfully the lights return, though so overly bright they hurt her eyes. Bulldog now sits on the floor—Midori has knocked him out of the booth.

But he isn't mad. He's laughing. "You're feisty," he says, still sprawled on the floor like an overgrown baby in his playpen.

Taffy rushes to his side. "Fujioka-san, are you all right?"

"Yes, yes," he says, getting up, brushing his hands over his worn pants. "Sheridan is just too beautiful. I couldn't help myself."

Midori whispers in Taffy's ear. "I can't deal with him. He grabbed my crotch. Can I take someone else?"

Taffy nods and Midori goes to sit with another customer, a rail-thin, forty-something salaryman in town for a computer convention who, Midori is relieved to find, only wants to talk about his admiration for Bill Gates. She sees Taffy speaking to Bulldog. He doesn't bother Midori the rest of the night. She's relieved but shaken up as the evening wears on. And at the end of the night her stomach turns when she sees Amber on his arm. How can this girl go off with someone like that? She shivers to think of him licking every inch of Amber's body, caressing her with that hand and its deformed digit.

Midori collects her money and takes a cab home. It isn't until she gets in the door that she feels the need to vomit. Once in the bathroom she can't throw up, but this isn't playacting like it had been over

Kevin; her nausea lingers for a while. She's glad Shinji isn't home. Even though she wouldn't have wanted him to know what had happened, she probably would have ended up blabbing every detail.

She fills the bathtub. Settling in, she lets the hot water cover her body. At first she can think of nothing but Bulldog's hand between her legs and that chopped-off finger. But eventually she's able to switch her thoughts over to ladyfingers, then to imagining the fluffy turrets of meringue she'll try to make for her next lemon pie. She stays in the bath for a long time. She dozes. Her head jerks upward when she awakens from a dream of bulldogs humping each other in Alta Plaza Park.

Once out of the tub she wraps her robe around her body. Although she's tired, she's too wound up to go to bed. Instead she goes to the living room.

Through the window she can see the moon shining above the rooftops, high in the sky like a bright white lantern. She sits in the easy chair where she'd been with Shinji and looks through the telescope, adjusting it until the orb is in clear view. What had he said about it? Oh, yes. He said it was majestic. And peaceful. And that he wished he could fly there to escape his troubles. She can understand those feelings now. She stares hard, searching for the man in the moon. But no matter how much she concentrates, she can only see the rabbit as he pounds the dough for his rice cakes.


It's a few nights later when Midori wakes up to the ringing of the telephone. She looks at the clock—it's just past two in the morning. It could be a wrong number, but even though she knows she's being irrational, Midori denotes a strange urgency to the ringing tone. She isn't sure if Shinji is home—he hadn't returned by the time she'd gone to sleep. Jumping out of bed, she throws on her robe.

"Mi-chan?"

It's her mother's voice.

"Yes? What is it, Mom?"

"Your father's in the hospital. He had a heart attack."

Midori tries to take a deep breath, but for a moment seems to have forgotten how to breathe. "Oh, no," she says. "Is he going to be all right?"

Her mother sighs. "He might need surgery. But I'm not sure yet. I'm waiting to talk to the doctor."

Midori brings the phone to the kitchen and sits at the table in the dark. She doesn't want to say anything to her mother, but her first thought is that maybe her father wouldn't have become ill if she hadn't upset him so much during their telephone conversation. She closes her eyes and rubs her now aching neck with her free hand. She dreads what she has to say next, but she says it anyway. "Do you want me to come home?"

"No, no," her mother says. "Let me find out first what's going on."

Midori is relieved that her mother seems calm, so unlike their last phone call. Her daughter not getting married seems more troublesome than her husband suffering a heart attack. She could have been hysterical, begging Midori to come home immediately. And then how would Midori explain to her that if she did that it would be discovered that she was illegal and she'd have to give up her dream of living in the United States?

"Are you all right, Mom?"

"I'm doing the best I can. Your aunt Tamayo has been a big help. And cousin Akemi-chan."

"Let me know if there's anything I can do," Midori says. "And tell Dad to do his best and get well."

"I will. I'll call you again."

Just as Midori hangs up, Shinji comes in the kitchen and turns on the light. He wears only a pair of running shorts. Midori is consumed with worry about her father, but takes comfort at the view of Shinji's chest.

"What happened?" he asks.

"My dad had a heart attack." Now she feels she has permission to cry. Shinji sits across from her and pats her hand as tears stream down her face. "I don't know yet how serious it is. I feel so guilty. I know I've upset him terribly."

"Well, it's a child's job to upset her parents. Just like it's his job to get mad at you because he cares so much."

"I know," she says, sniffling.

"But I'm sure it has nothing to do with what you said."

"I feel so bad, though, because I know I'm selfish. I want to see him, but I don't want to leave here. If I do, I won't be able to come back."

"Yeah, I know. But it's premature to think about that now. Maybe he'll be fine. Don't worry about something until you have to."

"Thanks, Shinji-san. I'm sorry the phone had to wake you up. Please go back to bed."

He nods. "Try and get some sleep too. Try not to worry too much." He gives her a smile, then returns to his room.

Back at the Miki Lounge, Midori wonders which would be worse— seeing Bulldog again or having Kevin return. Neither is appealing, but being felt up by Bulldog is probably better than seeing Kevin. Luckily, neither shows his face.

As usual, Tako arrives. And as usual he wants to sing "*Matsumi no Onna*" with her. Loyal, sweet Tako, who has never done more than put his hand on her thigh, and who has never uttered one salacious comment. Even his lectures about the insurance industry have become rather charming.

"I have some news," he says to her once they return to the booth after their duet.

"Really?"

"In six weeks my company will be transferring me back to Osaka."

Midori can't move. Why does she suddenly feel a lump in her throat? Tako is just a customer. She doesn't even remember his real name. Matsuda? No. Matsuoka? No, Teraoka. That's it. But his musty cologne and his eyeglass frames have always reminded her of her father. At first that seemed so unappetizing, but now it's practically endearing as she thinks of her dad lying helplessly in the hospital. Tears stream down her face.

Tako's eyes widen. "What's the matter, Sheridan?" he asks gently.

How ridiculous this looks. He's probably flattered to death to have this young woman crying over the news of his imminent departure. She can't tell him he reminds her of her father—no man wants to hear that from his favorite bar hostess, the one who brings him drinks, laughs at his jokes, and sings duets with him about secret love affairs.

"Silly me," she says, dabbing her eyes with a cocktail napkin. "I just get a little emotional when one of my customers has to leave."

Tako beams. "Don't worry, Sheridan. It's still not for a while. We still have some time together." He pats her thigh. "How about another whiskey and water?"

# 15

"MIDORI, YOU SHOULD COME SEE YOUR OLD DAD ONE LAST TIME BEFORE he croaks."

Midori's father's voice is weak, almost unrecognizable over the phone. So different from the usual bark. The doctors had implanted stents to keep his heart arteries open, which would hopefully prevent another heart attack. Now he's home and off work for a month, four weeks that will drive her mother crazy. Mrs. Saito has help from her sister Tamayo and Midori's cousin Akemi, but Midori feels the guilt and dread in her shoulders upon hearing her father's words. If she goes to see him, it means giving up her life in San Francisco. She's selfish, but she can't help it.

"You're not going to croak, Dad," is all she can say to him. "You better get your rest. I'll talk to you again soon."

Her mother comes on the phone. "I don't know what I'm going to do, having him around twenty-four hours a day. He's like a wet leaf stuck on the broom," she says, though her tone is more of an affectionate resignation than pointed complaining. "So how is Shinji-san?"

Why is she saying this? "He's fine."

"Such a nice-sounding young man."

"Have you heard anything on your dad?" that nice-sounding young man asks Midori that night. Shinji and Tracy are preparing to watch another drab video for one of her classes, this time about Commodore Perry's first visit to Japan.

Midori sighs. "He really wants me to come home and see him. I feel so guilty . . ."

Shinji nods, but Tracy looks confused. "You can't go home?" she says in Japanese. Maybe she doesn't know anything about Midori's illegal situation.

"It's complicated," Shinji says in English.

Tracy places the video in the player.

"Wait a minute," Shinji says to Midori. "Do your parents have a computer?"

"Yeah," Midori says. "But they barely know how to use it."

"Well, I have a Webcam, you know, a videocamera for the Internet. And if we could somehow get one hooked up on your parents' computer, you'd be able to talk to them face-to-face."

Midori's eyes are big. "Really?"

Shinji jumps up from the sofa. "It would be the next best thing to being right there. Is there someone who can help them set it up on their side?"

"My cousin Akemi could probably do it."

"Yeah? I could tell her what to do."

Tracy wears a cranky, pained expression and Midori hears her sigh. "I'll call later. You're busy right now and Tracy needs your help."

Tracy looks straight ahead, holding her arms to her chest.

"It won't take long. Just see if I can talk to your cousin," Shinji says, looking like a little boy who can't wait to get his hands on his new chemistry set. This is how he looks when he's at his telescope.

"Well, okay." Midori doesn't really understand what this is all about, but she dutifully calls her mother, who calls her cousin Akemi, who calls Midori back and then talks to Shinji. In just a little more than an hour Midori, Shinji, and a sulky Tracy are gathered around

Shinji's computer, in front of the Web camera and looking at Midori's parents and her cousin. The picture is surprisingly clear. Midori feels a catch in her throat when she sees her father's thin, drawn face.

"Dad, you're looking well," Midori says.

"He's well enough to demand his whiskey," Midori's mother says. "It's nice to finally see you, Shinji-san. Thank you so much for going to all this trouble." Midori's mother looks overly cheery, as if she's come face-to-face with *Longing to Hug* heartthrob Hiro Yamada.

Shinji introduces himself. "It's no trouble."

"This is Tracy, Shinji's girlfriend," Midori quickly puts in.

Tracy offers her introduction in perfect Japanese.

"Ah!" Mr. Saito's eyes bug out in surprise. How impressed he is with Tracy. "You . . . speak . . . Japanese?" he says in heavily accented English.

"I study Japanese in college," Tracy answers. "How are you feeling, Saito-san?"

*"Wah!"* Mr. and Mrs. Saito exclaim in unison, as if they have just witnessed a talking rabbit.

But Midori hears the weakness in her father's voice. There's no bellowing, no barking. It isn't just because Shinji and Tracy are here; his voice has lost its edge. She never thought she'd feel this way, but she actually misses it.

"Do you cook Japanese food?" Mr. Saito asks Tracy.

"A little. I like to make miso soup."

*"Miso soup?"* Mr. Saito says incredulously, as if Tracy has invented it. "So wonderful. Shinji-san, you are some lucky guy. You should marry this girl soon."

"Dad!" Midori butts in, noting that Shinji has answered with just a laugh as Tracy blushes.

"Now my daughter, on the other hand. Who knows when she'll ever get married?"

Midori isn't sure whether to be angry or relieved that her father has miraculously seemed to regain his familiar, complaining tone.

"Midori is picky," Shinji says. "And she should be."

Midori does not want to see Tracy's reaction. "That's enough of this talk," she says. "Dad, I want you to take care of yourself. Relax."

"It's so dull here being with your mother all day," he says as Mrs. Saito puffs out her cheeks and shakes her head. "I should be on the golf course."

"No golf. Just rest," Mrs. Saito says. "That is what the doctor said. But you never listen to the doctor, do you?"

"Listen to the doctor," Midori scolds.

"So when are you coming back home?" her father asks, actually sounding gentle.

The room seems to dim, as if the lights have flickered. But they haven't. "I wonder when . . . ," she says, being vague on purpose.

"Well, we thought this Webcam would be pretty convenient," Shinji says, trying to be helpful. "It's the next best thing to Midori-san being right there with you."

"Thank you, Shinji-san. We really appreciate it," Mrs. Saito says. "This must be very expensive."

"Not at all," Shinji says. "This is much better than a telephone call because we get to see you."

"Yes, I get to see Tracy-san. Such a pretty girl," Mr. Saito says as Mrs. Saito rolls her eyes.

Tracy blushes. "Thank you."

Midori hopes that her father's flattery is enough to keep her from sulking about how she and Shinji still haven't gotten to her homework assignment.

"Well, we don't want to keep you," Midori says. "Dad, get your rest. And don't give Mom too hard of a time."

"Yeah, yeah," he sputters, sounding more like his old self, as Shinji disconnects the camera.

"Shinji-san, thank you so much for all the trouble. That was really nice of you," Midori says.

"It worked well, huh?"

"But please don't spend any more time on this. Tracy has to watch her tape."

"Thank you, Midori-san," Tracy says, though Midori has felt a coolness from her the entire time. She most likely didn't like her boyfriend's enthusiasm for a project that had nothing to do with her. And what had she said before about the quickest way to get to a man's stomach? Or rather, the fastest way to get to a man's heart? Or whatever it was.

"Hopefully your dad will get well soon and you can avoid a trip to Japan," Shinji says.

If only this will be the case.


Even though the thought of returning to the Miki Lounge brings up mixed feelings, Midori can't discount the money. Maybe a new wig will ease the pain. She makes another trip to Hair Apparent.

"Ah! The lady in need of a disguise." The clerk seems happy to see her. This time his T-shirt says PUT ON YOUR BIG-BOY PANTIES AND DEAL WITH IT.

After trying on several wigs, she decides on an ash-blond pageboy model.

"Stunning, just stunning," he says excitedly. "Very Marilyn Monroe circa *The Misfits*."

Marilyn Monroe? Midori smiles. Such a high compliment.

Afterwards she stops by the Japanese bookstore in the Japan Center. Once inside she might as well be back in Japan. Japanese pop music plays over the sound system, and the sea of black heads signals that most of the customers are Japanese. They hang around in front of the shelves, buried in books, their fingers fluttering through magazines. Are they settled here in the States but homesick? Does coming here help them feel less lonely, less isolated? Is she the only illegal alien in the store?

Midori bypasses the fashion, computer, and movie magazines and goes straight to the cooking section. Just as she picks up a copy of *Sweet Times* with a chocolate soufflé on the cover, she hears a familiar woman's voice.

"Midori-san."

She turns around to see Tracy dressed in a denim skirt and blue tank top, clutching a Japanese dictionary.

"Hello, Tracy."

*"Ogenki desu ka?"*

"I'm fine. How are you?" Midori answers her in Japanese.

"Fine. Been shopping?" Tracy looks in the direction of Midori's Hair Apparent bag.

Midori nods. "A little." She isn't about to tell Tracy that she had just bought a second wig to wear to her bar hostess job. But maybe Tracy already knows about her poor excuse for an occupation. It's possible that Shinji has provided Tracy with a blow-by-blow account of each pathetic incident she'd experienced since moving here. It probably made for interesting conversation.

"So you're buying a dictionary?"

"Yeah. I never have enough." She pauses. "Do you want to have coffee or something?"

Midori is glad to see Tracy smiling and offering an invitation. Maybe she has recovered from her sulkiness over Shinji's enthusiastic setup of the Webcam. Even though Midori would like to browse longer, she says yes to having coffee. She doesn't want to be rude to Shinji's girlfriend.

They go to the counter to make their purchases. The Japanese clerk immediately speaks with Midori in Japanese, but greets Tracy in English. Tracy returns the greeting in Japanese. The clerk tells Tracy the amount of the dictionary in English and Tracy thanks her in Japanese. "Thank you," the clerk says again in English. It's just like how it goes with Shinji.

"Shall we go to Coffee Stop?" Tracy says in Japanese, pointing to a café Midori had of course noticed before because of the huge dessert assortment she could see through the window.

Tracy buys only a small bottle of sparkling water and finds a table. Midori carries her order of black coffee and a thick slice of dark chocolate pound cake topped with whipped cream. She sits across from Tracy as she flips through her dictionary.

"Sorry to put you and Shinji to so much trouble with the Webcam and everything." If Tracy is still in a snit about Shinji's helping Midori with this, it doesn't show.

"Oh, it was nice to meet your parents," she says, then adds, "I have a big kanji test tomorrow."

It's a quick change in subject. "I admire you for studying Japanese," Midori says. "It's so difficult."

"Yes, it is, but I really like it. It's fun."

It's hard to imagine studying Japanese as "fun." Midori certainly never found it pleasurable to study English, even though the language itself excited her. Trying to master it, however, has been a constant headache.

"I only have a few more weeks of the summer semester left," Tracy goes on, taking a drink from her water bottle. "Then I go to Japan for fifteen days." Her eyes sparkle at the mention of it.

So she's going to Japan? When did that come up?

"How great," Midori says, still speaking in Japanese but wishing that she could practice her English. But it would be rude to request this so early in the conversation. "Will you go to Tokyo?"

"Yes, I'll visit the homestay family I lived with before. I can't wait."

"September can be hot there, you know," Midori says. "I'm so glad to be here in cool San Francisco."

"Oh, I don't mind the heat."

Midori smiles. This girl would even withstand the most insufferable humidity known to man to be in her beloved Japan. "Is Shinji going with you?"

Tracy's face falls. "No. He can't take time off; he's got some big project at work. Besides, I don't think he'd want to go even if he had the time."

Maybe she shouldn't have asked this. Midori decides not to take a picture of the pound cake, even though she'd brought her camera. Instead she pushes the plate toward the middle of the table. She's brought an extra fork for Tracy.

"Would you like some?"

"Oh, no thank you."

She should have remembered—the pound cake is likely made with ingredients that don't comply with Tracy's high standards.

"Shinji's always talking about how good your pastries are," she says. "You should work in a restaurant."

Why is she bringing this up all of a sudden? "I'd like to," Midori says. "But it's a little difficult now . . ." She wonders if Danielle from Lupine ever gave her phone number to Kate the caterer, but it's possible that nothing good is likely to come out of the Graham fiasco.

"I guess you need a green card, huh?"

Tracy knows that much. Midori can only imagine what else Shinji has told her. *Don't get mad, Tracy, but this poor girl got dumped by her fiancé, and was crawling on her hands and knees begging me to help her because I stupidly gave her my business card at her engagement party. And since she would have ended up in the gutter if I didn't offer her shelter, and because I somehow felt partially responsible for her plight, what else could I have possibly done but ask her to move in with me?*

Midori's not in the mood to go into any details about her immigration status and lack of green card. She gives Tracy a smile. "Can I ask you a favor?"

"Sure."

"Do you mind if we speak English for a little while? I don't have much chance to practice."

"Oh! Okay. I'm sorry," she says in Japanese. Then in English, "You know, the easiest way to get a green card is to marry an American citizen."

Maybe Tracy doesn't know everything about her after all. Yes, Midori is well aware of the benefits of marrying an American. "That is true."

"I have this friend, you know? He married a girl from Japan just so she could get a green card."

Tracy speaks faster in English than she does in Japanese, but Midori can basically understand her. "Really?"

"She paid him, like, five thousand dollars."

"Lots of money."

"They lived together, but just as roommates. It was a marriage in name only."

"Name only?"

"Yeah. A fake marriage." Tracy fiddles with the cover of the dictionary. "He had a girlfriend and everything. And I think she had a boyfriend. Then a couple of years later they got divorced. Pretty simple."

Midori doesn't think it sounds so simple, but it's a scenario that has never occurred to her. Of course she knew marrying someone would solve her problem, but she figured it was best to fall in love first. "Is the Japanese girl doing a job now?"

"Last I heard she was working at a fabric store. She was into making clothes. I think she wanted to be a fashion designer. I don't really know her. I just know Damian, the guy who married her."

*Damian. Brent's brother and possibly the father of Kendall's baby.* Obviously this isn't the same person, but it's the first thing that pops into Midori's head. "That is interesting."

"Maybe you'd want to marry him," Tracy says, the tone of her voice elevating. "Damian might do it again. He said it was the easiest money he ever made."

"I don't know." Midori takes a bite of cake. "Seems to be a little strange." However, if this Damian looks anything like the Damian on *Farrington Falls*, it could be quite pleasant to be married to him, even in a fake way.

Tracy shrugs. "Think about it. It could solve your problems." She pauses. "It's technically illegal, but it's not easy for Immigration to figure out if a marriage is fake or not."

"Illegal is not good."

Tracy laughs. "Maybe not." She grabs her cell phone and punches a few buttons. Then she takes a pen and paper from her purse. "Here's his number," she says, handing her the piece of paper. "In case you want to consider it. His name is Damian Forrester. Tell him you know me."

"Thank you." Midori puts the paper in her wallet.

"But I guess you always have the option of going back to Japan," Tracy says.

Midori shakes her head. "No. I do not want to go back."

Tracy sighs. "Just like Shinji."

Midori sips her coffee, then offers Tracy a sympathetic smile. "I guess we are the two beans in the pod."

Tracy cocks her head, giving Midori a quizzical look.

Midori frowns, feeling her face turn red. "No? Oh, wait. I mean . . . let me think." She pauses, pressing her finger to her temple. Then she says slowly, "Shinji and I—we are like two peas in a pod."

If she were on an English idiomatic expression game show, she might win a trip to Las Vegas or at least go on to the next round. But when she sees the crestfallen look on Tracy's face, Midori senses it may not have been such a good idea to come up with the right answer.

# 16

"IT WOULD BE A FAKE MARRIAGE," MIDORI SAYS TO AKINA ON THE phone that evening.

"Fake?"

"Yes, we'd get married but there wouldn't be any sex. No relationship. But we'd have to live together just in case the authorities came to visit."

"Is there any reason not to do it?"

"It's illegal. And it would deplete all my money."

"Ah. Have you met this guy?"

"No. Do you think I should consider it?"

"Mmm. I don't know."

"If this works out I could quit the Miki Lounge and work anywhere I wanted. I could save up money and go to cooking school."

"Well, Mi-chan. I guess there isn't much to lose." Akina pauses. "But I just thought of something."

"What?"

"It would be good if *this* guy were gay."

The next morning Midori takes out the piece of paper from her wallet where Tracy had written Damian's phone number. How should she start the conversation? *Hello, I heard from a reliable source that you marry women in order for them to get green cards. Or, Hello, my name is Midori Saito, will you marry me?* She picks up the phone and punches in the number.

As the phone rings she suddenly feels nervous. She'd been hoping for the opportunity to just leave a message, but on the third ring a male voice answers, "Yeah?"

"Ahhh," Midori says. "Ahh . . . may I please speak to Damian?"

"You've got him."

She doesn't understand. "I beg your pardon?"

The voice is friendly. "I'm sorry. This is Damian speaking. And who is this?"

In halting English and in a quavering voice, Midori introduces herself and explains how she received his number from Tracy and how Tracy mentioned about the green card marriage.

*"Saito-san, konnichi wa! Yoroshiku onegai shimasu!"*

Here is another American speaking to her in Japanese. She can't get away from it. But, like Kevin, once Midori speaks back to Damian, he returns to English in a hurry.

"Saito-san, I would love to talk to you, but I'm in the middle of something. Can I call you back in a few minutes?"

Should she give him her phone number? Maybe instead she'll say she'll call him back and then just not call. But shouldn't she check it out before giving up? What was it that Kevin always said? *Don't be a pimp.* Is that right? Anyway, she tells Damian her phone number and hangs up.

In about five minutes he calls back.

"Hello, Saito-san? I'm so glad you called." His voice is warm, sincere. "You know, I think I may be able to help you," he goes on. "Things worked out very well for my ex-wife Yuko."

Ex-wife? She was a fake wife, so isn't it odd for him to refer to her as his ex-wife? Or maybe that's acceptable; Midori really doesn't know what the correct term is for a former phony marriage partner. "Really? Does Yuko-san live in San Francisco?"

"No, she moved to New York. Now she works for a fashion company there."

This sounds promising, especially since Tracy had said she only worked at a fabric store. But she wishes Yuko were available so she could talk to her. "Oh, I see. Ahhh. . . ."

"Would you like to get together to discuss this further?"

Damian seems to have an abundance of free time because he's able to see her that very afternoon at his apartment. After she hangs up she wonders if making this plan was a mistake. She doesn't know him. Maybe he's a creepy thug like Bulldog who only wants to suck on her suckable tits. But that may not be a problem if he looks like the *Farrington Falls* Damian. Anyway, he didn't sound scary and he *is* a friend of Tracy's, after all. Even if Tracy has been a bit miffed at Midori from time to time it isn't likely that she'd introduce her to an American gangster. And Damian lives in the same general neighborhood as Amber, which seems respectable enough.

Still, Midori searches for the bottle of Tabasco sauce she'd noticed the first time she looked through the kitchen to see what, if anything, Shinji had in his cupboards. Seiko-san on *Longing to Hug* had stopped a burglar from attacking her when she tossed Tabasco sauce in his face. Midori makes sure the cap is secured tightly, then puts it in her purse.

But it's probably silly to assume she'd have a problem with Damian, she thinks during the bus ride to Ninth Avenue and Clement Street. He seemed normal enough on the phone. She pictures the TV Damian's dark hair, the cleft in his chin, the stud on his ear. But as she walks to the apartment building, she digs into her purse to ensure her Tabasco bottle is in easy reach.

"Saito-san, *irrashaimase!*" Damian says, welcoming her as he opens the door.

It's silly to feel disappointed, but Damian does not look at all like the *Farrington Falls* Damian. First of all, instead of thick, chestnut hair, this Damian has wispy reddish brown hair, the texture of which reminds Midori of a scouring pad. He also weighs more than the other Damian, by about one hundred pounds. The only thing they have in common other than their name is their age—both look to be in their early thirties.

But Midori reminds herself that this would not be a real marriage. She doesn't need to be attracted to Damian, she doesn't need to fall in love with him. In fact, it's better that she *not* be attracted to him. So this shouldn't be considered a problem.

But there is another potential problem. From the extreme décor of his apartment, she can tell that Damian is obviously a complete Japan freak. Midori had met a few of these types at the conversation lounges back home. They were foreign men obsessed with traditional Japan who figured all Japanese women were subservient geisha who would cater to their every whim. She remembered one named Donald who had asked her if she would walk naked across his back for some kind of weird massage. She assured him she would not.

Midori removes her shoes—at Damian's insistence—and immediately notices the strong smell of jasmine incense, a fragrance one might encounter at a Buddhist temple. And Damian's cubbyhole could be called a temple—a temple in honor of Japanese culture. The apartment is small—basically one room and a kitchen—and decorated in an odd Japanese style—a Japanese style as conceived by an American.

In the middle of the room is a futon on the floor and a portable shoji screen next to a low Japanese table and desk. A Sony television set sits on a large tansu chest. On the walls are posters for Japanese animated movies, as well as pictures of famous Japanese movie actresses; Midori is relieved to see that they aren't nude poses and nothing overly sexy. A display shelf houses Japanese geisha dolls, and an elaborate red-and-white kimono with gold trim hangs on the wall as a piece of artwork. A poster tacked on another wall is one a Japanese child might have—a chart of *hiragana* and *katakana*, the syllabic Japanese writing systems.

"Would you like tea?" he asks.

"Yes, please."

He goes to the kitchen as she sits on the floor at the low table. Next to her is a stack of Japanese women's fashion magazines. They're outdated by a few years, their covers wrinkled, the pages curled at the corners. It's like being in his waiting room.

"So how do you know Tracy?"

"I, ahh, I rent a room in her boyfriend's apartment."

"Oh, I see." He carries a black lacquer tray topped with a ceramic teapot painted with Japanese characters, and two matching cups. There's also a bowl of fancy rice crackers, a type Midori is surprised to see outside of Japan.

He seems harmless enough. Summoning her Tabasco bottle will probably not be necessary.

"So you have a little immigration problem," he says.

"Uh, yes."

"Are you working under the table?"

Midori is surprised he's asked this. "Um, yes."

"At a restaurant?"

She nods. That sounds better than a hostess bar.

"Well, you have to be careful. Sometimes they raid places."

"Raid?"

"The authorities will come in looking for illegals. If you get busted, you get deported. Getting married to get a green card will solve all your problems. Not to mention you'll be able to get a higher quality job."

"I see." He seems to have his sales pitch down. Midori bites into a rice cracker. It's hard and stale.

"As I said, it worked out for Yuko. We got married at city hall and she stayed with me here."

Midori again notes that there is only one room. So they didn't even have separate bedrooms? Did they use the portable shoji screen as a partition?

"And we passed all the Immigration interviews with flying colors," he goes on.

She doesn't know what a flying color is, but it's pleasant to visualize a series of rainbows soaring through the air.

Damian pauses, then reaches for what looks like a photo album from a shelf filled with books on learning Japanese, the history of Japan, as well as volumes on topics in Japanese culture: tea ceremony, sumo, Zen gardens.

"This is Yuko," he says, opening the album. He shows Midori a picture of himself with a Japanese woman who looks to be her own age, smiling for the camera, their arms around each other. Yuko is holding up her right hand, giving the V sign.

They appear to be a typical married couple. Had they taken this photo to fool the immigration officials? But as Damian shows her the rest of the pictures in the book, he seems wistful; it's as though he misses Yuko. And most of the photographs—including those of the two of them dressed up at city hall taking their marriage vows—look like what you'd see in a happily married husband and wife's scrapbook. A trip to Disneyland. A campout at Yosemite. A romantic moment at an ice cream parlor. It's perplexing. This marriage looks real, not fake. And Damian's downturned eyes and slight smile seem to say that he wishes Yuko were still living with him.

"This was no-name marriage?" Midori asks.

Damian gives her a puzzled look. "I beg your pardon?"

There she goes again, bungling the phrase Tracy had used. She thinks hard. "Ah! Marriage in name only?"

"That's right, but with Yuko, well . . ." Damian smiles, but it's a smile aching with regret. "We got close, but . . ." He snaps the book shut, then pulls another off the shelf. His cheerful mood returns quickly. "Anyway, here's Aya, my first ex-wife."

There was another? It's like a collection.

"Yuko-san was number two?"

He nods, sipping his tea. "That's right. So you should feel secure about this. I know all the ropes."

*All the ropes.* She thinks of him as an expert at tying knots, perhaps a hangman's noose. The phrase repeats in Midori's head as she looks at pictures of Aya and Damian, which are similar to the ones of Yuko and Damian. Eating cotton candy at an amusement park. Standing on the walkway of the Golden Gate Bridge. Sharing a microphone and singing karaoke. Marrying illegal alien Japanese women seems to be Damian's hobby, perhaps even his career. But maybe she's being too critical of him. Hadn't she been crazy for gaijin when she was in Japan? Perhaps Damian didn't plan on falling in love with Aya and Yuko; it just happened when he tried to help them.

He sighs. "Aya had the most beautiful singing voice. But she ended up going back to Japan after our divorce. She missed her family."

Why would someone go to all the trouble of securing a green card just to return to Japan? There had to be more to the story than that. But Midori doesn't want to discount the idea of marrying Damian to get a green card just yet. Perhaps she would be able to put her foot down with him. Maybe she isn't even his type.

Again, he looks pensive, but suddenly snaps out of his nostalgic trance. "At any rate, this is strictly a business transaction so there are no obligations."

"I understand." Can he really live up to this side of the bargain? She knows she could. There's no chance of falling in love with Damian, and marrying him could solve her problem.

He talks on about his studies in Japanese at a school called Soko Daigaku, his job at a Japanese video store downtown, and his lessons at the Urasenke tea ceremony school. He seems to be a much better match for Tracy, though they probably wouldn't be attracted to each other in the least.

"So is this something you'd like to pursue, Midori-san?" he finally says.

She doesn't know what "pursue" means, but she can guess. "Let me think about it."

"It would be six thousand dollars," he says. "But we might be able to make some arrangements."

Midori isn't sure what he means by "arrangements." She wonders if the price has gone up due to inflation.

She sighs as she walks out the door. She isn't sure what to do next. And now she has one more thing to worry about—a possible "raid" at the Miki Lounge.

Midori remembers that Amber's house is only a few blocks away. She walks by and lingers at the gate, not sure what she's doing there nor what she expects to find. She walks down the alley at the side of the house and takes a breath as she stands in front of the yellow door marked 213A. It would be nice to talk to someone about her encounter with Damian, the serial Japanese woman marrier. She rings the bell and waits, but no one answers.

Catching the California bus, she rides it until it reaches Fillmore Street, then heads straight toward My Sweet Heart. Contemplating her unsettled situation, she starts with a slice of apricot strudel coffee cake, progresses to a crème caramel, and finishes with a piece of huckleberry pie topped with a generous scoop of vanilla bean ice cream.

The carrot cake is made up of whole wheat flour, honey, natural cream cheese frosting, and organic carrots. The orange frosting letters read BON VOYAGE, TRACY! Midori has spent the whole day making it. If Tracy refuses this cake, there's nothing more that can be done.

Tracy seems nervous when she comes over to watch her videotape that evening with Shinji. Midori knows things are hectic for her; Shinji had explained that she needed to write one more essay, take one more final test, and then would be off on Thursday morning for her trip to Japan. Midori brings the cake to the living room where Shinji and Tracy are sitting and places it on the coffee table.

"I hope you will try this," Midori says, after explaining the special ingredients to Tracy.

Tracy stares at the cake, blushing. She seems emotional, her eyes teary. "Thank you, Midori-san," she says in Japanese. "That was so thoughtful of you. Of course I'll have a piece."

Shinji gives her a gentle poke in the ribs with his elbow. Then Tracy repeats the same thing in English, which Midori figures is to be the language for the night since even Shinji begins speaking in English to her.

"What a beautiful cake," he says. "Thank you for going to so much trouble."

"Not a trouble." Midori beams and cuts three pieces. She doesn't know if the cake will taste any good—it's her first time to work with whole wheat flour.

"This is delicious," Tracy says.

"Sure is," Shinji says, his mouth full.

The cake doesn't taste too bad, but it wouldn't be Midori's first choice if she were putting together a dessert menu. Still, she's glad to see Tracy happy, knowing this makes Shinji happy as well.

"Take the cake with you," Midori says. "Take a piece for your long plane ride."

"You take the cake, Tracy," Shinji says.

Tracy rolls her eyes at him.

"What?" Midori says. It's the title of her pastry cookbook.

"It means I'm either great or outrageously bad." Tracy returns the poke in the ribs to Shinji.

"And Midori-san bakes the cake." Shinji smiles at her.

"Ha-ha. You're a poet and don't know it," Tracy says.

Midori doesn't understand why Shinji is a poet.

"Anyway, yes, Midori-san. I'll be sure and take the cake."

"I met Damian the other day," Midori says to Tracy. "Thank you for introducing me to him."

Tracy's eyes brighten. "Oh! So do you think things will work out?"

Midori shakes her head. "I don't think so."

"Who is Damian?" Shinji asks.

"Don't you remember that guy I knew from school? Who married that Japanese woman so she could get her green card?"

Shinji's face turns cloudy, but he doesn't say anything.

"I think he is not always doing fake marriage," Midori says.

"What do you mean?" Tracy asks.

"I think he fell in love with the women."

"Women? There was more than one?"

"He told me about two women."

Tracy laughs. "Oh, I see. I didn't know that."

Midori takes a last bite of carrot cake. "So good luck for your homework. And have good and safe trip."

"Don't you want to watch the video with us?" Shinji asks.

Tracy and Shinji must want to be alone since she's leaving for Japan soon. "No, thanks. I will read a cooking magazine."

They say their good nights.

Having barely read her magazine, Midori promptly falls asleep. The sound of the video from the living room hadn't bothered her, but she wakes up with a start when she hears muffled voices coming from Shinji's room. The clock says one-fifteen. She can't make out what Shinji and Tracy are saying, but their voices are raised—they're arguing.

If only she could understand; she would love to know what they're fighting about. Why is it that she could hear every sound when they had sex, but can't make out a thing now? She gets an idea when she notices the juice glass she'd left on her bedside table. On *Farrington Falls* when Ashley had gone to make a phone call in the conference room next door to Sheridan's office, Sheridan had eavesdropped on the conversation by putting a drinking glass up to the wall and listening through it. Somehow Sheridan feared that Ashley was plotting something against her.

Midori grabs the glass and tiptoes over to the wall her room shares with Shinji's. She holds the glass against it as Sheridan had done, pressing it to her ear. The reception isn't much better, though now she can understand that the language of choice for their fight is English. She can only hear the intensity of their voices rise, then fall; quicken, then slow. After a long break of silence the argument starts again. Removing the glass and putting her ear against the wall improves the sound quality.

Shinji: Why would you tell Midori to go meet with a guy so she can marry him to get a green card?

Tracy: I was just trying to be helpful.

Shinji: You know it's illegal. She could get in a lot of trouble if she did that and the authorities found out.

Tracy: Maybe you just don't like the idea of her getting married.

Shinji: What is that supposed to mean?

Tracy: It means whatever you think it means.

Shinji: Oh, we're back to that.

Tracy: Don't worry, Shinji. I'll be out of your way soon enough.

Shinji: Tracy, don't say that.

Tracy: Why not? It's true, isn't it? It's true you want me to go to Japan.

Shinji: I didn't say I wanted you to go.

Tracy: Yes, you did.

Shinji: I did not.

*Silence.*

Tracy: I don't care anymore. I don't want to stay here now.

Shinji: Tracy, come on.

Midori hears the bedroom door open, footsteps, then the opening and slamming of the front door. After a few moments Shinji goes to lock the door, then his bedroom door closes gently.

Midori stands by the wall, unable to move. It had been like a scene right out of *Farrington Falls* and she'd had no problem understanding the gist of the argument. Why would Tracy think Shinji wanted her to go? Surely he had no interest in Midori; Tracy was the perfect girlfriend for him. Is Tracy jealous because Shinji likes her pastries? Because Midori is finding the quickest way to get to his stomach? But that's so silly. There must be more to it than that. Is Tracy just being mean because Shinji refused to go to Japan with her?

Midori gets back in bed, but can't fall asleep. All she can hear is Tracy's voice saying, "I'll be out of your way soon enough."

# 17

MIDORI EVENTUALLY FALLS ASLEEP, BUT DOESN'T WAKE UP UNTIL A little before nine. Shinji is long gone to work. In the living room she finds Tracy's cake still sitting on the coffee table, only half remaining. BON VOY is all it says now. She figures Shinji probably ate most of it. Next to the cake is the videotape. The cover is blank and there is no label. It's sure to be about something dull, maybe Japanese Zen gardens or tea ceremony, like one of Damian's books. But Midori is curious and pops it in the player anyway.

She brings the cake in the kitchen and cuts a piece for herself. With a cup of tea to go with her cake, she plops on the couch and turns on the video player.

The title credits are deep red, like dripping blood—*Japan's Most Wanted!* Dramatic, intense music plays and the announcer's voice gives off a feeling of great urgency. "There are some 2,500 fugitives on the run," he says breathlessly. "But tonight we show you the top ten—the most dangerous, the most heinous, the most cold-blooded— Japan's most wanted!" This is definitely not a video about Japanese flower arranging.

Midori's neck chills as the music turns scarier, all dissonant horns and shrieking strings. She was never one to watch such programs back home, but she'd seen the wanted posters at the police boxes and the post office. They never failed to give her the creeps. Why would Tracy receive such an assignment and actually have to write a report about this? It's such an unbecoming subject for college class homework. It's enough to make Midori feel ashamed to be from Japan, at least temporarily. But it doesn't mean she's going to stop watching.

As the top ten counts down beginning with the criminal at the lowest end of the totem pole, it seems obvious that most of the fugitives would have some kind of gangland ties. Could they be Bulldog's cronies? Or would *he* even show up on the list? It wouldn't be surprising, but maybe lowly Bulldog isn't in this league.

Introduced first is forty-five-year-old Haruo Tamura, eluding authorities since 1994, for the murder of two police officers who had tried to stop a confrontation between him and a rival gang of *yakuza* in the streets of downtown Osaka. Tamura's pockmarked face and cold eyes make him look the perfect image of a wanted man. "Tamura is considered armed and *extremely* dangerous," warns the narrator.

Mitsuo Takahashi is fifty, wears his hair in a crew cut, and is being sought for the murder of an innocent bystander as he attempted to assassinate a crime boss in the lobby of a Kobe hotel. One of his distinguishing characteristics is a missing pinky finger on his left hand. Ugh! No finger? What's worse—having a stub like Bulldog's or nothing at all? Midori isn't sure which would score you more points in the *yakuza* world.

A robber of an armored car from a Tokyo bank who murdered the driver and made off with 55,000,000 yen; an angelic-looking young salaryman accused of murdering his wife and infant son in Sapporo, chopping up their bodies into little pieces; a bushy-haired, bespectacled college student who'd kidnapped a ten-year-old girl and raped and strangled her—they're all horrible people and horrible crimes, as would be expected.

Midori's curiosity is losing out to the terror she feels as she continues to watch. Maybe it's just time to turn the tape off. The music, the photographs and videos of the wanted men and their crimes, and the announcer's voice are all so frightening that every creak and crack in the apartment makes her jump. At least it's morning; she can't imagine how much scarier it would be to watch this alone at night. But she can't deny her morbid fascination either; it's like driving slowly by the site of a traffic accident to gauge just how bad it is.

As the program turns to the top three most-wanted fugitives, the music becomes even eerier. These three are followers of the Ten-Dō-Kyō—Heaven's Path—doomsday cult. Charismatic guru Jun Mizumori had started the group by concocting his own religion, which combined Eastern philosophy with the Western concept of Armageddon. With his self-published books and lectures he managed to recruit many bright Japanese scientists, students, and just ordinary people into his paranoid world. The cult at one time had 50,000 members in at least five countries, but the majority were based in Japan. Its most spectacular crime was the dispensing of poison gas during the morning rush hour on several Tokyo subway lines. A dozen people died and more than six thousand were injured. Most all of the culprits were now in jail, including the guru, who was indicted and found guilty of numerous murders and abductions carried out by his followers, along with weapons and poison gas manufacturing. He was imprisoned for life.

Midori remembered it well—the cult was front-page news for several years. But during the arrests and subsequent trials, Ten-Dō-Kyō had pretty much disbanded. Most of the followers hadn't been involved in the crimes—they were just lost souls looking for the meaning of life or something. Midori didn't realize there were still fugitives on the run.

Number three on Japan's Most Wanted is a Ten-Dō-Kyō member named Koichi Kudo, who is accused of the murder of a lawyer who had tried to negotiate with the cult on behalf of a group of parents whose children had vanished into the clutches of the guru. The other followers who had killed the attorney had been caught, but Kudo remained at large.

"Now we present number two of Japan's Most Wanted!" says the announcer. "Number two is the only woman to appear in the top ten. Wanted for kidnapping and conspiracy to commit murder, number two is Ten-Dō-Kyō follower Harumi Matsumoto!"

Midori gasps. The back of her head stiffens as she sits upright. On the screen is a picture of an attractive young woman who looks like someone you'd see working in a bakery or a flower shop. Not a criminal, just a regular person. The photo shows her sitting in the front row of a Ten-Dō-Kyō rally. The people sitting closest to her are made up of pixels, digitized to disguise their identities. Midori stops the tape, rewinds it for a few seconds, then plays it again. She doesn't want to believe it at first. It isn't possible, is it? But yes, this woman who is number two on *Japan's Most Wanted!*—this Harumi Matsumoto person—looks very much like Amber at the Miki Lounge.

The narrator, his voice growing direr, continues the story. "Fifty-five-year-old Kotaro Uchida, a clerk at the Adachi-ku ward office in Tokyo, was lured by Matsumoto to a love hotel where he was abducted by cult members who wanted to question him about the whereabouts of his brother, who'd wanted to leave the group. Uchida-san was injected with general anesthesia that led to his death from heart failure. Followers burned his body and disposed of the remains in a steel drum, which they buried in a mountainside hundreds of miles north of Tokyo.

"Harumi Matsumoto is twenty-eight years old and is considered an extreme flight risk. She is charged with being an accessory to murder and harboring a fugitive, and has been on the run for four years. Matsumoto joined Ten-Dō-Kyō when she was only seventeen. She vanished from home one day after leaving this homemade videotape for her parents."

A grainy, slightly blurry tape begins to play. The girl looks directly at the camera, a solemn expression on her face. She's sitting on the edge of a bed, probably in her own bedroom. Midori can make out a shelf behind her, crowded with an assortment of stuffed toys, including several of Hello Kitty. Midori stares intently at the screen, still unsure if this is really Amber. She probably can't even correctly identify her voice since the girl has spoken so seldom. And this tape was made eleven years ago.

"*Okaasan, Otousan,* please forgive me because there is something I must do. I am leaving you today. I have known for a long time that I do not belong here. I'm not interested in boys, pop music, or fashion. I'm no good at sports. Subjects at school bore me, and I don't see the point in studying hard just so I can get into a good college and get a good job. Because I don't think that is where happiness is. I don't think I've ever been happy. But now I have the chance to find true happiness, eternal happiness. I am joining with Mizumori-sensei to become truly liberated, which will lead to happiness, and the supreme path to heaven. Please don't try to find me. I am sorry. Forgive me. Good-bye."

The camera freezes on the girl's face. Big, black animated letters proclaiming NUMBER TWO MOST WANTED! are now stamped across her forehead. Midori grabs the remote and rewinds the tape to play the girl's video again. She shivers at her words. Whether this is Amber or not, the girl obviously felt at odds with Japanese society. But why had she picked such a wayward path out? Or did she have good intentions but was corrupted by the cult's members? Midori thinks of Amber's Hello Kitty wallet. Her spine tingles and it's then that she abruptly turns off the video player. She can't bear to see any more.

Harumi Matsumoto's mouth isn't crooked like Amber's, but that seems to be the only difference. Maybe she'd been in an accident since then. Maybe one of the Miki Lounge customers had hit her. Midori shudders to think that Amber *had* looked familiar to her from the first time she had met her. That's significant, isn't it? And she could never place her. Had she seen her face on a wanted poster? Had she seen her on the news?

If Amber is this person, Midori should tell someone—the police or maybe the Japanese consulate. But what if it isn't her? What if it's someone who just kind of looks like her? After all, Amber's driver's license has her name as Li Mei Yang. Maybe she's just a shy woman of Chinese descent, born and raised in Japan, who somehow made her way to San Francisco and now is just trying to make ends meet by being a bar hostess. *And a prostitute.* Maybe she'd even been dumped by her American fiancé right after her engagement party.

Midori wishes she could invite Taffy or Crystal or Britney to come over and get their opinions. But maybe they're *all* Ten-Dō-Kyō members! That's why Taffy doesn't mind that Amber won't make conversation or perform many of the tasks required for the job of bar hostess. They're all in it together! And maybe each one of those customers Amber has gone off with at the end of the night has been murdered. Wait. Have any of those customers ever returned to the Miki Lounge? Midori thinks hard. Yes, some did. It's difficult for her to understand the San Francisco newspaper so she doesn't read it too often, but she's sure there hasn't been a headline about a series of missing Japanese businessmen.

*Get ahold of yourself.* She puts her hand on her chest, taking a deep breath. She is going way too overboard. Hadn't there been the time she rushed up to that young woman at the Maruyama train station back home thinking she was her old high school classmate Kana-chan, only to have the girl look at her as if Midori had asked what planet she was from? Didn't her friends make fun of her in junior high when she always mixed up those two rock stars and would say Bryan Bon Jovi? It's true that she's not always good at recognizing faces.

Midori takes a shower and gets dressed, but she can't stop thinking about Harumi Matsumoto. And she can't help but turn on the video player once more to watch the rest of the show; after all, she had yet to see who had been designated as number one.

"This brings us to the number one fugitive on *Japan's Most Wanted!*—Hideshi Sawada. Sawada, a graduate of the finance school at Waseda University, joined Ten-Dō-Kyō after being recruited by Jun Mizumori as his chief financial officer. Number two fugitive Harumi Matsumoto's boyfriend, Sawada is wanted for the murders of Kotaro Uchida, the Adachi-ku ward office clerk, and his brother, Shige Uchida, a former member who had left the cult. Sawada is thirty years old and is considered extremely dangerous. He may be armed.

He is also considered an extreme flight risk and may or may not be with Matsumoto."

Midori can't be sure if Hideshi Sawada was the man she had seen with Amber at her apartment. She can't remember his face. But it certainly is a possibility. Midori rewinds the tape once more to watch the portions on Harumi Matsumoto and Hideshi Sawada. She still isn't sure if these are the same people.

After watching a few more times, she has to make herself stop. A walk to My Sweet Heart and the downing of a profiterole croquem-bouche filled with thick cream choux and topped with caramel sauce helps calm her. But still, she needs to talk to someone about what she'd seen on the tape. She doesn't want to bother Shinji at work but who else is there to call? She can't phone Akina right now—it's the middle of the night in Japan. Shinji might not even come home to-night and she'll have to wait until the next time she sees him. Al-ready she's about to burst. When she returns from the café she decides to telephone him.

"Sean Nishimura."

"Shinji-san?"

"Midori-san? Are you all right?"

"Yes, I'm fine," she says, now wondering if it had been such a good idea to call. Why does she always have some kind of weird news to re-late to him? That Kevin had dumped her; that she'd taken a job as a bar hostess; that Kevin had come to the Miki Lounge; and now he even knew that she'd considered marrying someone in name only to get a green card. Midori Saito: "Crisis" is her middle name. Shinji may like her pastries, but he must have finally come to the conclusion that she's nuttier than a pecan tart. And here is one more nutty thing he's going to hear from her. He must be sick of it by now.

Midori tries to make her voice calm and relaxed. "I'm sorry to bother you at work. I know you're busy . . ."

"It's okay. What's going on?"

"Were you going to be coming home tonight?"

"Probably. Tracy's too busy with her studies. Why?"

Of course he doesn't say they were in a fight. But maybe they'd talked by now and were all made up. How nice for them. "There's just something I wanted to talk to you about."

"Oh, okay." Shinji sounds somewhat concerned, but not overly so. It's a relief that she apparently doesn't sound to him as if she were having her regular meltdown du jour.

"Why don't you meet me after work and we'll have dinner?" he continues. "I'll treat you in return for all those nice pastries you've made."

She's surprised at the invitation. The tingling feeling throughout her body now isn't the result of fear as when she'd watched the video, it's of happy anticipation.

"Thank you, Shinji-san. Are you sure?"

"Of course. It will be my pleasure."

On the phone Akina knows very little about Harumi Matsumoto and Ten-Dō-Kyō.

"I guess I should keep up more with the news," she says. "But are you really sure this is the same person?"

"No. I mean, yes. I mean, I just don't know. She looked familiar when I first met her, but . . ."

"That would be so weird if it were her," Akina says.

"I just need some verification from someone. I was so freaked out I called Shinji."

"Has he seen her before?"

"No, but I have to tell someone. I just told him there was something I wanted to talk to him about. He ended up inviting me to dinner."

"A *date?*"

"Well, kind of, I guess."

"Midori Saito is going on a date with a Japanese guy?"

Midori laughs. "I guess I won't join your loser dogs club yet."

"*Ah-woo!*"

Midori laughs. "It's so weird to feel this way about Shinji."

"Maybe he's the right guy for you," Akina clucks.

"Well, he has a girlfriend."

"Who is going to be away."

"So what does that mean?"

Akina doesn't answer that but instead sighs and says, "Mi-chan, I'd give anything to have your exciting life, even my status as a loser dog."

The anxiety Midori is experiencing thinking about Amber being a possible fugitive from the law, and the prospect of going on a kind of date with Shinji, is almost too much to bear. What if she fingers the wrong person? And what would Tracy think?

Midori tries on three outfits before finally making a decision—a crisp pink blouse with a matching print scarf, a black skirt that hits an inch above the knee, and some black strappy sandals. The black skirt is snug around her waist, which should come as no surprise. Although she'd always eaten a multitude of desserts in the name of research back home, she's been eating even more now. And the portions here are bigger.

The reception desk at Sawyer & Jones is closed since it's already six-thirty. Shinji had said he'd meet her in the waiting area and he's right on time. She can see him sitting on the couch as she exits the elevator.

He smiles. "You look so nice," he says. "But you shouldn't have dressed up. It's just me."

Just him? Midori's heart lifts at the compliment and his humbleness. Shinji looks his regular cute self. He wears a tie with a print of tiny daisies, a pale lime-green shirt, black jeans, and black athletic shoes. But no, this isn't really a date, she has to keep reminding herself. Even if Shinji and Tracy are fighting, they're still together. And to Shinji this is obviously just dinner with a friend. His roommate.

"It's a special treat to have dinner with you," Midori says. Did his face just turn red?

"Do you like Chinese food?" he asks.

"Sure."

"Good. I made a reservation at this restaurant near the waterfront—China Village. It's kind of an Asian fusion place."

China Village's atmosphere is one of simple elegance. Their table looks out at San Francisco Bay and the Bay Bridge. The food is beautifully presented with special attention to the balance of color. The flavors are fresh and light and about as good as Lupine, the restaurant employing Midori's once future husband who so rudely turned out to be gay.

"This is a wonderful place," she says.

"I'm glad you like it." He fingers his chopsticks. "So what's going on?"

Midori looks down at her lap. "You know, I'm really sorry that I always seem to be pestering you with my problems."

"I don't think it's pestering." He takes a sip of wine. "I like to think that we're friends and that we can help each other."

"Well, you've certainly been a big help to me, but I don't know if I've been any help to you."

"You're a responsible roommate who happens to make fantastic desserts." He grins at her. "So I think that's very helpful. And I really appreciate how nice you've been to Tracy."

Couldn't they have dinner without her name coming up? It was probably unreasonable to think so. Tracy is important in Shinji's life and that's an undeniable fact. But what does he think about the fight they had last night? Do they have arguments like that all the time or is it something serious? Did Tracy really mean any harm when she advised Midori to go meet Damian? Midori doesn't have the nerve to bring any of this up.

"So anyway . . . I found Tracy's video on the coffee table this morning so I watched it."

"You did? Pretty creepy, huh?" Shinji's eyes are wide, his face animated. "I thought it was so weird that Tracy would have to watch something like that for school. But she had to write about comparing Japanese tabloid TV with American, or something."

"Really? I'd wondered about that too." Midori gulps her wine.

"Anyway, it was really strange because—do you remember the part about the woman who's on the most wanted list?"

"Yeah. The one from Ten-Dō-Kyō."

"Well, I know this is crazy, but I think that woman— that Harumi Matsumoto might be Amber, the hostess at the Miki Lounge."

"You're kidding!"

"It really looks like her, except for her mouth. But then I think maybe I'm crazy. I don't know. Sometimes I'm really bad with faces and I'd hate to turn her in if it wasn't even her!"

"You mean that bar hostess who never says anything but goes home with all the customers?"

"That's right."

"Oh, yeah. You said she looked familiar to you."

He actually remembers this.

"But do you really think she would have been able to get out of Japan?" he goes on. "I'm sure every authority was on the lookout for her."

"I know. Maybe I'm way off."

"But I guess she could have used a fake passport." He thinks for a moment. "But wouldn't the customers recognize her? Hasn't she been on wanted posters all over the place?"

"Well, that's what I thought, but then I was thinking that most of the customers are people who've been living here for a while. They might not be up on all this and they're not watching Japanese television. But I don't know." Midori grabs a slice of orange beef with her chopsticks. "But the other thing is that I saw Amber's driver's license."

"You did?"

Midori explains how she'd found Amber's Hello Kitty wallet in the bathroom and returned it to her.

"So you know where she lives."

"Yes, but the driver's license said her name is Li Mei Yang."

"It could be a fake license. Those are fairly easy to get, from what I understand." He offers her more rice; so different from her father, who would have stuck out his bowl, demanding it to be filled.

"And when I went to her apartment, a guy answered the door," Midori says. "And I'm not sure, but maybe it could have been the number-one fugitive, Hideshi Sawada. The one they said is her boyfriend."

"*Really?*"

"He acted kind of strange when he opened the door. Like he was suspicious or something. But I don't know for sure at all . . ."

"Wow. Now I want to watch that tape again." Shinji pauses. "I know what all those people did in Ten-Dō-Kyō was horrible, but I have to say that I was really struck by that girl's video to her parents."

"What do you mean?"

"It was obvious to me that she was unhappy with the expectations of what her life had to be in Japan. And she was searching for some alternative. But the only alternatives there seem to be to join some crazy cult or leave the country." Shinji pours more wine in Midori's glass. "I know that's kind of an exaggeration, but there's no safety net in Japan for people who are a little out of the norm. Who want an alternative life. You either play by the rules or you suffer."

"I know," Midori says, wiping her mouth with her napkin. "She was so young. She could have become corrupted by Mizumori or that boyfriend."

"Did you catch that part about the boyfriend?" Shinji says excitedly. "The guy graduated from Waseda with a finance degree. Just like my brother Toshi wanted to! That was a bit strange."

Midori nods. "That's right. What a coincidence." She pauses. "Even someone that bright was somehow mesmerized by Mizumori."

"That's so hard for me to relate to—to be taken in by some guru. I've always been so skeptical. Even from the time I was a little kid. There was this baseball coach at my elementary school who was so popular with all the little boys. He bought them toys, gave them candy. I never went near him—and I loved baseball." He pours more wine in Midori's glass. "But I was always suspicious," he continues. "I instinctively knew something wasn't right but all these other boys didn't give it a second thought. Sure enough, he ended up being arrested for child molestation."

"How awful." Midori drinks her wine, catching the view of the twinkling lights on the Bay Bridge from the corner of her eye. "I guess I was always a little more gullible. But I was never attracted to those weird religions."

"I guess you were too busy worshipping at the altar of the perfect gaijin man."

She laughs, but is surprised he came out and said this. Maybe he's a little drunk. "And you were too busy worshipping the blond high priestess Gina Torrance, Miss 'Kissing Lips.'"

He laughs. "You got me there."

"Let me pay my half," Midori says when the server brings the bill.

"No, that's okay." Shinji grabs the check and takes a credit card out of his wallet. "You've made so many desserts, Midori-san, that have been so delicious. This is my thanks to you for that and everything else."

"Thank you, Shinji-san." Her thoughts instantly turn toward dessert. "I guess we can have some carrot cake when we get home. I noticed Tracy didn't take the cake with her."

Shinji's face seems to darken. He nods slowly. "Yeah. She left late last night. We had a fight."

"I know." Now why did she say that? Is she also going to tell him about the glass she held up to the wall?

"Oh, sorry! I hope we didn't wake you up with our arguing."

"I heard the door shut, but I didn't really hear anything else," she fibs.

"Sorry. She was mad so she slammed the door. That was rude of her." He signs the bill.

Midori waits for him to tell her all the juicy details, how he had been mad at Tracy for telling Midori to go see Damian, but this doesn't happen. Instead he says, "Shall we get going?"

Back at the apartment Midori cuts some pieces of carrot cake while Shinji makes tea as they prepare to watch the last part of *Japan's Most Wanted!*

"So you think it's really her?" Shinji says as they watch the video of Harumi Matsumoto's message to her parents.

"I'm not positive."

"Well, why don't I come to the Miki Lounge and give you a second opinion?"

"What? *You* want to come to the Miki Lounge?" Midori laughs at the thought.

"Well, if it's good enough for Kevin Newbury . . ."

She laughs.

"I'll be your customer," he goes on, grinning. "I promise not to act too sleazy."

She isn't drunk enough to say that she'd welcome a little sleaziness from him. Instead she smiles. "Okay."

Shinji ejects the tape from the player and put it back on the table. "So when do you go back again?"

"Thursday night."

"Okay. Let's do it." He jumps up from the sofa. "Ah! I think it's a waxing crescent tonight."

She likes how at dinner he can be an intellectual adult philosophizing about Ten-Dō-Kyō followers and their feeling of inadequacy in Japanese society, and a couple hours later a little kid excited to look at the moon. He turns off the lights and moves the telescope in front of the easy chair. They sit together as he peers through the lens, making adjustments. "There," he says. "Look. It's so delicate. Like a sliver of one of your pastries."

She laughs. Yes, it looks like a slice of something or other. Her heart pounds as his hand brushes hers when he adjusts the telescope. Does he feel it? Is it on purpose? Or is he completely oblivious? Midori has to take a breath to calm herself.

"What are you going to do if it's her?" Shinji asks.

"Amber?"

"Yeah. Call the police? Or the Japanese consulate?"

"I don't know. If I identify myself they might come after me for being illegal."

"But there might be a reward."

"I hadn't even thought of that. The whole thing is just so creepy to even think about. What if Amber finds out I called the authorities and she sends Hideshi Sawada to kill me?"

Shinji smiles and squeezes her arm. "Don't worry. I'll protect you." He laughs.

It's like a heating pad has been gently wrapped around her forearm. And the arousal going on between her legs is only too noticeable. Without a doubt Shinji Nishimura ranks number one on her most wanted list. Maybe Tracy has a right to be worried. But Midori would never act on her feelings. Besides, Shinji doesn't feel the same way. He has his dream girl and once she returns from Japan, they'll be a happy couple once more.

# 18

MIDORI AWAKENS THE NEXT MORNING WITH A START, WONDERING IF she's crazy to think Amber is Harumi Matsumoto. Maybe it has all been in her imagination. She can't watch the tape again; Shinji has already returned it to Tracy.

Maybe the tape had been old, out-of-date. She hadn't thought of that. Maybe some of those people have already been caught, including Harumi Matsumoto. How can she find out? She could look on the Internet. Why hadn't she thought of that before?

She goes in Shinji's room, thinking about how he had mentioned he was taking the morning off work to drive Tracy to the airport. Obviously they had made up. And he had ended up staying over last night at her place.

Searching in Japanese on the computer, she finds plenty of Web sites that refer to Harumi Matsumoto. She even sees a few more photographs, but still isn't certain they are of Amber. And there are Web sites where you can play the video message she'd left to her parents.

But none of the information is conclusive as to how recent it is, though she doesn't find any indication that the woman had been caught. It's the same for Koichi Kudo and Harumi's boyfriend, Hideshi Sawada.

Maybe she should call her mother and ask her. Somehow bring up Ten-Dō-Kyō in the conversation. She needs to check up on her father anyway. Mrs. Saito is always up on the latest news and gossip in Japan. The television is her best friend.

After watching *Farrington Falls*—with Damian in a coma in the hospital from his fight with Brent, Sheridan arrested for a mysterious illegality having to do with the stock market, and Ashley overhearing an argument between Kyle and Mandy, which made her hopeful they would be breaking up soon—Midori calls her mother.

"Are you doing all right, Mi-chan?" Her tone is warm and caring.

"Yeah. How are you? Is Dad doing okay?"

"We're doing fine," she says. "Your father's back at work. He's feeling well. Right now he's out playing golf with Tomita-san."

"Oh, yeah?"

"And I'm going to *ikebana* class this afternoon. We're preparing for a display at the cultural center for next Sunday."

Midori is relieved to hear such mundane normality, feeling almost nostalgic for family life back home. *Almost.* And feeling relief that it doesn't appear she'll be called to come back home any time soon. "That's nice. And how's the weather there?"

"Just beautiful."

Imagine being able to just talk about the weather. It's such a relief to no longer have to come up with lies about Kevin and the wedding, and to hear that her father is fine.

"And how is Shinji-san?"

"He's good," Midori says.

"That was so nice of him to put the camera on the computer."

"Yes, it was nice." Now it's surely time to change the topic of conversation. "You know, the other day an American friend of mine brought over a tape about Ten-Dō-Kyō."

"They know about that over there?"

"Well, it was a video from Japanese TV. She wanted me to help translate it."

"For your job?"

"Uh-huh." Even still, it seems necessary to lie to her mother about something. "Anyway, I was wondering . . . I watched this part about the three followers who are still wanted by the police."

"How despicable that group was!"

"Yes, it was. Quite despicable. But do you know, Mom, if they're still looking for those people? My friend is curious."

"Oh, yes! Koichi Kudo, Hideshi Sawada, and that woman, Harumi Matsumoto. They're all on the run."

Midori is stunned to hear her mother say this. But on second thought, it's not that surprising. This is coming from a woman who can recite the titles, names, and ages of every member of Japan's royal family, and who had committed to memory the entire guest list for Princess Diana's funeral.

"They haven't been caught," Mrs. Saito goes on. "They're probably out of the country by now. Their pictures are everywhere so I don't know how they could go on living here. Someone would be sure to tell the police if they saw them."

"Maybe they could get plastic surgery."

"Maybe. But everything I've heard is that they've most likely escaped from Japan. They could be in Russia. Or Albania. Or North Korea. Who knows? But thank goodness most of the people from Ten-Dō-Kyō are in jail."

At the Miki Lounge Midori told Taffy that a customer will come in asking for her. Shinji said he would stay until closing time so he can take Midori home. He raised his eyebrows and said, "You'll be going home with a customer—just like Amber." It would be a nice scenario, but Midori has blocked any further fantasy out of her mind.

Midori told Shinji to come after eleven-thirty, otherwise he'd end up spending too much money on drinks.

Midori is on edge waiting for Shinji to show up. She's tried hard not to be obvious in staring at Amber, but she looks at her constantly. She still can't say 100 percent, however, that she *is* Harumi Matsumoto. What if this is all just one big mistake? And to make things even more nerve-wracking, Bulldog has returned—deformed pinky finger and all. He smiles and waves to Midori with that depraved hand, but thankfully is holding court with Britney, who has extremely suckable tits.

When Shinji finally arrives in the bar shortly before midnight, she sees him look straight at her, as though he doesn't seem to recognize her.

"*Irrashaimase!*" Taffy says, welcoming him, then rushes to assist with his coat.

Shinji is actually wearing a business suit.

Midori gives him a wave and excuses herself from a disappointed Tako.

"That's *you?*" Shinji says, looking shocked.

She nods. "Yes, it's me—Sheridan."

"No wonder Kevin didn't recognize you."

Is Shinji thinking that she looks sexy and sophisticated, or sleazy and cheap?

"And you're wearing a suit," Midori says.

His embarrassed expression endears her. "I wanted to look the part," he says shyly.

Midori laughs. As she takes his arm and guides him to one of the booths, he gazes around the place wide-eyed, a five-year-old on his first day of kindergarten. "So where is she?" he says in a low voice.

"Don't be obvious," Midori says. "But she's standing at the bar. The one wearing the short purple skirt and black ankle boots. I'll go get you a drink and ask her to join us."

Shinji cranes his neck, trying to look in Amber's direction.

"And over there," she says, nodding toward Britney, "is Bulldog." She goes on to tell him about his stubby finger and the pass he made at her.

Shinji again stretches his neck to get a look. He sticks out his tongue in sympathy. "Pretty gross."

Midori nods in agreement. "So what do you want to drink?"

"Um, how about a whiskey and water?"

"Coming right up." Midori goes to the bar and orders the drink from Jiro. Her heart pounds as she approaches Amber. Is this the girl who'd been cold enough to lure some poor middle-aged man to a love hotel and then to his unspeakable death? But what if this person had nothing to do with any of this? Midori has an idea. She'll tell Amber that Shinji's last name is Sawada, the same as Harumi Matsumoto's boyfriend. If she really is Matsumoto, she'd be sure to have some kind of reaction, wouldn't she? Midori clears her throat and folds her arms in an attempt to hide her shaking hands. "Amber, do you mind joining me over at the far booth? The customer's name— the customer's name is Sawada-san."

The girl is either really Li Mei Yang or a very cool and collected Harumi Matsumoto because no visible reaction registers on her face. "Mmm," is all she says as she saunters over toward Shinji's booth.

Midori grabs the waiting drink and hurries over to make sure she'll get there at the same time as Amber.

"Sawada-san," she says, enunciating clearly and looking at Shinji. "Here's your whiskey and water."

Shinji gives a slight smile and nods. He seems to understand that he has been given a pseudonym.

"This is Amber," she says.

"How do you do, Amber?" Shinji says. "You're so pretty."

Shinji is doing his best to play his part at pretending to be a customer, but is it necessary to be so realistic?

"Thank you," Amber mumbles as she sits next to Shinji on one side while Midori sits on the other.

"Well, I sure had a hard day at work today," Shinji says, stretching his legs and loosening his tie. "But I feel rejuvenated seeing you two lovely ladies." He takes a big gulp of his drink, trying to act cool, but has to catch the glass when it nearly slips out of his hand as he puts it on the table.

Midori senses his nervousness. Yet he looks cute trying to mimic the behavior of a flirtatious salaryman visiting a hostess bar. Acting so Japanese seems somehow out of character for him, which in itself is ridiculous.

Midori watches Shinji straining to get a good look at Amber while trying not to look as though he's gaping at her.

"Well, just sit back. We're here to keep you relaxed and re-freshed," Midori says.

She wonders if perhaps Amber will contribute something but, as usual, she is distracted, staring straight ahead, absentmindedly shak-ing her foot. Midori continues with the masquerade. "So what line of work are you in, Sawada-san?"

"Me? Oh, I'm a vacuum cleaner salesman."

Shinji is very well prepared, isn't he? He has remembered her complaints about boring customer talk.

"Oh, how interesting." Midori has a hard time keeping a straight face. Her customer is on the verge of cracking up as well.

"You'd be surprised how fascinating this line of work is." He takes a swig from his drink and smacks his lips. "Ahhhh."

"It must be *quite* fascinating."

"For example, I'm sure, Sheridan, you've often wondered which is better, a vacuum with a bag or a bagless vacuum."

"As a matter of fact, I *have* often wondered about that."

"Well, I'm here to tell you that neither one is better. They both clean equally well. It's your personal preference. It's all up to you."

"Well, I guess I prefer a vacuum with a bag."

"I could show you some wonderful models if you're in the market. Be sure and get my card before I leave."

For a moment his hopeful look convinces Midori that he is actu-ally yearning for a sale. She nods. "I'd be honored."

"And another thing I'm sure you've been concerned with is what the difference is between a canister and an upright vacuum."

"Yes, I've often wondered about the difference between a canister and an upright vacuum." Midori has to clutch her stomach to keep from laughing. How did he come up with this? Not only is it hysteri-cal, it's downright charming. She glances at Amber who isn't paying any attention, acting her usual comatose self.

"A vacuum with a canister is more versatile by far. It not only handles carpets, but it's perfect for cleaning bare floors, sucking up dirt from corners, and vacuuming stairs." Shinji downs his drink. "Amber? Excuse me, Amber?"

Amber looks at him. *"Hai?"*

Shinji shakes his glass, the ice cubes rattling like a maraca. "Another, please?"

She nods, takes the empty drink, and trudges toward the bar.

"You are so funny," Midori says in a low voice, smiling. Then turning serious she continues, "So do you think it's her? She didn't react when I called you Sawada-san."

"She's got it down, I guess. But I'm ninety-eight percent sure it's her," Shinji says. "I could call the police right now on my cell phone, but I'm afraid they'd bust everyone here for one thing or another. Including you. And we don't want that."

"I know." Midori sighs. What is the right thing to do? A thought comes to her. "Your cell phone has a camera, right?"

Shinji nods.

"When she comes back, ask me to take your picture together."

"Got it."

Amber returns with Shinji's drink.

"Thank you, Amber," he says, grinning at her. "You know, you look a little familiar to me. Haven't you been on TV in Japan?"

Midori stiffens. What will Amber say to that?

Amber shakes her head, giving him a tiny smile. If she's hiding something, she doesn't show it.

"Are you sure?" he says in a teasing voice.

She nods.

"Well, I guess you're just an exceptionally pretty girl."

*Can't he stop with the pretty girl stuff?*

Amber shrugs.

"Do you mind if Sheridan takes a picture of the two of us together? It would make a nice memory for me."

Amber shrugs again and moves in close to Shinji. Midori is forced to grit her teeth as she watches Shinji put his arm around the girl, squeezing her shoulders. Midori takes his phone. "Say cheese!" she instructs the two, who suddenly strike a pose for the camera that one could call downright lovey-dovey. Midori checks the picture on the screen—a perfect snapshot, with Amber in clear view.

"So, Sawada-san," Midori says, sitting on Shinji's right. "Getting back to your area of expertise, how often should I vacuum to keep my house clean?"

"I'm glad you asked me that, Sheridan." Shinji folds his arms, trying to look authoritative. "I'd say that in areas with heavy traffic you should vacuum every day. But with our busy modern lives, many of us don't have the time. So once or twice a week is a reasonable goal to aspire to."

"Well, I'll try my best."

"Please do."

Just then Taffy comes by. She smiles at Shinji, then asks Amber to take care of another customer who's just arrived.

"She sure acts calm for a fugitive," Midori says after Amber leaves. She shakes her head.

"Perhaps she's just a clever criminal. Or do you think she's on some kind of drug?" Shinji looks at the picture displayed on his cell phone screen.

"I don't know. I can't really believe it." Midori's eyebrows knit together in worry. "Maybe there's a tiny chance that it's not her, but I really think it must be. I'm not sure what to do, but at least I have her photograph."

Shinji gives her a sympathetic smile, pats the top of her hand, then squeezes it. Is he still playing the part of Sawada-san or is he back to being Nishimura-san? He keeps his hand there longer than one would for just a friendly gesture, at least that is how she interprets it. She turns her hand over, clasping his. Now they are officially holding hands. Her heart thumps big, practically skipping beats; she can't remember ever feeling this excited about holding someone's hand.

It seems to last for minutes. Shinji then puts his other hand lightly on her shoulder, gently releasing his hand from hers. "Excuse me, Midori-san," he says. "I need to use the restroom." He gives her a sweet smile.

She points in the direction of the bathroom and flops back in the booth, limp from what has just occurred. She gazes at him as he walks away. Did that mean something? Or is he playing a part? Or is he a little drunk?

Midori watches Crystal take the stage with her customer to sing a duet. They are halfway through when Shinji returns to Midori's side.

"So is that part of your job description?" he asks.

"What?"

"Singing karaoke with your customers."

She nods.

"Then let's go next."

"You're kidding."

He grins. "No, I'm not."

Midori brightens. "Okay." She grabs the binder that lists the songs in the karaoke system.

"Ready?" she says to Shinji when Crystal and her customer return to their booth.

"I'm ready."

Shinji and Midori walk to the stage. "I'm going to pick your song for you," Midori says.

His eyes go wide in anticipation. "Okay. But nothing too difficult."

She smiles. "Don't worry." She punches in the number on the screen and the intro starts, a bouncy melody accompanied by synthesizers and a mechanical disco beat.

Shinji bursts out laughing. It's obvious he recognizes it. The song is none other than "Kissing Lips" by one-hit wonder Gina Torrance, the Japanese-singing American blond bombshell he'd worshipped when he was thirteen.

Shinji and Midori each hold their respective microphones and look at each other.

"Oooh, you've got me on fire with your kissing, your kissing lips," they sing together. "You're my one heart's desire with your kissing, your kissing lips."

Taffy, Crystal, and Britney whoop and holler. "Sheridan, do your best! *Gambatte!*"

"I'm under your spell, and I can tell," Shinji sings in a not-too-shabby, reedy voice. "That you're the one, the one for me."

"And I know so well, that if I fell, with you forever I'd always be," Midori sings back.

And together, "Kissing, kissing lips! Kissing, kissing lips! Oooh-wow!"

Toward the end of the song Midori notices Amber is already wearing her coat and whispering in Taffy's ear. She looks at the clock—it isn't quite one o'clock, but Amber is leaving early. Midori shudders as she sees her walk out with Bulldog in tow.

Shinji and Midori sing the ending chorus, then bow to enthusiastic applause.

"Sheridan! Sheridan, please!"

Midori turns around. She's about to sit down, but Tako is intercepting her. "What about 'Matsumi no Onna.' Please?"

Old Tako, bless his heart. This is his favorite song to sing with her and he's due to leave San Francisco soon.

Her face burns with embarrassment, thinking of Shinji watching her sing this corny old song with this pudgy middle-aged man, his shiny bald head as bright white as the full moon viewed through Shinji's telescope. Out of the corner of her eye she can see his sympathetic grin as Tako puts a sloppy arm around her shoulders, crooning earnestly into the microphone, his eyes closed in a kind of rapture.

"Tomorrow will be my last night," Tako says to Midori after the song is over. "Then I'll be back in Japan."

"Then we must celebrate our last night together," Midori says. Tako beams.

Shinji claps the loudest as the song ends. Midori returns to his booth. "Looks like you have a big admirer," he says.

She sighs, rolling her eyes. "Yes, and he's just my type."

Shinji pouts. "You're making this customer jealous."

"Oh, really?"

Shinji looks around the room. "Where's Amber?"

"She left with the *yakuza*."

"Wow." Shinji shakes his head. Then he smiles and holds up his empty glass. "One more?"

———

"Well, that was the most expensive bar I've ever been to," Shinji says when they get back home around two-thirty. He hangs his coat up in the closet, tosses his suit jacket on the couch, and pulls off his tie.

"Thanks for coming."

"But it was a lot of fun." He sits on the couch and yawns. "And I think we've got ourselves a fugitive from justice."

"I guess it really is her."

"Not much doubt in my mind."

Midori sighs. "I know." She pauses. "Can you print out her photo for me?"

"Sure. But what are you going to do with it?"

"I'm not exactly sure yet, but I want to have it on hand."

Shinji goes to his room. It's only minutes later that he comes out with the photo of him and Amber blown up full size to fit an eight-by-ten piece of paper. "I wonder why no one else has ever noticed her," he says, handing over the picture.

Midori shakes her head, gazing at the couple's pose, something that could have come out of Damian Forrester's scrapbook of *Memories of Japanese Ladies I've Ripped Off and Married*. "Thank you, Shinji."

Midori is tired, but wound up. Maybe this would be a good time to fix Shinji a piece of carrot cake. Or maybe he'll suggest that they look at the moon. And then they could hold hands again. Or more. She's about to suggest they go to the telescope when the beeping of Shinji's cell phone stops her. Who would be calling him at this hour?

When he answers, it couldn't be more obvious. It's Tracy, telling him she's arrived safely in Japan. It's the next day there, early evening. Shinji's face lights up and, sounding excited to hear from her, he waves to Midori. Mouthing a "Good night," he retires to his room and shuts the door.

# 19

Midori tossed and turned during the night, wrestling with thoughts of Amber in her sleep, but by morning she is clearheaded, determined. She has come up with a plan. Yes, it could be considered far-fetched. Even insane. And, yes, it's a long shot. It may even garner the same result as the ill-conceived plot to experience connubial bliss with Graham Striker, the chef who had the audacity to be perfect in all ways except the most important one. And it could render her American Dream as flat as a failed soufflé. But there comes a time when you just have to take things into your own hands; when you possess information someone wants badly enough, you should be able to gain something valuable in return.

The Japanese consulate is located in a tall skyscraper adorned with smoky glass windows in downtown San Francisco, not too far from Shinji's office and Ferry Plaza. Wearing her gray business suit and clutching a manila envelope with the photo of Shinji and Amber, along with one of Harumi Matsumoto she has printed from the Web, Midori enters the elevator, aiming to blend in with the office workers who are about to start their day.

In her head she runs through what she hopes to say. Perhaps the clerk at the consulate will be male. She'll charm him to get what she wants, like a femme fatale in one of those old American detective movies. One who wears a trench coat and bursts into the private eye's office when he's just about to close for the night.

Detective: What can I do for you, sweetheart?

Midori (ducking in, as if being followed): I have something you're looking for.

Detective: And what might that be?

Midori: The scoop of the century. The location of the number two most wanted fugitive in Japan.

Detective: Sit down, sister. Let's talk.

Midori: I don't have time for talk. I want action. I'll give you this info on one condition and one condition only.

Detective: And what might that be?

Midori: That you get me a green card.

Detective: Now, wait just a minute, sweetheart.

Midori: A green card. In the brightest green you can find. Now. And make it snappy!

It probably won't go exactly that way. But even though Midori knows that the Japanese consulate is not in the business of giving permanent U.S. residency to Japanese citizens, certainly there must be some legs they could pull, couldn't they? Or is it that they could pull strings? Whatever. She sighs. Maybe this is just another Cinderella dream—something that requires fairy dust sprinkled Midori's way, a commodity that has been in short supply ever since the spate of bad luck that started when she was first introduced to Kevin Newbury. Still, what has she got to lose? Well, she could be deported. Oh, is that all?

Midori's stomach bounces up, then down, as the elevator settles on the thirty-second floor, the doors parting. Perhaps portraying herself as being in distress would be a more productive tactic. After all, this is why many people come to a consulate—for help. She approaches the young woman sitting at the reception desk.

"How may I assist you?" the woman asks pleasantly in Japanese.

"Well, I'm having— I'm having an emergency. I've, um, had my handbag stolen. I'm stranded here in San Francisco with no passport. . . ."

The woman fixes her gaze on Midori's purse hanging on her shoulder, but her eyes are still wide. "Oh? Well, you should speak to the duty officer. Please have a seat over there."

Midori thanks her and sits down. Well, it could be a temporary purse. But maybe this has all been a stupid idea. Why did a criminal have to pick Midori's hostess bar to work at? And why did Midori have to meet Crystal and end up working at the Miki Lounge in the first place? But why ask why? She could be here all day going over the long list of mishaps in her mixed-up life.

"Miss?"

Her thoughts are interrupted by a tall Japanese woman, her blue-black hair cut in a sleek pageboy. She wears a black pantsuit with a starched white blouse and sensible, flat shoes. Her middle is wide and her stomach protrudes—she seems to be pregnant. Midori notices a large diamond wedding ring on her left hand.

"I'm the duty officer," she says, smiling. "Won't you come this way?"

Holding tightly to her envelope and her supposedly stolen handbag, Midori follows the woman into an office that has a view of Ferry Plaza and the Bay Bridge.

"Now how may I be of service?"

The woman looks so friendly and caring and has such a warm smile that Midori decides to come clean. She forgets about the story of the snatched purse, takes a deep breath, and shows the duty officer the pictures of Amber. She tells the woman everything she knows about her, including her home address. She tells her that she understands there's reward money for the capture of Harumi Matsumoto, but she wonders if it is at all possible that somehow she can get a green card instead. Midori doesn't mention the Miki Lounge or the fact that she's illegal, but she does say that she's in the country on a fiancée visa but won't be getting married after all.

The woman's expression has changed from kind and concerned to one of extreme puzzlement. She hasn't said one word during Midori's rambling monologue. It looks as though this has been a mistake. Midori figures she must be thinking, *This woman is out of her mind— should I throw her out right now or call in the authorities? I better play it cool, though, because she could become violent. It's obvious she's a Ten-Dō-Kyō member too.* But it's too late to run away. Midori's heart sinks. This has not been a good idea.

The woman's eyes bore into Midori's. Her forehead is creased as if she is thinking hard. "Mi-chan?" she finally says.

"*Eh?*"

She breaks into a smile. "Is that you?"

Midori is confused, but then notices the name plate on the woman's desk: MIYUKI TANAKA. She stares hard at her face, then realizes who she is. It's Miyuki, the girl from her school, the girl who everyone refused to be friends with except Midori.

"Yes!" Midori cries out as the woman reaches out for her hands with hers, then squeezes them.

"I can't believe it's you," Miyuki says, her eyes shining. "After all these years."

Midori can't speak, her throat is dry. "How long have you been working here?" she finally croaks.

"About three years," she says. "When my husband and I moved from Tokyo." She points to a framed picture on her desk that shows her and a dark-haired Caucasian man clinking two champagne glasses. "This is my husband, Mark Johnston."

She didn't change her name, Midori thinks. That's just like Miyuki. "How wonderful for you." Miyuki's American Dream came true.

"We live in Palo Alto," she says. She pats her stomach. "And we're expecting our first child pretty soon." She giggles. "I'm getting as big as a house."

"Congratulations," Midori says, still stunned. "You know I brought that little cable car music box with me to America. The one you gave me. For good luck."

"*Wah!* The one that plays 'I Left My Heart in San Francisco'!"

Midori nods vigorously. From the corner of her eye she can see the silvery Bay Bridge glistening in the sunlight.

"I never forgot what you did for me, Mi-chan," Miyuki says. "And now I can finally thank you."

"She's going to give my information to the authorities," Midori tells Shinji on the phone. "And if there's an arrest, I'll get the reward money. Ten thousand dollars."

"That's fantastic."

"Yes, but the best part is that her husband is a lawyer in a big firm in Silicon Valley. She says he can introduce me to a top immigration attorney and there should be no problem with him helping me to get a green card. Miyuki will see to it."

"Midori, your luck is finally changing! It's about time."

"Yes, it is."

Midori has considered not showing up at the Miki Lounge tonight. Why should she go? Only to have the opportunity of being felt up by Bulldog once more? She'll be getting her green card soon, hopefully, so why should she bother? But it's the last time she'll see Tako and for some crazy reason she feels obligated to say good-bye to him. So she might as well go once more, for old times' sake. And she wonders if she'll see Amber as well or whether she has already gotten an unexpected visit at her apartment.

It's amazing how different a night can feel working at the Miki Lounge when you know you really don't have to be there anymore. The regular routine can even be perceived as something slightly fun. Jiro is his old untalkative self, while Taffy can't stop her chatter. Possum sits with Crystal, most likely enrapturing her with his latest insights on Bill Gates. Bulldog isn't around and Midori sees no sign of Amber. She asks Britney if she knows where she is.

"Taffy says she hasn't heard from her." Britney glances at the clock. "She's almost two hours late."

Midori feels a chill on her neck as she imagines the police breaking down the door of that little apartment, the smell of boiled cabbage wafting through the alleyway. They drag Amber away, clad in her overalls, looking more like a college freshman studying abroad than Japan's number two most wanted. Midori has some sympathy for Amber, though. She was a naïve girl, someone led astray, just one more person who wasn't a right fit for Japan. But Midori knows it was only right to turn her in.

As Tako enters the bar, his bald head and shining eyes are a happier sight. Midori gives his arm a squeeze, takes his coat and hangs it in the closet, then goes to retrieve his usual whiskey and water from Jiro.

"So this is the last night," she says to him as he sits back in the booth and takes a sip from his drink. "I'll miss you."

"Sheridan, I'll miss you too!" His expression is sincere as usual. "What am I going to do without you?"

"I'm sure you won't have a problem," she says. "There are hundreds of hostess bars in Osaka."

"Not with anyone like you."

She can't help but feel somewhat complimented. "Still, I guess you must be sort of homesick."

"Yes, I am. I can't wait to get my hands on a good chicken katsu curry," he says wistfully.

Midori laughs. It's one of her father's favorite dishes too.

"Don't you get homesick?" Tako goes on.

"Not really," she says. "I'm here to stay."

"Guess you've turned into an American."

Midori smiles at his words.

Taffy has cued up *"Matsumi no Onna"* on the karaoke system.

Tako gives Midori a sad smile. "Shall we? For the last time?"

She takes his arm and they walk up to the stage. She remembers the look on Shinji's face as he watched her sing this song with Tako the night before.

*Yes, we keep our love secret, it's a secret forever, a secret that will never be told.*

Tako gets a catch in his throat on the last line and coughs instead of sings. Midori is charmed by his emotion. He holds her hand once they return to the booth. "Thank you, Sheridan," he says. "Thank you."

Midori smiles, then excuses herself to go to the bathroom. She looks at her watch. It's still early—only a few minutes before eleven-thirty. She gazes in the mirror and dabs at some errant eyeliner. *Ouch!* She nearly jabs herself in the eye, startled when she hears the shouting of men's voices. It's not joyful, not the sound of partying. It sounds more like a fight. They're speaking in English, but she can't understand what they're saying. She hears women's screams, not unlike the time when the power went out and Bulldog made his move on her.

What is going on? Her heart pounds as she opens the door a crack, then peers out. The lights are still on, but they're blazing superbright. Her body freezes. The place is swarming with police and other official-looking men wearing dark blue parkas.

"Isn't it Amber you want?" she wants to shout, then instantly realizes this can't possibly have anything to do with her talking to Miyuki at the Japanese consulate. She didn't breathe one word about the Miki Lounge. Could it have been Kimberley? Maybe 36–double D Kimberley Hobbs called the authorities because Midori had practically written her a map of where Kevin had made his salacious visit that night: *"He's at the hostess bar in Japantown. The Miki Lounge."*

They're shoving everyone into a corner, but none of them are near the restroom—yet.

Midori doesn't have to give it any thought. It's as if the powerful winds of a typhoon have pushed her out of the bathroom as she lunges toward the back door exit. Pushing the door open, she runs, the cold night air hitting her body through her clothes that feel much too thin without a coat. She doesn't look back, scrambling through the alley, past the Dumpster, then stumbling on the cobblestones of Buchanan Street. Her feet turn and twist—high heels are highly inadequate as running shoes. One foot hits the pavement with a bang, the heel on her shoe has broken off. Stopping, she quickly steps out of her shoes, tossing the pair into a trash can. For a brief moment she thinks of the bronzed shoes in Shinji's bedroom.

Now running in her stocking feet it's easier to sprint, though she breathes heavily as she makes a left onto Sutter Street, crossing against a red light, her eyes darting as she checks for oncoming cars.

Once she's reached Fillmore, she turns her head to look for any police. Maybe she should stop running now, she will only look suspicious. Panting, she walks stiffly passing Bush, Pine, then California Street.

"Hey, geisha girl!"

There are whistles and hoots from a group of rowdy young guys who step out of a bar, but she ignores them and continues toward Sacramento Street, then on to Clay. How weird she must look being out in the streets in her Miki Lounge getup, heavy makeup, and wig. She pulls off the fake hair and shakes her own hair loose. It sticks to her sweaty face.

Reaching the apartment building, she fumbles with her purse. Her hands shake, but she finally locates her keys. Unlocking the front door to the lobby in the dim light she sees a figure coming toward her. It's a man. *Shinji*. Wearing a jacket, he seems to be on his way out.

At first he looks surprised, then relieved to see her. He pulls her to him, taking her in his arms.

"Midori," he says urgently. "Are you okay?"

"I think so," she answers, her breath still short, wondering why he has come down to meet her. He couldn't have seen her from the apartment.

"I was on my way to the Miki Lounge," he says, still holding on to her.

"*What?*"

"It was on the news. There was a raid."

"Raid." She feels her shoulders go numb. "Yes, the police came while I was in the bathroom. I heard shouting and I just left out the back door," she says as he leads her up the stairs, his arm around her.

"How lucky! Looks like they arrested everybody."

"Because of something to do with Amber?"

"I don't know. It just said that there were raids on a bunch of businesses in Japantown. They were looking for illegals."

Midori has difficulty staying on her feet when she realizes indeed how close she came to getting arrested. She knew the police wouldn't think much of her promise of a green card from Miyuki Tanaka, the duty officer at the Japanese consulate. Her heels and the balls of her feet burn, her raw toes ache.

"Where are your shoes?" Shinji asks gently as he opens the door to the apartment.

"I couldn't run in them. I threw them away."

Shinji brings her a glass of water as she flops on the sofa. He turns on the television and flips through the channels until he finds the local news.

"In our top story, the Department of Immigration has detained at least twenty-four illegal workers after raids tonight in Japantown as part of a crackdown on illegal immigration. With backup from San Francisco police officers from the Northern Station, workers were picked up and arrested from establishments including Kintoki restaurant, Kyoto Massage, Miki Lounge, Club Starlight, and Silhouette Bar. The workers were made up of Korean, Chinese, Mexican, and Japanese nationals who were found to be unlawfully in the United States or in breach of their visa conditions. An Immigration Department spokesperson says more raids are expected in other parts of the city."

Midori watches in shock at footage of workers being hustled into police vans, the glaring lights of the television cameras blinding them. She thinks she recognizes Britney, though it is difficult to be sure.

"That could have been you," Shinji blurts out as they look at each other.

Midori bursts into tears and feels Shinji's arms encircle her. "I guess that means Amber is caught," he murmurs as he continues to hold Midori, gently stroking her hair.

"No," Midori says. "She wasn't there."

"She didn't show up?"

"I'm hoping they already caught her at her apartment. Along with maybe her boyfriend too."

"They must have alerted the TV stations right before they did this. How else could they have filmed it?" He shakes his head. "It's like a reality show."

Midori buries her face against his chest. It feels so good to be in his arms. The authorities conducting the raid didn't have German shepherd attack dogs as in her long-ago fantasy back at the Fairmont Hotel, but if she hadn't been in the bathroom, she might be on a plane to Japan right now. How would she explain it to her parents? And what would it have been like to know she couldn't return to the United States for years, if at all? She thinks of Britney, Crystal, Taffy, and Jiro. It really wasn't fair. They weren't such bad people.

Midori's throat burns as if it's on fire, and her nose is more stuffed than a Thanksgiving turkey. She has caught a cold from being out last night without a coat, a coat that must still be hanging in the closet at the Miki Lounge. The shouting of the police and the screams of the women during the raid were constant in her dreams, but the ringing of the phone has awakened her. She looks at the clock. It's already two-fifteen in the afternoon, at least she thinks it's the afternoon. The sun *does* seem to be shining through the curtains. She should just let the phone go—it's most likely only her parents or a wrong number. But she can't ignore it any longer.

"Hello, is this Saito-san?"

It's a man's voice, a voice she doesn't recognize. Maybe it's the colleague of Miyuki's husband. The immigration lawyer.

"Hello, Saito-san, *ogenki desu ka?*"

*Who is this? The guru from Ten-Dō-Kyō?* "Um, yes . . ."

The man laughs gently. "This is Damian Forrester. You came and visited me, remember?"

*Damian?* Why is he calling? And how did he get her phone number? Her woozy head is the source of the slowdown in her thought process, but then she remembers that she gave her number to him so he could call her back that one time. She clears her phlegm-coated throat, but her voice still resembles that of an old lady who smokes too many cigarettes. "Oh, hello, Damian. How are you?"

"I'm fine, but you sure sound stuffed up."

It seems way too personal for him to comment on the state of her nasal passages. "I'm sorry. I have a cold."

"Oh, that's a shame. Hope you're getting lots of rest and drinking plenty of fluids."

Fluids? She can't pinpoint it, but there's something unappetizing about that word. "Yes."

"Well, I was just calling to see if you'd made a decision."

"A decision?"

"Yeah. If you've decided about our marriage."

*Our marriage.* The hairs stand up on the back of her sweaty neck. Thank goodness she doesn't need to have anything more to do with this loser. She sneezes.

"God bless you!"

"Thank you. But, Damian, I'm sorry. I think I will not do."

"Oh, really? Are you sure?"

"Yes, I think so."

"I see." He pauses. "Did you see on the news last night about that big raid on illegals in Japantown?"

She certainly did. "Yes."

"Looks like they're cracking down heavy right now."

She isn't sure what "cracking down" means, but it must be unpleasant.

"Yes."

"Didn't you tell me that you work under the table at a restaurant?"

"Yes."

"You'd better be careful." He sounds like a little girl's daddy.

"Uh-huh."

"A green card is really necessary to have any decent life here in the United States, you know," he clucks. "And because I like you so much, Saito-san, I'd only charge five thousand dollars instead of six as I originally said."

It may be because she's sick, or that she's still traumatized from
the previous night, or it could just be the fact that Damian is acting as
pushy as a vacuum cleaner salesman, but she feels her blood turning
bad. Is that right? Maybe it's that her blood is boiling. Or at least sim-
mering. Had he not understood her answer? Had she been too vague?
As Kevin had told her long ago, being vague didn't work with Americans. It's better to be more direct. Forthright. To the point.

"Damian, thank you for call, but I would rather catch myself
dead than marry you. Do not phone me again!" She slams down the
receiver.

Her scratchy throat and plugged-up nose remain, but how good it
feels to have told him off. Returning to bed, she falls back asleep only
to wake up once again to the sound of the telephone. The room is
dark and this time the phone quickly stops ringing. She can hear
Shinji talking but can't make out what he's saying. Surely Tracy
wouldn't be calling him on the phone in the house. Midori looks at
the clock. It's almost seven-thirty.

She hears a knock on her door.

"Midori-san? It's your mother on the phone."

Midori puts on her robe and tries to fluff her hair, a feeble attempt
at changing her appearance from bag lady to Sheridan Hamilton. She
could always put on one of her wigs. Then Shinji's hunch that she is
crazy would be confirmed.

"Shinji-san is such a nice man," is the first thing her mother says
to her. "Too bad he's not single."

"Mom . . ."

"What does he do again?"

"He works for an advertising agency." Midori brings the phone
into the kitchen and sits at the table.

"And how long has he lived in the United States?

"I think about six or seven years."

"Where was he born?"

"I guess in Tokyo."

"Oh, really? Midori, are you all right? You sound stuffed up."

Yes, it's a fact that she's stuffed up. Everyone's been talking about it. "I have a cold. But it's getting better." As soon as she says it, she launches into an uncontrollable coughing fit.

"You sound terrible. Be sure and drink lots of tea and miso soup." Mrs. Saito pauses. "And Shinji-san's father, what does he do?"

"I don't know. Mom, did you call for a specific reason?" Midori grabs a napkin from the counter and blows her nose. Yes, it would be nice to have Shinji Nishimura as the candidate for her mother's next marriage arrangement meeting. After all, he was so caring about her that he was ready to try and rescue her from the Miki Lounge. But it wasn't a scenario likely to happen.

Her mother laughs. "I almost forgot. Guess what?"

"What?"

"They said on the news that Harumi Matsumoto was caught. In San Francisco!"

Midori's heart pounds. "You're kidding!"

"No! They're flying her to Tokyo now where she'll be arraigned. She'd been working as a bar hostess!"

"Really?"

"Just like Namie-san on *Longing to Hug*."

"I thought she worked as a prostitute in a massage parlor."

"Well, same thing."

Midori gulps. "What about the others? Did they find them?"

"Apparently Sawada was living with her but when the police arrested her at their apartment, he wasn't there. So they went to the hostess bar where she'd been working to see if they could find him." Her mother is out of breath with excitement. "And Kudo, I haven't heard anything about him. Can you imagine? You might have met them!"

"Yes, I guess I could have," Midori says. "If I were the type to hang around in hostess bars."

# 20

PACKS OF PHOTOGRAPHERS VIE TO GET A SHOT OF HARUMI MATSU-
moto as she arrives at the courthouse in Tokyo. Dressed in a plain
white blouse and gray skirt, her hair tied back in a simple ponytail,
she emerges from a black sedan, escorted by two stern-looking women
police officers. Unlike most criminals caught in Japan, she doesn't
wear a sweater or jacket over her head to hide herself, or cover her
face with her hand. Instead she looks straight ahead, her eyes steely,
focused. Midori never saw her wear such a cool expression when she
worked at the Miki Lounge. Amber had disappeared.

"Amazing," Shinji says as he stops the tape and rewinds it to take
another look. The American media isn't giving the story much cov-
erage, but Midori and Shinji are able to keep up with the latest news
on the Internet and the local San Francisco Japanese television programming. Shinji makes an exception and deigns to watch the Japanese channel this time.

"Matsumoto has been interred in a special, high security holding
cell," says the newscaster. "She has refused to cooperate with authorities in regards to information on the whereabouts of Ten-Dō-Kyō
cult members Hideshi Sawada—also her boyfriend—or Koichi
Kudo."

————

On *Farrington Falls*, Sheridan Hamilton is convicted of something called insider trading. "We find the defendant, Sheridan Hamilton, guilty of insider trading," says the jury forewoman.

Midori hasn't seen Shinji for several days—he religiously leaves early and returns late when she is already asleep. Tracy is due to come home from Japan tomorrow. While watching the TV, Midori works on decorating a lemon poppy seed cake with blueberries, raspberries, and edible flowers.

Midori pops a blueberry in her mouth as the scene changes to Ashley and Kyle. Ashley sits behind the big desk in Sheridan's office at Elegant Lifestyle.

"You've done such a great job filling in for Sheridan," Kyle is saying, sitting across from her.

"It's been challenging," she says.

"Life is full of challenges." Kyle gazes at her face. "Ashley?"

"Yes, Kyle?"

"Ashley, I— I've been wanting to tell you . . ."

"Yes, Kyle?"

"I've been wanting to tell you that I've grown— I've grown to have feelings for you."

Ashley looks as stunned as Midori feels.

"Oh, Kyle," Ashley says. "But what about— what about Mandy?"

"As of yesterday, Ashley," Kyle says, "Mandy is history. And, you, Ashley, I hope you can be the future." Kyle rises from his seat, slowly walking around the desk. Ashley jumps up and they fall into each other's arms.

"*Wah!*" Midori exclaims as they kiss, resting her elbows on the table and leaning toward the television to get a closer look. Suddenly she hears a thud. The blueberries scatter all over the floor, rolling like marbles. But it doesn't matter. Ashley and Kyle are together now and nothing will pull them apart.

————

Midori had left Shinji a note on the kitchen table in front of the lemon poppy seed cake that now had fewer blueberries than originally planned.

Bring this cake to Tracy and tell her welcome home from me. It is all-natural with no refined sugar or white flour.

Midori

The cake is gone the next morning. "Thank you!" Shinji has written on her note.

Right before *Farrington Falls* is to start that afternoon, the phone rings. Midori is surprised to hear Shinji's voice.

"Midori-san? Are you terribly busy?"

"No."

"I know this is all of a sudden, but do you think you could make three more of those poppy seed cakes?"

"Three more?" She can't believe such a request. Has she misunderstood him?

"I brought it to work and it was a big hit as usual. But turns out there's a special luncheon meeting tomorrow for some visiting executives and someone here wants to serve your cakes. They'll pay you."

"Really?" Her voice is so loud, it echoes in the kitchen.

He laughs. "Yes. You'll finally get some compensation for your hard work, though I don't know how much it will be."

Midori is stunned. "Yes, I'll do it. Do they need to be made with whole wheat flour and no sugar?"

"No. Just make them the regular way. We can take a taxi to work tomorrow and bring them in."

It isn't until after she hangs up and is in the middle of making her grocery list that it dawns on her. Shinji had mistakenly brought the cake to work instead of giving it to Tracy as a welcome home present. She'll have to ask him why.

Midori has never made three cakes in one day, but she manages to have them done just before dinnertime. She buys special cake boxes at the kitchen supply store. Everything looks so professional, as if she's running a real bakery.

She's been so busy she's almost out of breath. If Shinji comes home earlier, will he bring Tracy over? Now there's no cake for her, but Midori can make one later. Maybe she'll try and make something completely new. She decides to look for another natural food recipe on the Internet.

Instead of turning on the computer, though, she goes over to Shinji's brother's bronzed shoes. She brushes her fingers gently over them. The metal is smooth and cool. She pictures Shinji packing the shoes in his suitcase, thinking how they traveled all the way here. Midori is no longer in the mood to look up recipes on the computer. She wishes she had been around to hold Shinji when he packed those shoes away, to tell him that everything was going to be all right.

Midori is reading *Sweet Times* in her room when she hears the front door open. She listens for Tracy's voice and laughter, but hears nothing. Tracy was probably too jet-lagged for a visit and Shinji thought it best she stay home and catch up on her sleep.

"Come in the kitchen," Midori says to Shinji when she goes to the hallway to greet him. She opens each box to show him the cakes.

"They look great," he says. "Can you come with me in the morning to help bring them to the office? I think Donna, the human resources manager, would like to meet you."

"Sure." A meeting with her first client. Midori feels like a genuine businessperson. "Thanks so much, Shinji-san, for arranging this."

"I didn't do much," he says. "It's your pastries that speak for you."

As usual, he's enthusiastic about her desserts, but the folds of skin under his eyes are only too noticeable. He looks tired. Cranky. She's never seen him like this. And in his voice she detects a different tone. He meant what he said, but he also seems preoccupied with something else. Distracted. He must have had a hard day.

Sitting down at the kitchen table he sighs as Midori fastens the cake boxes shut.

"Thank you for bringing the cake to your work," she says, sitting across from him. "I don't know if you misunderstood, though. I made that cake for Tracy as a welcome home present."

Shinji's face flashes sad, the same expression she'd seen on him when he recounted how the subway authorities came to visit his family after his brother's suicide. He looks directly at her face. "I didn't misunderstand."

Midori doesn't know what to say.

He looks down. "I couldn't give the cake to Tracy because she didn't come back from Japan."

"*Eh?*" Her voice bounces around the room. Why can't she keep better control of her reactions? She sounds as shocked as her mother did when she first told her the wedding was being postponed. And that hadn't made her feel good.

"She said she wants to stay there. She's dropping out of school."

"Oh!"

Shinji holds his arms against his chest. Even though Midori is instantly curious about what happened, she knows she shouldn't pry any further. Right now it's best to just give him her sympathy. But before she even has time to analyze this further, she blurts out, "How long is she going to stay there?"

He shrugs. "I don't know. Six months, a year. Forever maybe."

Forever. This is serious. "Oh, I see." She waits for him to say more, but he's quiet. "Shinji, I'm so sorry to hear that."

He nods, but still says nothing.

Silence ensues for what seems like a long time. Midori wants to take him in her arms, but isn't bold enough to do it.

"I think she wanted me to get on a plane and beg her to come back or something. Ideally she wanted me to go there and be with her," he finally says. He shakes his head. "It just didn't work out."

Her heart aches for him. He looks so dejected. Is she the first person he's told? The irony isn't lost on her. A girl who loved Japan fell for a Japanese guy who represented everything she loved, but one who had no desire to have Japan play any more part in his life. But maybe Tracy hadn't really loved Shinji for who he is. She fantasized that he was someone else and wanted him to be someone he couldn't be. That wasn't something completely unknown to Midori.

She looks at the cakes sitting in the pink boxes. Too bad there's no dessert for Shinji to make him feel a little better. Should she take him to My Sweet Heart? Maybe not—he looks too tired to go out. Then she thinks of something else. "Isn't it a full moon tonight?"

He gives her a little smile. "Not quite."

"I want to look," she says, trying to be cheerful, hoping he'll follow her to the living room. He does.

They sit together in the big easy chair, but this time Midori takes charge, adjusting the telescope and looking through it. "Well, if it's not a full moon, it might as well be—it's so big and fat."

He gives a short laugh. Maybe she's cheering him up.

"It's kind of yellowish, isn't it?" She concentrates hard on the image before her. "You know what?" she says.

"What?"

"I think I finally see it!"

"See what?"

"The man in the moon." She squints. "Yes! I can see him."

He laughs again and she feels warm as his head rests lightly on her shoulder, his body leaning against her side. She's about to ask him if he wants to take a look at the moon himself, but it feels so good to be here with him like this. She slowly leans back so her head touches the cushiony top of the chair while he keeps his head in place. She places her hand on top of his and they sit there silently.

"So when are you getting your green card?" Shinji asks. "Everything going okay with that?"

"Yes. The lawyer is setting the paperwork in motion and I'm on the waiting list."

"That's great."

They're silent for a long time. Shinji finally gets up. "Thanks for listening to all my troubles, Midori," he says. "I'm tired. I'm going to bed." He pats her shoulder, then goes to his room and shuts the door.

The next morning Midori makes sure to wear her gray business suit to bring her cakes to Sawyer & Jones. It was a lucky suit to wear to the Japanese consulate, so maybe it will be her lucky suit this time as well.

"You look nice," Shinji says when he sees her. "So professional."

"Thank you." She blushes but can't help staring at Shinji's face. He's dressed and ready to go, but his five-o'clock shadow seems to be closer to midnight.

He must have noticed her expression because he says, "Is something wrong?"

"Are you growing a beard?"

"Huh?" His face still looks drawn, as if he tossed and turned most of the night. He grasps his chin with his thumb and forefinger, then shakes his head. "Shit. I forgot to shave. Hang on a minute."

Midori's heart aches for him. She's never seen him so distracted. But she actually likes his cute, rumpled look accompanied by the stubble. She hears the buzzing of the electric razor from the bathroom as she gazes at the row of three pink boxes lined up on the kitchen table.

Shinji told her that he usually takes the number three bus to work, but this morning they would take a taxi to transport the cakes.

Now with his skin smooth and the shadow gone, they go downstairs to wait for the cab he called.

Shinji carries two cake boxes and Midori one when they arrive at Sawyer & Jones. They go to meet Donna, the human resources manager, an African-American woman with a round, friendly face.

"So this is the famous Midori," she says, grinning as they place the cakes on her desk.

Midori has never been called famous before. "How do you do?" Midori says, shaking Donna's hand.

"Thank you so much for doing this at the last minute. We've had trouble with our caterer and I needed something quick. And your sweets are so popular with everyone here, including yours truly."

"Thank you," Midori says, opening one of the boxes to show her. "This is fine?"

"Just beautiful. And I'm sure absolutely delicious." Donna is obviously pleased. "So I'd like to know how much we owe you so I can write you a check."

Midori looks at Shinji, hoping her face relays to him that she has no idea how much to charge.

"Sixty-five dollars," Shinji whispers to her.

Midori thinks that's not enough.

"Seventy-five dollars," Midori says, thinking now that she'd seen cakes priced at twenty-five dollars at My Sweet Heart.

"I'll make it one hundred," Donna says, writing a check. "Since this was a rush job."

"Thank you so much," Midori says, grinning as she holds the check.

"I'd like to use you again so I'll keep your name and number on hand."

"Thank you."

Has Shinji taken down the picture of Tracy from his cubicle wall and torn it into pieces? Midori doesn't have the chance to check. Shinji tells her he has to get to work and hurriedly bids her good-bye.

# 21

Kendall is carrying Damian's baby, all right—she's as big as Shamu the killer whale who had jumped out of his pool, splashing Midori and soaking her clothes at her fourth grade field trip to SeaWorld.

On *Farrington Falls*, Damian has been in a coma for forever it seems. But even in an unconscious state he looks sexy with his perfectly styled hair, long eyelashes, and cleft chin. And he still wears his earring. He lay in his hospital bed hooked up to various monitors that blip and beep. Midori is busily whipping egg whites for a pumpkin meringue pie in honor of Halloween, a pie requested by Donna at Sawyer & Jones. Midori's been getting regular orders from her as well as from some other offices where Donna has referred her. Even Kate's Katering, the place Danielle at Lupine told her about, finally called, and she's making pastries for them too. Midori has turned into a one-woman bakery, her wares so popular they seem to be selling like pancakes.

Midori jumps as she hears the doorbell ring. No, it isn't on *Farrington Falls*. It's her own doorbell. She peers through the peephole. It's a surprise to see Graham's face.

"Hi, Midori. How are you?" he says.

He still looks so cute. It's such a waste.

"I am fine."

"Haven't seen you around for quite a while."

"I am so busy."

He peers over her shoulder. "Baking?"

"Yes. I'm having some jobs now."

"Good for you," he says, smiling. "Anyway, the trusty old U.S. post office screwed up again. These two letters were in my box. One's for you and the other is for your roommate."

"One for me?"

She has never received mail here, something actually addressed to Ms. Midori Saito. She tears open the envelope.

"Ah!" she says, smiling.

"Good news?"

"My friend Miyuki. My good friend. She had her baby. A girl."

"That's always good news."

"Yes!" Midori says. "I'm sorry. Would you like a tea?"

"Sure. If you're not too busy."

They step into the kitchen. "Looks like you *are* busy," he says, eyeing her pie preparations. "And busy watching *Farrington Falls*." He says the title with an amused tone.

She feels her face turn red. She reaches for the remote.

"No, you don't have to turn it off," he says. "Don't you think that Damian is such a dreamboat?"

"Dream boat?" Midori says, puzzled.

Graham smiles. "Means he's cute." He takes a seat at the kitchen table.

"Oh! Yes," she says, feeling they at least have something in common now. Midori puts Miyuki's announcement and the letter for Shinji on the table and goes to start the tea.

"You should come back to Lupine sometime."

"I like to." She takes out two mugs from the cupboard. "You must be so busy."

"Yeah, luckily the restaurant's doing well. But there've been a lot of closings lately. It's a tough business."

"It is very nice restaurant. Number one."

"Thank you."

She brings the cups to the table and sits across from him. She stares at the envelope addressed to Shinji. There's something curious about it. It's oversized and ivory-colored, and Shinji's name and address are written in elegant black calligraphy with an abundance of loops and curlicues. He doesn't usually get handwritten envelopes in the mail, only bills or those letters addressed to Resident or Occupant.

Hearing the *Farrington Falls* theme in the background, she absent-mindedly picks up the envelope and turns it over. Suddenly a chill blankets her neck.

"Are you all right?" Graham asks, sipping his tea, a curious look on his face.

Does she look crazy? Because she feels crazed. The return address on the back flap says: Mr. and Mrs. Byron Hobbs, 25191 Winding Way, Hillsborough, California.

*Hobbs?* Does this have something to do with Kimberley Hobbs? Why would Shinji be receiving this? She rips into the envelope.

"Isn't that addressed to your roommate?" Graham says in a quiet voice. "Are you okay?"

"Arghh! Arghh!" She's uttering a cross between a growl and a burp. She's too upset to feel embarrassed in front of Graham. Shaking, she pulls out the card and reads:

MR. AND MRS. BYRON HOBBS

AND

MR. AND MRS. DURWARD NEWBURY

REQUEST THE HONOR OF YOUR PRESENCE

AT THE MARRIAGE OF THEIR CHILDREN

KIMBERLEY REBECCA

AND

KEVIN DONALD

AT THE SAN FRANCISCO GOLF AND COUNTRY CLUB

SATURDAY, DECEMBER 2

AT SIX O'CLOCK IN THE EVENING

RECEPTION AND DINNER TO FOLLOW

"Ahhhh!"

"Midori? Is it bad news?"

She stares at Graham. He must think that she looks like a wild-eyed witch. "It is wedding invitation," she says. "Of Kevin. My old fiancé."

"Oh," Graham says. "Yes, I remember you told me about him. I'm sorry to bring you such bad news, Midori. If I'd known, I would have thrown it in the trash."

"It is okay. But I feel so, so strange."

"Well, of course you do," Graham says. "I know all about bad breakups."

She's grateful for his understanding.

"Do you think your roommate will go?"

"Go?"

"To the wedding," he says.

"Oh. I don't know. He is mad at Kevin too. Like me."

"Maybe *you* should go."

"*What?*"

"Go to the wedding. Freak him out. Make him feel a little guilty." His grin is wicked. "Go with some fabulous guy. Show him up."

Midori smiles, but shakes her head. "Oh, I don't know."

"It sounds absolutely perfect. Like something right out of *Farrington Falls*."


The rest of the day Midori can't stop thinking about Kevin's wedding invitation. She stares at it so much she has almost memorized the text.

MR. AND MRS. SNOBBY HOBBS

AND

MR. AND MRS. DISTURBING NEWBURY

REQUEST THE HORROR OF YOUR PRESENTS
AT THE MIRAGE OF THEIR CHILDREN
KIMBERLEY VENDETTA
AND
KEVIN DEADHEAD
AT THE SNOOTY GOLF AND COUNTRY CLUB
SATURDAY, DECEMBER 2
AT SIX O'CLOCK IN THE EVENING
APOLOGY AND DINNER TO FOLLOW

Will Shinji want to go to the wedding? He'd said to her how he wanted nothing more to do with Kevin. Maybe she should just throw the invitation away; tear it up into little pieces just like how Shinji ripped up the photograph of him and Kevin. Even Graham said he would have done that.

Shinji doesn't have to know anything about it. And he's really going to think she's insane when he sees that she couldn't control herself and opened his mail. But instead of jamming the card down the garbage disposal, she places it back into the envelope, which is now nearly ripped in two. On a sticky note she writes in Japanese, "I have no excuse but to ask you to forgive me for opening this. I'm so sorry, Midori," and affixes it to the invitation, placing it in the middle of his desk.

"I'm sorry, Shinji-san," Midori says, as soon as he walks in the door that evening.

"What about?"

Shinji still looks drained, though it has been a couple of weeks since he learned that Tracy isn't coming back. He has been uncommunicative, sulky. Midori can't blame him, but she has missed the bright and cheerful old Shinji. He looks thinner, too; his pants are looser around the waist and don't hug his thighs as tightly.

"I opened your mail."

"You did? Why?" He looks too tired to be exasperated.

"I'm sorry, Shinji-san," Midori says again. She goes to his room, takes the invitation with the sticky note still on it, and hands it to him.

"What the hell?" he says, pulling the card out of what's left of the envelope. He shakes his head. "I don't believe this."

"Please don't be mad at me," she says. "I shouldn't have touched it."

Shinji sits at the kitchen table in silence.

"You can go if you want," Midori continues, wondering if he's angrier at her indiscretion than at Kevin marrying that horrible Hobbs woman. "I don't mind."

"What makes you think I want to go?"

"I don't know."

He taps the corner of the card against the table. "It says I can bring one guest."

Midori's heart sinks, the kitchen chair turning into a wooden plank shoved up against her back. Is he really going to go? Yes, she said she didn't mind, but she really does. She minds a tremendous lot. Would he have considered bringing Tracy if she were here?

"Maybe we should go together," he says.

"*What?*"

"Maybe we should go together."

"That's kind of what Graham said."

"You told Graham?"

Midori explains how he brought over the invitation. "He said I should go with some fabulous guy. Show Kevin up."

Shinji laughs. "Well, I don't know if I fit that description. But I think it's a good idea. Let's give Kevin a shock."

"Really?"

"It's the least you can do to get back at him just a little bit," he says. "And, besides, it's a free dinner, right?"

"I don't know if I could do it."

"Why not? Buy a new outfit, some new shoes. Make him see what he missed."

"But won't it ruin his wedding?"

"Isn't that the point?" Shinji laughs. "But, no, it's not going to ruin it. I'm sure they're having a huge affair with hundreds of guests. It's possible they won't even see us. At least he didn't ask me to be a groomsman. You know, I was going to be one for your wedding."

"You were? I didn't know." Midori feels a headache coming on. "So he never contacted you after he broke up with me?"

Shinji shakes his head. "I guess he was too embarrassed. Or else I was no longer a necessary friend." He pauses. "Funny that he sent this to me, though. Maybe they just forgot to delete me from the original list."

"Okay," Midori says. "I'll go with you."

Shinji grins and pulls a pen out from his jacket pocket. "All right. Now you can't change your mind. I'm writing on the RSVP card that I'm bringing one guest." He puts the card in the return envelope, licks the back, and seals it.

"It's a done deal now," he says in English.

"Done deal," Midori repeats.


Midori has taken Shinji's advice and bought a new dress. It's sexy, something that would have pleased Taffy if she'd worn it to her old job. And with her figure filling out due to the consumption of so many pastries, the dress fits better than it would have before. Now it's time to buy some shoes since she'd thrown out her best pair on Buchanan Street during her escape from the siege at the Miki Lounge.

Midori spends several hours downtown perusing shoe sections in the department stores around Union Square. The only ones that attract her cost hundreds of dollars, but a small shoe store on Grant Avenue seems to offer somewhat lower prices.

She makes her way to the dress shoes and finds some black heels with pointy toes that are reasonably priced and appealing. Looking inside them, trying to read the size, she's startled when she hears a male voice say, "Sheridan?"

For a moment Midori can't move. Who would be calling her *that*?

She isn't even wearing her wig. It had been sitting lifeless in her chest of drawers, like a dead squirrel snuggled next to the one snatched from Marilyn Monroe. She slowly turns around and sees a Japanese man smiling at her. He seems to be a shoe salesman, one with too much pomade in his hair. It takes her a moment to realize that this is Jiro, the bartender at the Miki Lounge.

"Ah! Jiro-san."

"I thought that was you."

"You work here?"

"Yes, ever since the Miki Lounge was shut down. I guess you got out. I didn't see you get taken away."

Midori nods, explaining how she was in the bathroom when the raid took place and then ran out the back door to freedom.

"*Tana kara bota mochi.*"

Midori smiles. It's a Japanese proverb expressing an unexpected piece of good luck: A sweet bean rice cake on the shelf. But maybe more like a chocolate soufflé in this case.

"Did you want to try those on?"

It feels so strange to see him, like someone from the distant past. The shoes on display in front of her now all seem to look identical. "Um, yes," she says. "Size seven?"

"I'll be right back."

Why is Jiro working here? Wasn't he arrested? This is the longest conversation she's had with him. He'd been almost as silent and sullen as Amber. Midori watches a tall, blond woman with a striking upturned nose consider a pair of boots on the other side of the room. She imagines Kimberley Hobbs picking out the shoes she'll wear at her wedding.

Jiro returns with two boxes. "I don't have this in a seven, but I've got a six and a half and a seven and a half." He removes the first pair out of the box as Midori slips off her shoes. He holds her foot, guiding it gently into the shoe. "You were sure lucky to get away."

"Do you know why it happened?" She doesn't want to mention anything about Amber.

"I have an idea," he says. "How do those feel?"

Midori walks toward the mirror. "They're a little tight in the toe."

"Why don't you try the seven and a half?" He takes out the pair from the other box. "I didn't have to worry," he says. "I don't have any legal problems. I have a green card."

"Oh, I see." She wonders why on earth he'd wanted to work at the Miki Lounge if he had a green card, but she doesn't ask him this. There are those who would ask her why on earth she'd stoop so low to work as a bar hostess, green card or not.

"I think it had to do with Fujioka," he says in a low voice. "You remember him, right?" The expression on his face says, How could you ever forget him?

Bulldog. Yes, he and his finger, or lack of it, will always warrant a page in her memory book. She steps into the next pair of shoes, but continues to be riveted to the chair. "Why would he . . . ?"

"I heard some rumors afterwards," he says. "That he knew about Amber." He pauses, then continues in a murmur. "You heard about that, right?"

Midori nods, suddenly feeling a little nervous. "Did you— did you know that was her?"

He laughs. "No. I didn't have a clue. I felt like an idiot after I saw it on the news. She didn't look much different."

Midori nods slowly. "So, Fujioka-san . . ."

"I heard he called the cops on Amber and they just busted the whole place. He wasn't there that night, you know. And while they were at it, they raided a bunch of other places in J-town. And Fujioka got some reward money."

Midori knows this isn't true, thinking of the ten thousand dollars she was able to put in her savings account, part of which helped pay for the immigration attorney. "You talked to him?"

"No, it's just the word on the street. He's probably back in Japan now, rolling in the dough. Everyone had to pay for Amber's crime. Those gals didn't mean any harm. Yeah, they were all illegal, but it was a legitimate business."

"So they were all deported?"

"Yeah. I don't know what's become of them other than they're back in Japan."

Midori sighs. "That's terrible."

She stands up but at first has difficulty balancing on the narrow high heels. But in a few moments she is able to stride toward the mirror. The shoes make her legs look longer, thinner. And they are a perfect fit.

"I'll take these," she says to Jiro.

She walks out of the store swinging her shopping bag, feeling relieved, though she's not sure why. But the Miki Lounge is over, she's at last a soon-to-be-legal pastry queen, and now she's going to be Shinji's date at Kevin's wedding.

The air is chilly, pricking her cheeks. She wraps her muffler around her neck. Waiting at the bus stop, she leans against a telephone pole and looks up at the sky. It isn't quite dark yet, but she can already see the faint imprint of the moon.

Japantown is on the way home and she decides to stop at the Japanese bookstore to buy the latest issue of *Sweet Times*. Maybe there are some new recipes she can use. Usually she heads straight to the magazine section, but a display table by the cashier catches her eye. It's filled with oversized books on different aspects of Japanese culture, most of them in English.

Flower arranging, teahouses, Kyoto temples—there's a wide variety of topics, all that would feel right at home in Damian Forrester's bookcase. She picks one up with a cover showing a samurai warrior leaning against a tree on the shore of a lake. He's blowing into a huge conch shell. The moon has risen behind a mountain, its reflection hitting the water.

The title of the book is in both Japanese and English: *Tsuki Hyakushi* or *One Hundred Aspects of the Moon*. Midori turns the pages. These are woodblock prints by an artist named Yoshitoshi who lived in the nineteenth century. According to the introduction it's a famous collection, but Midori has never heard of it. Traditional Japanese woodblock prints have never interested her, but these are stunning. Each one is of a scene where the moon plays prominently. In one print, *Enjoying the Evening Cool at Shijo—Shijo Noryo—*a geisha sits on a bench under the full moon and dips her foot in the streambed of the Kamo River in Kyoto. A fox preens herself under the moonlight in *Moon on the Saga Moor—Sagano no Tsuki.* She turns the page and sees a depiction of farmers celebrating the full autumn moon, which makes her think of her great-grandparents. "This is the night they have been waiting for," the caption says, "ever since the crescent moon."

This book would be perfect for Shinji. She's so excited to buy it for him that she forgets all about looking for the latest issue of *Sweet Times* and dashes off to the cashier.

# 22

THE BRIDE IS REGAL, ON THE ARM OF HER HANDSOME FATHER AS THEY walk down the aisle. The familiar wedding song plays as she joins her groom at the altar in front of the minister. He speaks in a lush baritone, saying everyone is gathered there today to join the couple together in matrimony. The groom smiles warmly at his bride.

"If anyone present can show just and legal cause why they may not be joined," the minister goes on, "let them speak now or forever hold their peace."

"I'm speaking up! I'm speaking up!" A woman's urgent voice rings out from the entryway to the church. The wedding guests gasp as the bride puts her hand on her chest, her face paralyzed with alarm. The minister's mouth forms an O as the groom glares at the intruder.

"You'll never marry her. Not as long as I live!" shouts the woman.

*Pop! Pop! Pop!*

The woman has pulled a gun from her purse and fires three shots at the groom. He clutches his chest and falls to the floor. The bridesmaids scatter. The guests are cowering, screaming.

"Kyle! Kyle!" the bride cries.

Why did the minister say such a thing? Midori wonders. That was pretty irresponsible, inviting someone to protest the marriage. But how could Mandy perform such an evil deed? Just when Kyle and Ashley were about to find true happiness?

Midori has been waiting for the right moment to give Shinji the moon book she bought for him at the Japanese bookstore, and decides now is the time. He's just come home from work and is looking through the mail she has left on the kitchen table. Mail that she has made sure to leave unopened.

"I want to give you this to thank you for everything you've done for me," she says to him.

"A present? Why?" He sits at the kitchen table.

"Well, to thank you for getting me the baking jobs for Sawyer and Jones. And letting me live here. And listening to all my problems."

"That's not necessary."

She has wrapped the book as a gift in a sheet of traditional Japanese *washi* paper printed with a cherry blossom pattern she found in a stationery shop in Japantown.

"Well, thank you." He's smiling as he carefully pulls off the paper. "*Tsuki Hyakushi*," he murmurs when he sees it. "One hundred aspects of the moon." He looks at her. "This is wonderful." He slowly turns the pages.

"I know Japanese things aren't your first choice, but somehow I thought this was perfect for you."

"It's beautiful, Midori-san. I've never seen this before. Thank you so much."

He clearly looks touched, his face slightly red, his demeanor quiet as he gazes carefully at each print. "Look at this one," he says, turning the book so that it faces her. He points to a piece depicting a beautiful, young kimono-clad woman framed by a trailing vine dotted with white flowers. The moon shines down on her, giving off a white glow. "This one has the wrong title."

"What do you mean?"

"It should be called *Midori by Moonlight*."

Midori blushes. It's a nice compliment. The kitchen feels warm and cozy.

Shinji has been sitting directly across from her but now moves to the chair that's next to hers. Slowly he takes her hand in his and holds it firmly. Then gently pulling her toward him he kisses her on the lips. She's so surprised she can't move. The chair she sits in is wooden and hard, but now it feels like it's upholstered with a soft cushion.

He seems to sense that she enjoyed receiving a kiss from him. She leans in as he kisses her once more.

"Midori," he says, his face close to hers. "I have a confession to make."

"Yes?"

"I've been in love with you for a long time."

Her smile seems to take up residence on her whole face.

Shinji wraps his arms around her and kisses her again. She clasps his neck with her hands and returns his kisses. By now the kisses have turned passionate.

"Is it okay?" he murmurs.

"Yes." Yes, it is *very* okay.

They can't stop kissing. It's as if she's watching one of those movies on the ceiling of her room. She begins to unbutton Shinji's shirt while he takes off her sweater, then her bra. He kisses her breasts as she leans back, slipping out of her skirt until she's wearing nothing. She can't believe it but she is now lying naked on the kitchen table.

He takes off his pants, his underwear. When he kisses her between her legs, her orgasms don't seem to stop. It's never been like this. When he's finally inside her she comes again. And again.

When they're done, they lie motionlessly on the kitchen table. She can't believe how comfortable it feels—it might as well be a comfy bed made with 700–thread count sheets. And it's not lost on Midori that making love in the kitchen, that holiest of places, signals how right this is.

"I thought you said you didn't like Japanese men," Shinji says in a teasing voice.

She hugs him tightly. "I love you, Shinji."


Midori puts on her new dress and shoes and examines herself in the full-length mirror in Shinji's room. Or, rather, their room. That's where they seem to be spending most of their time now, and a lot of that time in bed.

Is she really going to go through with it? Attend Kevin's wedding?

Shinji hugs her from behind, kissing her neck. "You look so beautiful."

Her face turns red as she thanks him for the compliment. She still can't get over the fact that they've confessed their love for each other, yet she realizes it's been there all along even when she couldn't get her mind off the deceptively gay Graham Striker.

Shinji is dressed in a black suit, probably the same one that he wore to her engagement party and the one that played the role of salaryman costume at the Miki Lounge. As usual, he's adorable.

"Do you feel okay about going?" he asks.

"I think so."

"I just had a crazy idea."

"It's already kind of crazy that we're going to this wedding."

He laughs. "We don't *have* to go, you know." He raises his eyebrows. "We could stay *here*." His eyes move toward the direction of the bed.

She smiles. "Well, that would be nice too, but I do want to go."

"Okay. But what if you wore your makeup and wig so you look like you did when Kevin came to the Miki Lounge?"

Midori laughs. "Are you kidding?"

"Not really."

"I don't know. I . . ."

"Come on."

Shinji's playfulness is one of the things she loves about him. The idea appeals to her. Why not do it? After about ten minutes in the bathroom she walks out in full regalia.

"Wow!" Shinji says. "I have a date with the glamorous Sheridan!"

"Have you been to an American wedding before?" Midori asks Shinji, as they hold hands, riding in the back of the cab taking them to the San Francisco Golf and Country Club.

"A few."

"Do they really have a part in the ceremony where someone can protest the marriage?"

"Protest?"

"Where they say something like, 'If anyone wants to come forward and say these two people shouldn't be married, let them do so now.'"

Shinji laughs. "Is that what you plan to do?"

Midori smiles. "No."

"Where did you hear that?"

"On *Farrington Falls*."

Shinji grins and kisses her neck. "I don't remember hearing it, but maybe they do."

"On *Farrington Falls* the woman who protested shot the groom."

"You don't have a gun in your purse, do you?"

She rolls her eyes.

It's no surprise that the San Francisco Golf and Country Club is a fancy and gorgeous place—it's not as if Kevin would be having his wedding at the local branch of the Rotary club. The grounds and golf course go on forever, their velvety green illuminated by strings of twinkling white lights and spotlights lining the footpaths.

A large hall serves as a kind of church, where Midori and Shinji are seated toward the back to witness the ceremony. Midori's half-geisha half-bar hostess makeup and wig have caused some stares but she doesn't care. And Shinji thinks it's hilarious.

The hall is filled with flowers and flickering candles surround the altar. At the end of the row in front of theirs Midori sees Consuelo, the Newburys' maid, sitting next to a Latin man who may be her husband or boyfriend. She's dressed as a guest, not a servant, in a flattering floral-printed dress. Once Midori catches her eye, she gives her a small wave. But Consuelo's puzzled look and halfhearted return wave make her think she doesn't know who on earth she is.

Piano and flute music begins to play, and a woman at the front dressed in an ice-blue evening gown sings in an operatic voice about finding your true love on top of a mountain. The bridesmaids wear lavender dresses with puffy sleeves. The large bows attached to their behinds would make even the skinniest person look hefty.

"It's like a herd of purple elephants," Shinji whispers to her. Midori has to cough to cover her laugh.

When Kimberley walks down the aisle in a lacy, form-fitting white gown with a long train held by two little girls, Midori notices that she looks heavier than at the party. Is she pregnant or is it just the dress?

"Are you okay?" Shinji says in her ear, squeezing her hand.

She nods. Yes, she is okay. More okay than she ever thought she could be. Listening to Kevin and Kimberley pledge their love to each other does not faze her. Any anger and resentment has dissipated. "I'm glad we came," Midori says to Shinji. He smiles at her and kisses her cheek.

The minister does ask if there are any protestors.

Midori looks at Shinji and laughs when he says, "Shh," placing his index finger to his lips.

The reception is held in an enormous banquet room, a short walk from the wedding hall. There are so many guests that it's quite likely that Kevin and Kimberley will not even see Midori and Shinji. It will be easy to avoid them.

They're seated at a table with four other couples.

"How do you know Kevin and Kimberley?" a distinguished-looking woman in her fifties asks Shinji, while trying hard not to gape at Midori.

"Kevin and I are old friends," Shinji says.

"Are you from the Orient?" she asks Midori.

Midori nods.

"Didn't Kevin work somewhere over there?"

"Yes," she says. "I met him in Japan."

"How nice."

"Not really."

The woman gives her a twisted smile, acting as if she must have misheard her, then turns away to speak to the man seated next to her.

There are many long speeches and dinner has yet to be served. Midori is so hungry all she can do is daydream about profiteroles and crêpe suzettes.

"This is kind of boring," Shinji whispers to Midori. "Do you want to just go?"

"What about your free dinner?" she asks, smiling.

"I'd rather go have wonton soup and kung pao chicken over at Uncle Chan's on Clement Street," he says, flashing a grin at her.

A small combo set up in the corner starts playing "I Just Called to Say I Love You."

"That's fine with me," she says. "But before we go I just want to give the couple my best wishes."

Midori cranes her neck. She can see that Kevin and Kimberley have started to talk to guests at one of the tables in front of the room.

"Come on," Midori says and takes Shinji's hand as she maneuvers her way through the maze of banquet tables and chairs toward the direction of the couple.

Kevin smiles as he seems to recognize Shinji, but looks puzzled at the sight of Midori. He can't stop staring at her.

"Hey, Kevin," Shinji says. "Congratulations."

"Thanks, Shinji." Kevin continues to stare at Midori, his face now turning pale. Visions of the Miki Lounge must be dancing through his head. After giving Shinji an air kiss on the cheek, Kimberley cocks her head and squints, giving Midori a quizzical look.

"Kevin and Kimberley," Midori says, smiling. "Make the best of it!"

"*What? Midori?*" Kevin gasps.

"And, Kevin," Midori says, turning toward him. "I want to thank you for introducing me to Shinji. I never would have met him if it weren't for you." It's just what Kevin had said to Shinji at Midori's engagement party. Shinji puts his arm around Midori's shoulders, and she places hers around his waist. Then they kiss, as if a minister has just pronounced them husband and wife.

Kevin's mouth is hanging open, but no words come out.

"*The Japanese girl?*" Kimberley says, with a scowl. She turns to Kevin. "How did *she* get an invitation?"

"Good luck to both of you," Shinji says. They break into laughter as they run through the hall, causing many of the guests to turn and stare. An attendant opens the door for them as they step out into the cold, clear night.

Out on the expansive lawn Midori kicks off her shoes. Taking off her wig, she shakes her head as her hair falls freely to her shoulders. Shinji grabs her waist, and they spin around until they lose their balance, giggling as they fall to the grass. The green blades feel like a cool, damp carpet against Midori's skin.

"Look," Shinji says, pointing toward the sky.

It's the moon. Bold. Bright. White. Even with the naked eye Midori can envision it as a big ball of pastry dough. A simple ball of dough that, if kneaded and shaped in just the right way, will turn into a beautiful and delectable dessert she'll savor forever.